RICK PARTLOW
WHOLESALE SLAUGHTER

AETHON
BOOKS

WHOLESALE SLAUGHTER

©2019 RICK PARTLOW

Print and eBook formatting, and cover design by Steve Beaulieu. Artwork provided by Filip Dudek.

Published by Aethon Books LLC. 2019

1

The guard huddled inside the heater coils of his jacket and muttered curses into the teeth of the north wind. Captain Lyta Randell couldn't see his face, couldn't quite make out the words, but she knew exactly what he was thinking. It was there in the shudders running through him, in the way he had his rifle slung over his back instead of held at the ready because his hands were stuffed into his pockets. It was universal.

He was cursing the cold, cursing the wind, cursing his sergeant for putting him on guard duty in the first place. He wished he was inside the main compound, impermanent and slap-dash as it was. He had to see it teasing him—he was even closer than Lyta to the floodlights piercing the midnight darkness, turning snow flurries into a meteor shower, warmth and comfort hidden behind walls of aluminum sheeting. He was undoubtedly upset about missing out on the entertainment as well. On a world like this, barren, barely habitable, with nothing around for three jump-points, entertainment was hard to come by, and there was a fresh batch of new prisoners on the other side of those walls. Women, men, children, whatever he was into and his superiors would let him get away with.

A feral rage surged upward from Lyta Randell's gut to her chest and she had to force herself not to give in to it, not to bring the muzzle of her carbine up and put a burst through the guard's head. It would have been easy, quiet even with the integral suppressor... but there was always the chance the floppy hood the man was wearing would throw off her aim, that she'd hit off to the side instead of right in the brainstem, that he'd get off a warning on the radio.

So, she waited, knowing what was going on inside those walls, what the captives would be going through. She tamped it down like a powder charge and saved it for later. A hundred meters away, on the other side of the perimeter fence, there was nothing, no activity all the way from the wire to the compound. On the far side of the cluster of buildings, she saw the faint motion of a pair of bird-legged mecha shuffling back and forth on a security patrol, while more of the ten-meter, bipedal tanks stood motionless and unmanned nearby.

"Shadow One in position," she subvocalized into her throat mic.

The answer was deep and male and nearly operatic in its smooth timbre.

"Roger, Shadow One. You are go in two mikes."

"Two mikes, roger," she echoed automatically.

Two minutes. The guard wouldn't wander off in just two minutes. She thought it at him, a mental command not to move, to stay right where he was and shiver. It was an old soldier's superstition, and she was a very old soldier. Old enough to count the two minutes down in her head without resorting to checking under the sleeve covering her wrist computer.

"Shadow Three," she murmured. "Take him out."

I used to do this sort of thing myself, she complained silently, to the only person who cared.

Still, Sergeant Marini was pretty good as a second choice. He made no sound, appearing like a wraith out of the blackness and snaking an arm around the sentry's throat, silencing him in the spare moments before his knife plunged upward into the man's armpit, a necessary weak-spot in the sort of cheap, basic armor the pirate troops could afford. The guard thrashed, trying to reach the rifle he'd slung for comfort, clutching through his heavy jacket for his equipment belt and the combat blade useless beneath it.

Blood spattered inky black on the powdered snow, Rorschach test patterns on the virgin white until the galvanic drumming of the dying man's heels scratched them away. A long thirty seconds before all movement stopped and Marini dragged the lifeless body out of the glow of the security lights and into a stand of skinny, balding trees.

The rest of the squad was moving without having to be told. Scherer was still attaching the alligator clips of the dampener to the fence wires when Lansdale yanked out the cutters, slicing through the first strand of fence just as the green indicator glowed in muted cheerfulness on the dampener's display. Captain Randell grinned beneath her face hood, unfolding from her spider-hole with a clicking and cracking of stiff, overworked joints, and waving the bulk of the platoon forward.

Off to the side, she made an approving note of Marini stripping the magazine and loaded round from the guard's rifle and tossing the weapon aside.

6mm caseless, Lyta judged with clinical precision. *Easy to fabricate the gun and the ammo even out here in Shitsville.*

Lansdale flashed a thumbs-up back to Lyta, pulling back the section of wire fence she'd cut as Marini prepared to crawl through, waiting for her signal. She thumbed the switch for her throat mic.

"Shadow One has a breach. I say again, Shadow One has a breach."

There was a long silence, and for just a heartbeat, she had the paranoid notion the Gomers had twigged to them and were jamming their signals. But then...

"Shadow One, execute."

She made a slashing motion at Marini, and the Rangers began scrambling through the hole in the fence, scattering to cover positions on the other side.

About damn time. It's been way too long since I killed some pirates.

Kathren Margolis shoved her hands tight against her ears and tried to shut out the screams. The walls of the storage closet were pressed particle board, the door hollow plastic; they might as well have not been there, yet they were her only defense from the fate looming on the other side, the only fate she could imagine worse than what had already happened. The screams were high-pitched, inhuman, but she thought it was the Captain of the transport. She'd spoken with him once on the voyage from Nike and recognized his pleasant tenor somewhere underlying the agonizing wails.

He wasn't the first. They'd started with the Navigator three days ago, then the First Officer yesterday. She hadn't seen it, but she'd heard every last, excruciating second, and still she'd preferred to concentrate on the screams than what was happening to her in that closet. But the screams wouldn't stop and she couldn't shut them out and the floor was ice-cold and rough against her skin and she was shivering and scared and she felt so dirty she might never feel clean again, and if that closet door opened again, she was going to just make them kill her.

The closet door opened.

Light flooded in from behind the man, but she knew him by

the massive shoulders, the heavy gut that might have been absurd on someone who was less of a sadistic animal. They called him Sergeant Kuschel, but she'd never met a sergeant with a gut like his, or an unkempt beard. They seemed afraid of him, and with her right eye swollen nearly shut and the bruises on her arms and legs, she understood that part well enough.

She scrabbled back from the door, leaning against the wall. Disdain battled pleasure across his scarred face; he liked to intimidate women, she'd seen it from the first.

Not this time.

She pushed away from the wall and lunged forward, intent on punching him in the balls, hurting him badly enough for him to lose control and beat her to death this time. Her legs betrayed her, wouldn't support her weight after three days without food or sleep, and she fell half a meter short, landing on her side hard, the wind gushing from her lungs.

Stars filled her vision and she couldn't see Kuschel's twisted, filthy smile, but she heard the laugh and she knew the loathsome smirk accompanied it. She heard his heavy footsteps as he circled around her, toying with her, and she tried to move away from them, bringing her knees up to her chest. He kicked at her, not hard, not like he had the first time, just a jab to sting her shin with the steel toe of his combat boot. He was playing with her, a fat, stupid cat to her mouse.

"What did you think you were going to do, flyer girl?" Kuschel mocked in an accent that was harsh, grating, metal scraping on metal. "You going to beat me up and fly away?"

His laugh was sharp and ragged and devolved into coughing. He coughed a lot; he'd probably damaged his lungs and never had access to advanced health care to get them repaired. She wished it had killed him.

"You won't fly away from this, little flyer girl." He bent over her, grabbing her face between the roughened fingers of his

5

beefy hand. "After we've had our fun, then you get to be the last one." He jerked a thumb back toward the door, toward the screams.

But the screams had stopped. Kuschel seemed to notice about the same time she had, and he straightened slightly, twisting around to look behind him. She tried to use the opportunity to wriggle free, but his fingers tightened on her face. She felt the painful compression on her cheekbones, the dull pain in the bruise over her right eye, and she couldn't see past his bulk, past the unwashed grey of what had once been a uniform from one military or another.

"What the..." Kuschel's exclamation was cut short and suddenly something warm and wet splashed across Kathren's face. She tasted copper and salt and spat reflexively. It was blood, but not hers.

Sgt. Kuschel toppled, an ancient oak felled by one storm too many, his fingertips scraping across her face as they slipped free. Kathren desperately wiped at her face, trying to get the big man's blood out of her eyes. A tall, black-clad figure stood in the doorway, a faint curl of smoke rising from the muzzle of a suppressed carbine still trained on Kuschel's inert form. Kathren's first thought was this was an attack by a rival pirate group and she felt a surge of hope they'd just kill her outright.

A long-fingered hand left the fore-grip of the carbine and pulled up the featureless black hood and night vision goggles, revealing the sharp-edged, not unpleasant face of a woman, somewhere in her late thirties or early forties, her hair dark brown and cut short and spikey. Her eyes glinted green in the faint light filtering in from outside the room, and a grim smile played across her lips as she finally concluded Kuschel was really dead. Behind her, other black-clad commandos spread out into a defensive formation, stepping over the corpses of the pirates to reach the captives they'd brought out of their cells. She saw one man pulling open a nylon bag marked with a small, subdued red caduceus, a medical kit.

"I'm Captain Lyta Randell, First Spartan Rangers," she announced, her voice slightly raspy, as if she'd spent too many years yelling at the top of her lungs. She extended a hand, a clear offer to help Kathren to her feet. "Are you all right?"

Kathren stared at her, at the hand, then down at herself, at the torn and filthy rags left from the Navy uniform she'd been wearing, the bruises and dried blood... and other things less pleasant. Gratitude and relief suddenly transformed into hard-edged anger.

"I was kidnaped," Kathren growled with surprising ferocity, "watched people around me killed and tortured, and I've spent the three days being... being... Of course," she screamed her throat raw, "I'm not fucking all right!"

"Good," the female commando smiled, grabbing Kathren's hand and pulling her up. "Realizing that's the first step."

Logan Conner cinched his harness tighter, clenched his teeth and stomped heavily on the jump pedals. Pressure slammed him down into the gimbal-mounted "easy chair," the padding of the headrest and the interior padding of his helmet warring with acceleration to keep his skull in one piece. The roar of the jets filled the mech's tiny cockpit, air sucked into turbines on the Vindicator's shoulders then superheated in the fusion reactor before screaming out of the exhausts in the machine's "backpack" at thousands of meters per second.

Forty tons of vaguely humanoid assault mech soared through the night sky, lifting over the dark line of the low ridge on streams of glowing fusion fury. Logan forced himself to ignore the confused jumble of lights and snow and steam outside his cockpit canopy, concentrating instead on the clarity of the Heads-Up

Display and the well-demarcated lines of the fence surrounding the bandit compound. Logan's teeth clicked together with the impact as the Vindicator landed just inside the wire, only a hundred meters from the two Hopper scout mechs on night patrol.

"Hopper" wasn't a production model or a military designation, not like "Vindicator." The design was too old for that, older than the Dominions, older even than the Empire, so simple even bandit trash like this could fabricate the parts to slap them together out in the middle of nowhere. They were named for the curious gait their ostrich-like legs imparted to the ten-meter tall machine, distinctive and unmistakable even in the scant seconds his mech had been in flight.

Not waiting to see whether the rest of his squad had followed, Logan immediately targeted the right-hand Hopper with a laser designator and launched a flight of Fire-n-Forget missiles from the pod mounted on his mech's left shoulder. The high-explosive warheads slammed into the light mech, covering the machine in a cascading series of fireballs and sheering armor away from its chest and legs. Smoke shrouded the machine, hiding it from view, and while Logan didn't exactly forget it, he suddenly had more important things to think about.

The pilot of the mech to his left had heeded the warning flare of the Vindicator's jump jets and used the time to spin his chin cannon around and line up a shot. The 25mm chain gun thundered and flashed, and a hail of tungsten slugs, each the size of a man's thumb, smashed into the chest plastron of the Vindicator and drove the assault mech back a step… but didn't penetrate. The bullets were big but slow, intended more for anti-infantry or anti-vehicle use, and they barely cracked the surface armor on a mech the size of the Vindicator.

Wincing at the jackhammer blows ringing through the cockpit, Logan squeezed a control and felt a shift in his machine's stance to compensate for the 30mm Vulcan firing off the right shoulder, nearly un-aimed, a desperation shot to distract the Hopper pilot. It would have been too much to hope for to score a hit on the Hopper's cockpit, or even its hip-mounted turbines, but luck was with him and two slugs from the ten-round burst sliced through the missile pod on the bandit's right shoulder. The shots didn't ignite the warheads, but they did jam the launcher before it could get off a salvo... and bought him the seconds he needed.

The Vindicator's primary weapon weighed down the right arm like some ridiculously outsized pistol, the electromagnetic coils connecting it to the fusion reactor covered by layered scales of flexible BiPhase Carbide running all the way up the arm. The aiming reticle for the gun floated over the cockpit of the Hopper and Logan touched the trigger pad on the mech's joystick. The Vindicator rocked backward, absorbing the recoil of a coherent packet of plasma shooting out of the muzzle at thousands of meters per second, a microsecond of sunrise in the darkness of midnight, polarizing the canopy surface to nearly opaque for nearly a second.

The HUD still showed him the view from the exterior cameras, images of the Hopper tumbling back, the cockpit incinerated along with the pilot and the gyros that could have stopped its out-of-control crash. Tons of charred, smoking metal slammed to the ground, gouts of steam rising up from snow sublimated directly into water vapor by the excess heat, joining the smoke and radiant heat from the plasma gun blast and the missile explosions in a roiling cloud, impenetrable to eye and sensor alike.

From the cloud emerged the first Hopper, a mutilated zombie rising from the grave. Its left arm was gone, along with the left-side turbine and most of the armor on its left chest and leg, but amidst those torn, charred, and ragged strips of metal, the cockpit was intact... and so was the missile launch pod on its right shoulder.

"Shit!" Logan blurted, simultaneously twisting the control to swing around the Gatling turret, taking a step to the side and trying to decide whether he should slam the jump pedals.

Before he could complete any of it, something streaked out of the night from behind him and slammed into the Hopper's missile launcher. The pod erupted with a starburst of secondary explosions as the propellant cooked off, followed closely by the warheads. A huge secondary blast tore what was left of the light mecha apart and sent debris spattering off the Vindicator's armor like a hailstorm. Bits and pieces of burning metal rained down across the compound, lighting up the night and throwing monstrous shadows from the huge Sentinel strike mech plodding up from behind him. The slender barrel of the Electro-Thermal Chemical cannon jutting out across its right shoulder still glowed red from the hypersonic round it had fired to take out the Hopper.

"Thanks, Colonel Anders," Logan transmitted, unable to hold in the deep sigh, relief at the rescue and disappointment it had been necessary.

"Wait for your platoon before you rush in headlong, Lieutenant," Donnel Anders chided him, his soothingly deep voice softening the impact of the words just a hair. "These may be bandit trash, but don't underestimate them."

"Yes, sir," Logan acknowledged, abashed.

They were touching down all around him now, jetting in only seconds behind him though it might as well have been days later. There were three of them, all in Golem assault mecha, just slightly smaller and lighter than his Vindicator. Always four machines in an armor platoon, that's what Colonel Anders had told him, a tradition dating back a thousand years.

"The compound is secure," Anders declared. "Captain Randell has the captives in hand and her Rangers have neutralized the dismounts." Neutralized was such a sterile word. The Rangers had killed them. "I want your platoon to run a patrol spiral out to ten kilometers, then circle back in to the landing zone for dust-off."

"Roger that, sir." He turned his mech away from the Colonel's fifteen-meter Sentinel strike mech, facing his people.

"Follow me, First Platoon," Logan said, heading for the wire with quick, tromping steps. "But keep your eyes open," he added, trying to take Ander's criticism to heart. "There's no way of telling how many of the bandits might have been outside the compound."

His Vindicator walked through the fence as if it weren't there, the remaining three machines following behind him in a wedge. In the tiny rear-view image at the corner of his HUD, Logan could still see Ander's tall, hulking grey mech standing, watchful as its namesake. He wondered if the man wished he could still go on patrols like this instead of ordering other people to do it. Logan led from the front and couldn't imagine doing it any other way.

The mechs ate up ground quickly, each plodding step covering twenty meters, their spiked foot pads ripping brush by the roots and sending up white sprays of snow. They passed by the main mech hangar, a ramshackle structure, barely more than three corrugated aluminum walls on a concrete slab, and Logan was beginning to think they'd been dead lucky and caught everyone with their pants down.

"Logan." Marc Langella, the platoon's Sub-Lieutenant and the only one of the three who could get away with calling him by his first name, was in the Golem to Logan's right and he automatically glanced toward his subordinate even though he could see the image of the other man's mecha in the HUD. "We got multiple thermal signatures out to the southwest, maybe one-five-zero meters."

Logan checked his own sensor readout and spotted the flickering red dots a moment later, fitful and intermittent through the snow. The flurries had turned into a full-fledged blizzard as the night wore on, the wind pushing the white-out snow nearly horizontal now, and he could make out little detail past the floodlights of the bandit compound, just a vague sense of the surrounding trees.

Same trees out here as back home on Sparta, some tiny partition of his thoughts devoted to inanities noted. *This place was terraformed way back when. Maybe the Empire, maybe before.*

And somewhere back there, behind trees transplanted from Earth fauna centuries or even millennia ago, were at least three heat signatures so big they could only be mecha. Not dead lucky, after all. Only one thing to be done about it.

"Prevatt, Coughlin," he snapped to the two Warrants who filled out his platoon, the decision made almost as he said the words, "put your backs against the main hangar back there and prepare to provide fire support. Marc, you and I are jumping two hundred meters southwest, fifty meters up."

"Roger that, boss," Langella replied easily, as if this were just a training simulation and they'd be heading out for a beer after.

Langella's Golem stepped abreast with Logan's Vindicator, twenty meters off to the left, shoulders hunched like a lineman preparing to rush the passer. The cockpit canopy of the Golem was flush with the chest, a jack-o-lantern of transparent aluminum carved into BiPhase Carbide, and Logan thought he glimpsed the motion of a thumbs-up through the surface.

"On three," he said, making sure he had his weapons systems ready to go. "One... two... three."

Both mecha rose on columns of hot gas, arcing over the camp to a wide, dirt trail leading up the plateau from the valley below. While still in mid-air, above the interference of the thick forest, Logan picked up half a dozen Hoppers bounding up the trail, coming back, he guessed, from a patrol.

And then he and Langella were in the midst of the ostrich-legged machines, landing back to back. Logan expelled a flight of missiles instinctively, without thought, all of them impacting on the center torso of a Hopper to his left and about forty meters out. The machine was consumed in an incandescent cloud of smoke as the armor-piercing warheads ate through the honeycomb boron, through the depleted uranium beneath that and into the fusion bottle. Plumes of plasma shot out from the machine and both shoulder-mounted, spiked-plasma MHD turbines blew outward, taking the machine's arms with it.

Logan turned his mech away from the blast and caught a brief glimpse of Marc Langella firing the Electro-Thermal Chemical cannon that was his primary weapon, mounted like an oversized rifle cradled in the Golem's right hand. The 100mm tungsten slug was invisible, a streak of light at six thousand meters a second, riding the flames of igniting gasses lit with an electrical pulse in front of the main charge, a plasma afterburner. The round cored one of the Hoppers like an apple, blowing its reactor in a starburst of plasma plumes and Logan was blind again, thermal and infrared useless, the optical cameras whited out for a moment. All he had to go on was active lidar and radar painting the best picture they could in his HUD.

But it rained, as his father liked to say, on the just and the unjust. The remaining bandit Hoppers tried to return fire at near point-blank range, but they were frightened and confused, and just as blind as he was. What missiles, lasers and cannonfire didn't go streaking off into the night actually wound up striking their own machines. For Logan Conner and Marc Langella, it was like hunting baby whales in a bathtub.

No bonus for coming back with unexpended ammunition, he thought, an echo of a phrase he'd heard over and over in the Academy and mecha pilot training.

Logan cut loose with everything he had, the fingers of his left hand stretching out to hit three firing controls at once. His Vulcan and the twin five Mega-joule chemical pulse lasers in the Vindicator's upper chest taking out the right-hand turbine and igniting the flamethrower fuel in one of the Hoppers. Sheathed in unquenchable flames, the Hopper's pilot ejected, his canopy blowing out and his control couch rocketing into the sky to come down kilometers away on a billowing white parachute. Logan ignored it; pirates were fair game in or out of the cockpit, but he just didn't have the time.

He squeezed the trigger pad on his right-hand joystick in an almost sympathetic reflex to the motions of the left and his main gun spat out what looked like a flash of ball lightning. The plasmoid exploded against another Hopper's right leg joint, severing the limb in a spray of molten metal and sending the small mech lurching over to crash heavily into the snow-covered ground. He had the space to breathe and he used it to check on his wingman —and best friend.

Langella was too close to the remaining two machines to use his missiles and he'd opened up with the twin Vulcans mounted just above his Golem's hips, chewing at the armor on one of the smaller mechs' left chest in a firework display of sparks. The other tried to get in close and use his left-arm flamers, but Langella jammed the muzzle of his ETC against the mech's "chin" and fired at contact distance. Logan flinched, worried the massive weapon would backfire and take the mech's right arm with it, but the huge round tore through the bandit's cockpit, vaporized the pilot within and soared upward into the sky. The headless machine tottered backward, fell with a shriek of tearing metal.

The last mech, battered by Langella's Vulcans, tried to jump out, the hydrogen jets in its broad feet carrying it about twenty meters off the ground before Logan expended his last flight of missiles into it. The warheads struck along the Hopper's right flank, stripping armor from the leg and chest and, most devastatingly, blowing out the right-leg jump-jet. The mech's left leg jerked upward from the unbalanced boost of the remaining jet, tore loose of the main body with a shower of hydrogen plasma and the Hopper spun crazily back to the ground. It laid silent for a moment before the hydrogen fuel went up, consuming the torso in a shower of flame.

Logan leaned back into his easy chair, his mech mirroring the motion as it straightened, and let go a long-held breath.

"White Leader, this is White One," he radioed Colonel Anders.

"Go ahead, White One," the Colonel replied.

"Neutralized six unfriendlies," Logan Conner reported. "All light scout types. Going to make a quick sweep of the area..."

Logan bit down on the next word as something slammed him against his seat restraints hard enough that he thought his shoulders might dislocate, sending his Vindicator stumbling forward, the gyros barely able to keep the mech upright. An incandescent cloud of smoke drifted across his view and by the time he heard Langella's uncharacteristically panicked shouting in his ear, he already knew what had happened.

"Missiles!" his friend was yelling.

"Where, Goddammit?"

Logan spun his mech, eyes flickering through one sensor after another, trying to determine the source of the launch, turned just in time to see Langella's humanoid Golem rock back, a phospherescent streak of red that could only have been a heavy ETC round catching it in the left shoulder. The tungsten slug tore off the mech's left arm in a shower of sparks, spinning the machine around and sending it crashing onto its back with the finality of thirty tons of cutting-edge technology turned to scrap.

Logan acted without thought, running on instinct, and slammed his booted soles down on the jump pedals, shooting his Vindicator into the air in the direction from which the cannon-round had come. He came down with an uneven, bone-jarring impact, feeling the metal taste of blood in his mouth. It was inconsequential; he doubted he'd live long enough to find out if he'd bit his tongue or busted his lip. He'd almost landed directly on top of a huge Scorpion strike mech.

Ostrich-legged like the Hopper, the Scorpion outweighed that light scout mech by at least half-again and mounted much deadlier weaponry. He could see them checked off on a list in one of the familiarization classes he'd taken: a large ETC cannon fixed to the top of its podlike torso, a chin-mounted Vulcan, a six-tube integral missile launch system on either side of the cockpit and a pair of five Mega-joule lasers on its lower torso. But the machine's deadliest armaments were the twin plasma cannons that each formed the end of a long, claw-like arm. It was fifteen meters tall and weighed nearly sixty tons. It was the most fearsome fighting machine in the human worlds, and Logan was staring at it nose to nose.

His jump, however, had taken the big mech's pilot by surprise; he could tell by the interrupted motion of the big machine's torso, as if the driver couldn't decide if he wanted to shit or go blind. Logan Conner was a lot of things, but no one had ever accused him of being hesitant. Moving in closer to the Scorpion, he fired his lasers directly at the mech's cockpit—the polished transparent aluminum diffused and reflected the thin red pulses as Logan had known it would, but the twin blasts temporarily blinded the enemy pilot and burned out the Scorpion's thermal and infrared sensors.

He'd bought himself time, now he could do something stupid with it. Logan gritted his teeth, grabbed the Scorpion's right-side plasma cannon with his Vindicator's articulated left hand, jammed the muzzle of his own plasma gun against the enemy mech's right-hand weapon and fired. The burst of superheated gas burned through even the thick armor like butter at that close a range, and a flare of actinic light enveloped both the mechs for just a moment. Heat washed through his cockpit like a physical fist slamming into him and he was barely able to retain consciousness.

Logan wasn't sure at first if the explosion was just the Scorpion's plasma cannon blowing or his own main gun going with it, but none of the yellow warning lights flashing in the periphery of his vision on his HUD had turned red, so nothing was that wrong yet. Yet. Logan scrambled to keep the Vindicator from tumbling forward as the Scorpion pilot jerked his mech back, freeing it from Logan's grasp and knocking the lighter machine off-balance.

Heat filled the cockpit and a sledgehammer vibration threatened to shake the Vindicator apart and Logan was dimly aware the maimed strike mech was hitting him with its Vulcan and twin lasers simultaneously, chewing armor from his machine's left arm and chest. Those yellow lights were beginning to show red and he knew he had less than a second before the damage would be too much to overcome.

"Bastard!"

The exclamation was guttural, instinctive, and so were his actions. Logan lunged forward, let the bigger mech have a wide hook with the Vindicator's armored left fist, smashing the Vulcan cannon and one of the laser projectors off their mounts, the laser falling to the ground in a shower of sparks while caseless ammo for the Vulcan spilled out like coins from a slot machine. The bandit pilot tried to back his machine up, knowing he was at a disadvantage at this close a range, but Logan stuck to him like a boxer trying to get under a bigger opponent's guard, grabbing at the Scorpion's remaining plasma cannon again to force it away from a firing arc.

Trying to apply his unarmed combat training to the situation, Logan received a sudden inspiration. Still controlling his opponent's right-hand main gun, he ducked his machine's shoulder under the Scorpion's torso pod, planted his mech's feet solidly beneath the enemy mech's center of gravity, and hit the jump-jets. The plasma flame melted snow and turned the sandy ground beneath it to polished glass, pushing the heavy Scorpion backward off its feet and slamming it to the ground with a crash of metal that was quite possibly the loudest thing Logan had ever heard… and then he heard nothing.

His vision swam, his ears were filled with a hollow ringing, and he wasn't quite certain if he'd passed out or which way, exactly, was up. His seat restraints cut into his shoulders through his tactical vest, though, and from that kernel of data, he realized the Vindicator was face down and so was he. Logan shook his head to clear it and tried to assess his situation.

His helmet was still on, and as his vision cleared, he could see on the HUD that most of his systems were operational, so he visualized the correct movements, letting the neural halo inside the helmet read the electrical activity in his brain. He tried to get the Vindicator's legs beneath it, tried to push down with the mech's left hand, but the foot pads couldn't get any purchase on the sandy earth and the articulated hand was tangled up with the Scorpion's arm. The big strike mecha was, at least, equally helpless, unable to roll over and regain its footing with the forty tons of Vindicator laying across it, and unable to reach Logan's machine with any of its weapons.

Then Logan saw the escape hatch beneath the strike mech's chin swing open, a rope ladder spilling out of it.

Damn, he thought, not even stopping to consider whether he might be concussed. *Can't let this guy get away.*

Logan yanked the quick-release for his safety harness and fell straight into the canopy of his cockpit. He stopped himself with an outstretched arm against the fuselage, reaching out with his other hand and hitting the emergency canopy release switch, allowing the transparent dome to swing outward on its hinges. Cold air slapped him in the face and with it, something resembling reason.

Gun. Need my gun.

He patted around his tactical vest with his right hand, finding the butt of his sidearm and trying to remember the last time he'd qualified with the weapon. Had it been a month ago? Two months? *Shit.*

Drawing his sidearm, Logan shifted his helmet back, tightened his chin strap and climbed cautiously onto the upper section of the Vindicator's chest, keeping his left hand tightly gripped around the safety handle built into the side of the cockpit. Charred, jagged bits of BiPhase Carbide pockmarked the chest plastron and he tried to keep his boot soles away from them, hooking a heel inside the cockpit canopy and wedging his other foot in the only maintenance step left unmangled. He looked down and found himself directly below the Scorpion's escape hatch.

It was pitch black outside, with not a hint of moonlight or starlight penetrating the snow clouds, but his helmet's visor had infrared and thermal optics built in, and through them, he could still make out the shape of a tall, rangy male climbing through the hatch. Bereft of a helmet, he looked to be in his late forties, with long, braided black hair. He wore a pistol in a shoulder holster, but hadn't yet tried to draw it.

Logan braced himself against the side of his mech's chest, brought up his heavy pistol and tried to draw a bead on the man with the targeting laser built into the weapon. With the IR sighting in his helmet's visor, he could see the full beam of the laser interacting with the moisture in the air and he brought it around to the enemy pilot's chest. Logan's gloved finger was squeezing on the trigger when the bandit's head suddenly whipped around and he threw himself away from the Scorpion's hatch, and caught the hanging rope ladder about five meters down. Swinging back toward the main body of the downed strike mech with an impressively acrobatic move for a mech pilot, the bandit drew his weapon faster than Logan thought humanly possible.

He ducked back inside his cockpit canopy just ahead of a full-auto hailstorm of small-caliber slugs, heard them ricocheting off the armor on the Vindicator's chest and flinched in anticipation of a killing shot, but it didn't come. Logan bit off a curse and swung back out, pulling the trigger of his large-bore semiauto slugshooter before he even had it lined up. It wasn't as loud as he remembered it being on the range, didn't seem to kick as hard, and he'd fired four rounds before he could let off the trigger.

Mithra alone knew how, but he managed to hit the bandit pilot, a visible impact in the upper chest. The tall man flopped backward off the rope ladder, mouth opening in pain and shock. Not dead though; he twisted in midair, again with more agility than any mech-driver had a right to, and rolled to absorb the impact before he hit about five meters below.

Logan cursed again, realizing the bandit's tactical vest had absorbed at least some of the round's energy.

I'm cursing an awful lot today, he thought as he jumped after him.

He tried to roll with the fall, but came to the conclusion about halfway down he was *not* as accomplished an acrobat as the bandit pilot. The impact half-knocked the wind out of him, would have probably broken his shoulder if it hadn't been for nearly half a meter of fresh snow. In the seconds it took him to stumble to his feet, the bandit opened up again with his machine pistol.

The burst of tiny tantalum bullets struck Logan in the left chest and he grunted, fell back heavily as a sharp stinging shot through his left arm, a tiny probe of fire burning into him. One of the rounds had missed his armored tactical vest and buried itself in his left bicep—not deep, thanks to the ballistic cloth of his fatigues, but it still hurt like hell. It didn't hurt so bad he couldn't hold onto his gun and he fired convulsively in the Scorpion pilot's general direction, two rounds, three.

The bandit tried to turn and run and Logan sighted the aiming laser carefully, fired. This time it kicked, this time it was loud. The 12mm slug smashed the pilot's right forearm in a spray of blood and the tall man screamed, dropped his machine pistol and stumbled to his knees, hair whipping around in the wind. Logan struggled back to his feet, blinking snow out of his eyes, and stepped cautiously up to the man, covering him with his sidearm. He knew he should just blow the pilot's head off, but shooting an unarmed man face-to-face was a few factors harder than shooting into a cockpit.

"You want to die quick," Logan said, his throat dry and raspy, "this is your one chance. Otherwise, you can come back to Sparta and stand trial—then be executed. Your choice."

By way of reply, the tall man lunged for his fallen weapon. He was fast; he had already wrapped his fingers around the grip before the 12mm slug slammed into his temple, exploded out the other side of his skull in a spray of blood and brains. The bandit dropped, twitched once and then lay still. Logan took a deep breath, fell heavily to one knee, his arm on fire with pain. He bit back the wave of agony, looked up in time to see Marc Langella walking toward him from his downed Golem, pistol drawn.

"You okay?" The Sub-lieutenant offered him a hand and he took it with his left, not wanting to put that much weight on his wounded arm.

"I will be." Logan nodded slowly. He shoved his sidearm into its shoulder holster, pulled off his helmet and let the snow cool him down. "You'd better call the Colonel, Marc. Looks like we're going to need a ride."

2

Logan Conner winced as the utility vehicle jerked to a halt in front of the main hangar. He was grateful the driver wasn't piloting a mech.

"This is where you get off, sir," the corpsman who'd put a field bandage on his injured arm announced. "They've set up a field hospital to take care of the civilians from the ship."

"Thanks." Logan nodded, stepping carefully out of the back of the truck. Langella had remained at the battle site to oversee the repair and salvage of their mecha, but Colonel Anders had insisted Logan get his arm checked out back at the camp. The Colonel had actually complimented him, impressed with Logan's successful attack on the strike mech, which had freaked him out a little.

He walked slowly across the open ground to the hangar, snow crunching beneath his boots. The storm had ended before reinforcements had arrived at the battle site and without the wind, it didn't seem nearly as cold anymore. The compound had been surrounded by arrays of spotlights, and was secured by the rest of Captain Danaan's company of assault mecha, including the half of his own platoon that still had functioning machines. A crew of workers were clearing the landing pad to allow their shuttle to jet in from the isolated valley where it had originally landed.

This would be a good mission for salvage, he reflected. The Scorpion was mostly intact, and at least half a dozen mecha and five heavy-lift shuttles were untouched. And, of course, anytime the Guard got to take out a bandit cabal, it made Sparta and all the Dominions that much safer. That was what Father always said.

Logan limped slowly into the hangar—*Damn leg hurts worse from where I jumped out of the mech than my arm does from getting shot*—and made his way to where a line of folding examination tables had been set up. The civilians and the transport crew were a ragged lot, most sporting at least minor injuries. Here and there, he saw a man shivering uncontrollably, or a woman hugging a blanket around herself and staring vacantly into space, or the pair of young, teenage girls holding each other and crying. He was suddenly glad he'd killed the bandit leader instead of capturing him.

Logan hesitantly took a seat beside a young woman who would have been beautiful if not for the haunted look in her eyes… her eye. One of them was swollen shut, the whole side of her face black and blue. Her short-cut hair was matted with dirt and blood, her face and neck scratched and every exposed centimeter of flesh bruised and coated with dust. Beneath the blanket she clutched around her he thought he saw the remains of a Naval uniform. He tried not to stare, tried not to attract her attention. He wouldn't know what to say to her if she tried to talk to him.

And then she turned, looked at him. She didn't say anything for long moments, stared at his face, then at the blood-stained bandage on his arm.

"You got shot," she said, more of a statement than a question.

"Uh, yeah." He nodded.

"Who shot you?" There seemed to be genuine curiosity in her voice.

"'Nother mech pilot," he shrugged. "Turned out to be the head of this whole bunch of assholes."

"Did you kill him?"

"Yeah." He nodded. "Didn't have much choice."

"Good," she said, her voice ruthless.

Logan looked away from her eyes, uncomfortable with the abject hatred he saw there, noticed her arms shaking, her hands clutching tightly at the blanket around her.

"Hey, are you okay, miss?" he asked her, starting to bring a hand to her arm to support her, but halting it in mid-reach as he saw her flinch away. He awkwardly pulled back the hand, let it fall into his lap. "Sorry."

"You know," the woman said, fixing him with a stare cold and frightening enough to make him wish he was back in his mech, "you're the second person who's asked me that question tonight. I was a little less than polite to the first. Since I'm a bit calmer now, I'll try to be a little more civil. How to put this..." she trailed off thoughtfully, staring into space.

"Say you'd just graduated from the Military Academy on Nike. You're twenty-one years old and all you've ever wanted to do is fly assault shuttles. You don't care what your parents or your friends think about the military, you just want to fly. You're heading for your first assignment after one last awkward visit home with your pacifist father and your doctor mother and thinking that's the worst thing that could possibly happen to you." She cocked her head to the side, staring at him the way he might look at some weird insect on some far-off planet.

"Then you find yourself shut away in a closet, listening to innocent people being tortured to death, and feeling their pain with every scream, wanting it to be over for them but also *not* wanting it to end because you know when it does, you're next.

25

Unless you're 'lucky' enough for them to sell you as a slave on the open market instead, because if they're not going to kill you, there's only one other use they have for you."

A long, steadying breath, as if she were fighting back against something, a memory that wanted to take her over.

"And then, when you have the incredible fortune to actually be rescued, you have a man's brains blown into your face. After this series of events, would you, by any stretch of semantics, call yourself 'okay?'"

Logan's ears burned and he felt a hot flush in his face, his after-battle elation fading away to a kind of emptiness. He got to his feet, his stomach twisting.

"I'm sorry," he said helplessly, then turned, heading for the hangar's exit.

"What about your arm?" the woman asked.

"It's not important," he mumbled, not turning back.

It wasn't important at all.

The Vindicator towered over Logan a monster forged from metal so black it was nearly swallowed by the shadows of the darkened mech bay. The damage from days ago was gone, scraped down and patched and smoothed over as if it had never happened. Just like the bullet wound in his arm, nearly gone but for a small scar. Some damage, though, wasn't quite as easily repaired.

"Been a busy few days, Lieutenant."

The voice was casual, conversational, but it nearly made Logan Conner jump right out of his skin. It took every ounce of self-control he had not to spin around and go for his gun, or alternatively throw himself down into the shadows and cower like a dog beaten too much. Neither would have been a good idea with Captain Lyta Randell. Her shoulders were wide and strained against the seams of the regulation Ranger Corps utility fatigues, narrowing at the waist and then solidifying once more into legs as big around as his. She always went armed, but he knew she wouldn't need a weapon to take him down if she were of a mind.

"That it has, Captain," he responded as if Ranger officers stalking through darkened mech bays under acceleration were a normal operating procedure on the Spartan Guard warship *Manannan Mac Lyr*. "Lots of salvage, lot of repair, lots of civilians to babysit."

"Not just babysit either," she corrected. "The Dominions are going to need intelligence, and they're going to have to run through us to get it."

"Oh, I think Starkad has all the intelligence they need on this one, Captain," he said, unable to keep the bitterness out of his tone. His eyes darted back to the Vindicator. "After all, they fund these bandits, don't they?"

"There's no *actionable* evidence of the Starkad Supremacy's involvement in piracy." He didn't even need to be watching her to tell her tongue was planted firmly in her cheek. "As I'm sure your father has told you. Officially, this cluster of loose nutsacks is part of something called the 'Red Brotherhood,' but that's more of a loose association than a real paramilitary organization. Their 'boss' is somewhere out on the Periphery and has probably never heard of these jokers. All we could dig up on the one you shot was an old wanted notice from the Shang Directorate. His name was Peter Che back in the Directorate but I understand he'd taken to calling himself Captain Cai Quian."

He snorted softly but still didn't turn. The lines of the Vindicator drew his eyes to them, the gaping emitter of the plasma gun, its electromagnetic coils a spiral nautilus shell turned inside out, the jutting barrels of the Vulcan. Beside it, secured in their cradles for space transport, the Golems of the rest of his platoon stood stalwart, ready to support their leader.

"What good is all this," he blurted, giving voice to the thoughts plaguing him, keeping him awake most of the last three nights, "if we can't use it to keep our people safe? People like the crew of the *Atlas?*"

He'd thought she'd chew him out, disabuse him of the childish notion it was even possible to keep anyone safe anywhere in the Dominions, but when she replied, her voice was almost gentle, understanding.

"We did the best we could for them, Lieutenant... Logan. Most times, if a crew is taken by pirates, there *is* no just-in-time rescue."

"Not in time for the three men they killed," he shot back, being insubordinate and just not caring. "Not in time for the poor bastard they tortured nearly to death." His mouth worked silently and he felt bile rising in his throat. "Not in time for those two little girls, that pilot..."

If she objected to his tone, she gave no indication.

"We saved those people from horrible deaths, or from lives even worse than death."

"It's not enough!" Logan shook his head, his voice filled with the fierce conviction burning up from his gut. "We should have hunted down that bandit trash and all the others like them years ago. We should have gone after the governments that supply them! Instead, we fuck around with meaningless raids, fighting for worthless pieces of rock in battles that nobody really wins. We leave our troops garrisoned on the frontier, sitting on their asses in case the Jeuta decide to attack. And the whole time, bandits are chipping away at everything we try to build, slowly tearing down anything we have left from the Empire." He stopped, took a deep breath, his hands shaking.

"We all feel that way, Logan," she tried to put a comforting hand on his arm, "but..."

"No, Lyta!" He spun away from her hand, fists clenched, and

tried to bring himself back under control. "Sorry," he corrected himself. "Ma'am. I know we all feel that way, but no one else can do anything about it! Someday, I'm going to be brought before the Council and they're going to vote me Guardian in my father's stead, and I'm going to have all your lives in my hands. I'm going to have the power to actually do something. But I," he emphasized each word, "don't know what to do." He shrugged helplessly. "I see the face of this woman I talked to back in the hangar on Ramman, and all I can think is that I don't know what I could tell her I'd do to keep it from happening again."

"That woman's name," Lyta told him softly, "is Kathren Margolis. She told me about you. She feels bad about coming down on you so hard—she wants to talk to you. She wants to thank you for rescuing them."

"You and your Rangers rescued them, ma'am." He dismissed the words with a negligent wave of his hand.

"And how long do you think we could have lasted against nearly two full squads of light mecha, plus a fucking Scorpion?" Lyta Randell shook her head. "Katy's already seen the holo of that fight from your mech's mission recorder—everyone has." She smiled. "They're already comparing it to your father's fight in the coup."

"Oh, God," he sighed, shaking his head. "It wasn't that big a deal."

"Who do you think you're kidding, Kel?" She laughed. "Look, don't torture yourself. You've done all you can." She put a hand on his arm, and this time he didn't flinch away. "Maybe, someday, you'll be able to do more, do something to actually bring a change. I think you will. You're a lot like your father. But for now, you need to go talk to Katy. She's in the sick bay and she needs to see you."

"I..." he trailed off helplessly. "I wouldn't know what to say."

"Just be yourself." She squeezed his arm. "Trust me, she

needs this more than you do. She's a fighter, but she's going to need friends to get through the next few weeks."

"All right," he said, surrendering with a shrug. "I'll try."

"Don't underestimate yourself, Logan Conner," Lyta admonished him. "Let the enemy do that."

"I've got a lot to live up to," he admitted. She jabbed a finger at him.

"You believe this, Conner: a hundred years from now, when your oldest child takes the throne, they'll be worrying about living up to your legend, not your father's."

With that, she turned and left him alone in the dark, speechless.

Logan Conner had dined with diplomats and Generals, been dressed down by Colonels, and sent to his room without dinner by the head of a government, but he couldn't remember ever being quite as nervous as he was stepping into the *Manannan Mac Lyr*'s medical bay. He'd waited three hours and might not have come at all if Marc Langella hadn't kept bugging him about it.

"You know we're going to be at the jump point soon," the younger man had said, stretched out on his bunk, eyes closed. As junior officers, they shared one of the smallest class of cabins on the cruiser, which usually didn't bother him except for Langella's tendency to snore in free fall, but now... "We'll lose gravity when they cut thrust and then it'll be harder to get around."

Logan had glared at Langella with as much antipathy as he could collect into one expression, but the Sub-lieutenant had studiously ignored him, pretending to be "resting his eyes." In the end, he'd decided to go through with it in the hope the woman might be on a different sleep schedule and at least he'd have an honest excuse to give Captain Randell if she asked about it.

No such luck. The medical bay wasn't crowded; it was designed to treat hundreds, and there had only been a handful of survivors from the *Atlas*. They were scattered here and there amidst dozens of unoccupied beds, some lying down, some sitting up and a few shuffling back and forth to the head. The giveaway was the glow of the active sensor display above each bed, showing the vital signs of the person assigned to it until they were officially checked out. And they were all being kept to ship-time during the four-day burn to the next jump-point, so the lights were on and patients were being encouraged to stay awake and active until the official bedtime.

He found her sitting cross-legged at the foot of the sickbay bed, reading intently from one of the folding tablets you could get out of the data-docks in any compartment on the ship. The white, ankle-length hospital gown Kathren Margolis wore reminded Logan of the matrons of the Temple in the hills back home, a marked difference from the last time he'd seen her. It wasn't the only change.

Her hair was blond. He hadn't been able to tell before; it had been matted with dirt and dried blood. The bruises and scratches and gouges were gone, faded to a faint, yellow-tinted memory after three days of treatment, and the zombie vacancy was gone from her eyes as well. Scrubbed clean, she could have been a university student… or a young officer, which was, he reminded himself, what she was.

She glanced up from the tablet as he approached , and she smiled.

God, she has a beautiful smile.

"Hi," he said, waving in lieu of offering a hand, remembering the way she'd reacted the last time he'd come anywhere near her. "How is… everything?"

"I'm feeling much better, Lieutenant," she told him, setting down the tablet, unfolding her legs and letting them dangle over the side of the bed. She was short, he realized, maybe four centimeters shorter than his meter-nine. "Or should I say, my lord?"

He winced at that. Sparta didn't have primogenitor, but being the son of the Guardian of the most powerful of the Dominions brought with it a position of its own, and far too many expectations, which was why he tried not to spread his parentage around his unit.

"You can just call me Logan," he assured her. "Lyta… Captain Randell, that is, said you wanted to talk to me."

"Sit down," she told him, patting the edge of the bed.

"Okay." Logan slowly and hesitantly sat so near the edge of the bed he was mostly leaning, as far away from her as he could get. His fingers drummed on his thigh and his eyes flickered toward and then away from her.

"I wanted to apologize for what I said back at the hangar."

"You've got nothing to be sorry for," he insisted, shaking his head. "After… what happened, you had every right to react the way you did. I was an idiot and I'm the one who should be sorry."

"I should have been thanking you, not lashing out at you. You saved all our lives."

"Captain Randell and her Rangers saved your life." He tried not to snap the words.

"She did," Kathren agreed. "But if you hadn't taken out that Scorpion, it would have circled back and caught us at the hangar with nothing but a few ground troops."

He was about to argue that Colonel Anders had stayed back with the command group, but he realized she was right; he'd read in the After-Action Review that the Colonel had fallen back to the landing zone to cover the cargo shuttles once he'd heard the Rangers had taken the compound. There would have been no armor at all guarding the ground troops and survivors.

He opened his mouth, shut it.

"I don't know what to say, Sub-lieutenant Margolis."

"You could call me Katy," she suggested, covering his hand with one of hers. "And you could say 'you're welcome.'"

He felt heat rising to his face.

"You're welcome."

She moved the hand away and he breathed again.

"Captain Randell was telling me," Katy went on as if she hadn't noticed his reaction, "you don't think Sparta is doing enough to interdict the bandits."

He scowled, suddenly feeling his earlier depression returning.

"You've seen it first-hand." He waved a hand around as if they were back in the pirate base. "You saw the arms, the ships, the equipment they were able to build up right under our noses. And this is just one, small sliver of a larger network of bandits and pirates and black marketeers who slip into any system the military is too busy to patrol."

"But you came." She shook her head. "You rescued us."

"It was just luck," Logan nearly spat the words out. "We were rotating back from a stretch on the frontier and we jumped into the transition system just about twenty hours after the bandits hit your ship. We could see them heading for the mid-system jump-point, but we were thirty-six hours behind. If not for that coincidence..."

"Thank Mithra for coincidences," she said softly, looking down as if she could see the future that might have been somewhere on the deck below.

"Those scum should've been hunted down months or even years ago, but we're so busy fighting each other and worrying about invasions from the Jeuta Confederation that we haven't the time or the troops to do it."

"So, what's the answer, Lord Guardian?" Her words weren't quite mocking, but they were a challenge, and he couldn't help but grin at the spirit behind them.

"The Dominions have to be united again," he declared without hesitation. "It's the only way we'll have the forces to guard against the Jeuta and hunt down the bandits at the same time."

She smiled, cocked an eyebrow. "I assume that sounds simpler than it is."

"If it wasn't, someone would have done it already. Hell, it's hard enough to keep our own Guardianship together. Political approaches are hopeless." He shook his head. "None of us trusts the others—we've all used pirates against each other in the past, although my father ended that practice for Sparta once he took power. And getting any two of the Dominions to agree to the speed of light is next to impossible.

"That leaves military conquest; but a lot of our troops are tied up on the frontier. Any major redeployment would be noticed and we'd be attacked. If we tried to build new machines... well, war materials and production facilities are severely limited and heavily spied upon. If we start punching out new mecha and ships too fast, we're sabotaged or attacked." Logan sighed heavily, shoulders sagging.

"Add to that," he went on, "the fact that all the established and mapped jump-points in the settled Dominion systems are pretty heavily patrolled, and it makes conquest nearly impossible."

"Secret facilities?" Katy suggested.

"I've thought of that," Logan admitted. "But if it would work, wouldn't someone have done it already?" He ran a hand through his hair. He normally kept it a close buzz, but it had grown out over the course of this patrol and he needed to get it cut. "Maybe I should talk this over with my father."

"I've always thought the Guardian was a very wise man," Katy replied with what seemed like carefully chosen words. "He seems to be genuinely concerned about the well-being of his people. But he's a man who's fought his battles."

"What do you mean?" Logan frowned at the unspoken implication.

"He's fought his war, won his throne." Katy shrugged. "He may be content with the accomplishments he's already achieved. Maybe what's needed is a new approach."

"I don't know what I could come up with that he hasn't already."

"Give it time. You're still young. I'm sure your father didn't dream up a way to take back the throne till he was a few days older than you."

Logan laughed, loud and hard. He knew people were looking at him from around the medical bay, but he didn't care.

"You know, Sub-lieutenant Margolis," he said, surprising himself with his own frankness, "I don't think I've met anyone quite like you."

"Call me Katy, Logan," she reminded him. "And considering the company you keep, I'll take that as quite the compliment."

"Is there anything you need? Anything I can do for you?"

She let out a breath, and with it the brash confidence he'd found so amazing.

"I don't know what's going to happen now," she admitted, staring into space as she gave voice to fears he was sure she hadn't wanted to admit. "I know they won't just let me report for my assignment on Sparta without psychological and emotional evaluation, and Mithra alone knows how long that will take." She met his gaze again. "I don't know anyone in Argos."

"I'd be happy to show you around the city," he volunteered. "Assuming I don't get sent out on another patrol right away."

"That'd be nice, but..." She glanced around her, eyeing the duty nurse carefully. The older man seemed suspicious, as if he'd already had to deal with trouble from Katy before. "I'd really love just to get out of this damned room."

"Give me an hour," he said, sliding off the edge of the bunk and holding up a hand, half a plea to wait, half an oath he was taking. "I've got just the place."

"But why won't you tell me where we're going?" Katy insisted, following Logan through corridors nearly jammed with ship's crewmen rushing to their jump stations.

He was preoccupied with the intricacies of weaving through the crowd, but he risked a glance back. She looked out of place in the utility fatigues he'd had fabricated to replace her hospital gown, though he couldn't say why. The clothes had been easy; talking the *Manannan Mac* Lyr's chief medical officer into letting him take her out of the sickbay, even for just an hour, had been several degrees more difficult. In the end, Logan had convinced the man it would do her good psychologically to get out of the sterile surroundings of the medical bay for a while. Dr. Severeid knew who his father was, and Logan glumly acknowledged that fact probably had held more sway than his arguments.

"It's a surprise," he repeated for about the fifth time since he'd led her out of the medical ward. "If I told you, it wouldn't be a surprise."

He led her through a corridor marked "Authorized Personnel Only," seeing the worried look in her eyes as passing crewman stared at them. At the end of the passageway was a set of double-doors, a red warning light blinking forebodingly on their security lock. Logan tapped a code in on the numeric keypad and the light flashed green, the doors hissing apart automatically. Beyond them was his favorite compartment on the ship… on *any* ship.

"Wow," Katy gasped quietly. "I've never been on the Observation Deck of a cruiser before."

"Most people haven't." He hit the control to shut the hatch

behind them and it seemed as if they shut the rest of the universe off as well.

Nearly every centimeter of any military ship was thickly armored behind centimeters of BiPhase Carbide, nickel iron, honeycomb boron or whatever the builders and buyers could afford, against man-made threats like lasers and railguns as well as more natural dangers such as cosmic rays and solar flares. But there was always the possibility of instrument failure, and in that event, there needed to be *somewhere* you could physically go out and look at the stars. At least that was the excuse they used; Logan suspected it was a perk Captains and Admirals enjoyed, a place where they could be alone with the stars and shut out everyone else.

Or, in this case, the perk of the son of the Guardian.

"Rank hath its privileges," he expanded, his own voice sounding distracted in his ears.

The Observation Deck of the *Manannan Mac Lyr* was a bubble of transparent aluminum positioned just above the forward hangar deck, nothing above it, nothing ahead, nothing at all to block the view. He'd seen the stars from uninhabited planets, with no light pollution to block them out, high in the mountains where the air was thin, and this was *still* better. You couldn't find a blank patch of space to stare at; just when you thought you had, your eyes would adjust and there'd be more stars. You'd see what you thought was stark blackness in your peripheral vision and you'd turn and hunt for it, but that would be full of stars, too.

He almost let himself be hypnotized by the view, let it take his mind out of the present and set it adrift in the universe... and then he felt warmth and pressure against his right side and realized Katy was leaning into him, maybe to keep her balance while she stared at the stars, and maybe not. He looked away from the universe and into her face and couldn't decide which was more beautiful.

The whooping of an alarm klaxon snapped him back to reality and started him breathing again. He could see her blue eyes refocusing, looking into his.

"That's the jump warning," she said. "Shouldn't we get out of here?"

"That's why we have the boots," he told her, clicking the heels of his ship-boots together to activate the magnets in the heels.

There was just the subtlest hint of connection to the metal deck-plates to let him know they were working; he noted hers were active too, and just in time. His stomach flipped and twisted at the sudden absence of acceleration-as-gravity and only the magnets in his heels were holding him down to the deck. The free fall didn't seem to bother Katy, but then it wouldn't; she was a pilot.

"We're going to watch the jump from here?" It was half a question, half a hopeful statement. She smiled broadly. "I've always had to be strapped into my berth in my cabin."

"My father," Logan said, for once not feeling the little tinge of resentment he usually did when he thought of the side-effects of being the Guardian's son, "brought me up to the Observation Deck the very first time I went with him and Mom on a starship. I try to get up here once every trip since then."

"Prepare for jump in ten," an automated voice announced over unseen speakers. "Nine, eight..."

Katy grabbed his hand, squeezing it tight. Her grip was firm, warm, certain. He wanted to meet her eyes, but he felt as if he'd be somehow breaking a spell. He lost track of the countdown, stopped paying attention, so when the jump came, it took him by surprise. Somewhere deep inside the ship, wrapped around the fusion reactor core like some parasitic worm, a giant spiral of superconductive wire was woven into a capacitor larger than most shuttles, larger than some in-system freighters. It took hours to charge, but it discharged in less than a second, venting its energy through the Kadish-Dean field generator, visible as a faint blue halo of Cherenkov radiation at the nose of the ship.

Space ripped, torn apart at a weak spot, a jump-point mapped out and recorded a thousand years ago, and through that hole, he caught the briefest glimpse of another universe.

"Oh!" Katy exclaimed, the same way he had the very first time he'd seen it. And then, "Damn!" which he'd also said, and gotten his ear boxed by his mother for swearing.

And then they were through and the stars reappeared, different stars in the midst of a different system, six light years away from the one they'd just left.

"It's…" Katy stumbled over the words. "It was…" He glanced away from the new starfield and saw the consternation on her face. "It's like I knew it was there, I could see what it was, but I can't remember it now. It makes no sense."

"It's always that way," he agreed, trying to sound sympathetic. "But you never get enough of trying." He laughed softly. "It's like a drug. You always think the next time is the time you'll understand, the time you'll be able to wrap your brain around it. I never get tired of it."

The klaxon sounded again, this time warning of the return of thrust, and Logan sighed softly, knowing it was time. One gravity of acceleration returned beneath the faint rumble of the fusion drive igniting, and with it the perception of gravity.

"I have a meeting with Colonel Anders in a half an hour," he told Katy. "And Doc Severeid'll tear me a new one if I don't get you back soon, anyway."

"I understand," she said, though he could hear just a touch of disappointment in her voice. She let her hand slip out of his, turning back to the hatchway out of the compartment. She paused and looked over her shoulder at him. "Thanks for showing me this." Her jaw worked, her eyes retreating inward for a moment as if they'd caught a glimpse of an unwelcome memory. "It's nice to see something beautiful after…"

"Katy," he told her, his guts churning as if they'd slipped back into free-fall, "I don't have to look out the window to see the beauty in here."

It was a huge risk and he was probably an idiot to take it. She was still recovering from a horrific experience, she'd had her whole life ripped apart. This wasn't the time to be…

She kissed him on the cheek, the corner of her mouth turning up at his obvious insecurity.

"Come see me on Sparta," she said, heading for the hatchway. A glance backward at him, those blue eyes he'd seen so cold before suddenly glowing warm. "Promise."

She was gone, but he was still nodding.

"I promise."

3

Argos was a gleaming jewel in the mid-morning light, its bleached white spires painfully dazzling beneath the cloudless sky. Logan Conner slipped on a pair of sunglasses as he clambered out of the car, grabbing his bags out of the back seat and resisting an instinct to pay the driver; the man was an employee of the Guardianship government, sent by his father or, more likely, one of his father's many aides to pick him up at the spaceport. Tipping him would be seen as an insult.

He nodded to the short, thick-necked man who'd taken him to the palace, offering a hand through the open driver's-side window of the limo.

"Thanks for the ride, Victor," he said, noting the surprise on the man's face at Logan remembering his name. It was something his father had taught him, though he was sure the old man did it to engender personal loyalty; he just did it because it made people happy when someone important remembered their name.

His duffle bag was light, another trick he'd learned long ago, though not from his father. He'd known Colonel Anders since he was a teenager and Anders had been a Captain and a favorite of the Guardian even then. Soldiers traveled light, Anders had told him. *Things* dragged you down, tied you to one place. He shouldered the bag and began walking up the steps to the palace.

He heard the chime of his 'link before he'd taken two steps, and stopped to check the message rather than trying to walk and read because he might wind up blowing past a General and getting an earful. The message "from" label was a stream of random numbers, indicating the 'link messaging him was unassigned, a free unit picked up at a public terminal.

It's Katy. Got orders. On psychological leave for two weeks, pending evaluation. Assigned quarters at Outpatient Center at Naval Medical Center. I hate hospitals.

He frowned, tucking the 'link away. He'd answer her later; he didn't want to stand too long in the middle of the square. It wasn't busy today; he tried to remember if it was a holiday but nothing came to mind. There were a couple dozen people flowing back and forth, some in civilian clothes but a few in uniform. He eyed them carefully, trying to determine whether he'd have to salute them, but they were NCOs, probably clerks to the brass running their daily errands. A couple of them stopped to salute *him* and he dutifully returned the motion, fist going to his chest.

At least none of them recognize me.

Saluting was part of his job; the bows were not.

The guards at the front gate knew him, though. They always did. Their ceremonial armor dazzled in the sun and he was glad he hadn't yet taken off his sunglasses. There was a double line of them, angled in toward the doorway, and if their armor was for show, their weapons were for go. They came to attention as he approached, their rifles going to port arms as their leader brought a fist to his chest, then bowed at the waist.

"Lord Guardian," the Captain said respectfully.

Logan fought against the frown trying to make its way across his face, not wanting to give the man the idea he disapproved of his uniform or his greeting. What he disapproved of was the idea of a Captain saluting him, a Lieutenant. He rebelled in his own, small way by coming to attention and returning the salute crisply, as was appropriate to greet a superior officer. He had to release it first, though; otherwise, the Captain would have stood there until hell froze over.

The sunglasses came off, secured in a thigh pocket of his mottled green-and-grey utility fatigues as he passed under the Arch of the Restoration, which served as both the entranceway to the Palace and a work of art commemorating Jaimie Brannigan's victory over his cousin Declan Lambert and the faction of the Sparta Guard under the rebel's command. The figures were carved into the stone archway by hand, stylized into creatures of myth with wild, flowing hair tossing in the wind and eyes wide with battle madness.

Dad hated the damn thing, but Mother had commissioned it before she died and he refused to have it torn down.

Beyond the arch, the artwork became less commemorative and more decorative, also a legacy of his mother. The world might be called Sparta, but Maggie Conner had insisted the atmosphere of the house where *she* lived was not going to be Spartan. His favorite was a five-meter tall bronze copy of Michelangelo's "David" standing like a silent sentry at the mouth of the hallway to the sections of the palace closed off to casual visitors and tourists, the part where the actual work was done.

He paused for a moment beside a tour group of school children and listened to their teacher describing the provenance of the piece and the history of the original.

"...was originally commissioned as one of a series of statues of Biblical figures," the young woman was reciting to the group of what he judged to be ten-year-olds, "meant to be positioned along the roofline of the cathedral at Florence, a city-state on Old Earth. Instead, it was placed in a public square outside the government palace in the year 1504 CE in the calendar of the

time, what we would call year 2686 of the Pre-Imperial period."
The woman smiled with a touch of sadness he thought she might
actually feel. "Of course, the original was lost in the Final War
and the great exodus of year 367 Pre-Imperial..."

He left them, dragged down himself by the loss despite the
centuries gone by. Old Earth was a distant memory, even its location lost to the years and he wondered sometimes if they were a
different species now than they'd been before they left it.

Another set of guards were stationed only a few meters past
David, flanking a biometric security scanner, but there was
nothing ceremonial about these men and women. Their armor was
functional and camouflaged and their weapons were always held
at the ready. He knew they were just the *visible* deterrent to
anyone who might choose to trespass in a restricted area.

They knew him as well, but they said nothing, faces concealed
behind visors as if they were the war robots of lurid science
fiction. They watched him just as closely as they did any minor,
anonymous functionary, weapons tensed until a scan of his retina
proved he was the same Lt. Conner his name tape advertised.
Only then was he waved through, and he supposed the whole
spectacle was intimidating to the school children watching from
the shadow of Michelangelo's masterpiece, but to him it was just
an annoyance.

Beyond the checkpoint, he took a branch to the left and the
well-appointed dress suits of the government service began to
outnumber the military uniforms, the quality and expense of their
wardrobes climbing higher the closer he came to the offices of the
Guardian. Conversely, the decoration seemed to become sparser
and plainer as he approached his father's chambers. The man had
little use for frivolities, and if he kept the art his late wife had
favored out in public, he made no such effort in the spaces where
he worked.

His private offices could have been the workspace of the city comptroller for all the pomp and circumstance surrounding it. The doors were polished oak, but unadorned with as much as the family crest, and the single receptionist sat at a desk about as large as his own back in the platoon area of Guard Headquarters.

Where I need to be in two hours, he reminded himself, *son of the Guardian or not.*

"Good morning, Lt. Conner," the receptionist piped up with bland cheerfulness. Logan had known the little man for years and still wasn't sure if his upbeat attitude was his real personality or an act he put on. "Your father is with General Constantine, but he said to send you in when you arrived." He motioned behind his desk where his one affectation, a leafy potted fern squatted forlornly. "You can leave you things here."

"Thanks, Phillip."

He dropped his bag behind the desk, returned the smile, whether it was genuine or not, and pushed the door open almost simultaneous with the audible click of the electromagnetic locks disengaging. The door did *not* squeak, didn't make a sound, either because of the impeccable maintenance in the palace or perhaps because it was afraid to disturb *the* Jaimie Brannigan in his den.

General Nicolai Constantine was a dangerous-looking man. He was tall, even sprawled out in the comfortable-looking chair across the desk, with the look of a coiled snake or a crouching cat ready to spring. He was in a dress uniform, which Logan really should have taken the time to change into, pressed and starched until every tan crease seemed a razor suitable for slashing throats. His face might have been put through the same laundering process, all hard, straight edges and harsh lines. Eyes as dark as a taxman's heart stared out from thick, black brows and someone who didn't know the General might have mistaken the natural intensity of his gaze with a murderous turn of mood. Logan had known him long enough to recognize it for boredom.

"Thank God you're here, boy," Constantine murmured,

waving a hand. "If I had to go over production numbers for Navy fusion thrusters one more time…"

"Good morning, General," he said with a respectful nod. Training made him want to come to attention and salute the man, but you couldn't do that when the other man in the room was the Guardian of Sparta himself.

"Son!" Jaimie Brannigan exploded with the joyful exuberance of a grizzly bear finding an elk carcass. He rose from his leather office chair and kept on rising.

The Guardian was a giant of a man, half a head taller than Logan and Mithra alone knew where *those* genes had gone because neither Logan nor his younger brother even approached their father's height, nor his width, nor his breadth. He seemed the sort of man who *should* have the wild, free-flowing mane of hair the artists tended to give him, but in reality, he was a soldier and a mech pilot and had always kept his hair regulation even after he'd made the transition from military officer to civil leader. He still wore a uniform of sorts, though not the one he'd worn when he'd piloted his Sentinel against Declan Lambert's Titan on the steps of the palace thirty years ago.

Jaimie Brannigan swept his son into an embrace strong enough to make Logan's ribs creak. The younger man did his best to return it, knowing he'd never be able to no matter how many hours he spent in the gym.

"I saw you take out that Scorpion, boy!" Brannigan enthused, holding Logan out at arm's length as if he were still a five-year-old. His father's face was always ruddy and flushed even at rest, and seemed positively inflamed at that moment. "God *damn*, that was a hell of a move, using your jump-jets that way!"

"It was smart," Constantine acknowledged with a diffident shrug. "This bandit trash, though, they have no discipline, no tactics, all brute force because they're usually fighting local militias with little to no armor." He raised a hand to forestall Brannigan's protest. "It was impressive to take out a strike mech one-on-one with a Vindicator, no mistake and nothing taken from your son, my Lord Guardian." He shrugged again, as if there were no other expression to convey his point. "I am only saying if *I* had been in that Scorpion, things would have turned out differently."

"I hope never to have to face you anywhere but the training simulators, sir," Logan told him, realizing he actually felt grateful at the General downplaying the fight. He'd been firmly convinced everyone was making too much of it.

"Not to imply I'm not happy as hell to see you, son," Brannigan said, big, meaty hand still resting on Logan's right shoulder, "but you don't usually run straight to the palace after a patrol without even reporting back to base first. Is something wrong?"

"Sort of," he admitted, falling into an "at ease" position automatically. "I kind of had a, well…" He hunted for the right words. "A policy question to ask you. For the future, you know."

"You mean when you're sitting behind this desk someday," his father deduced with his usual canny intuition. He cocked an eyebrow at Logan. "Don't make any assumptions, boy. Just because you're my son doesn't mean the Council will automatically choose you to succeed me when the time comes. Military experience is fine, for a start, but eventually, you're going to have to dip your toe into the politics of this game."

Which was all a load of bullshit, and they both knew it. His father had never spent one second worrying about politics prior to the coup, and the Council had picked him to take over from his late father because he was the man who'd stopped the Lamberts from seizing the government. If Jaimie Brannigan was still breathing and gave up the Guardianship willingly, it would damn well go to the successor he hand-picked.

"Yes, sir," Logan said anyway, because arguing with his father was about as useful as head-butting a bighorn sheep. "That's sort of what I'd like to talk about, the politics of it."

"Well, then, pop a squat, lad!" Brannigan motioned to the chair beside General Constantine and fell heavily back into his own seat, the ancient office chair groaning in protest as it nearly wilted under his bulk. "Tell your father what's on your mind."

He hesitated, trying to come up with a way of putting his feelings into words without making it seem like an emotional appeal. His eyes darted around the office, as if there were some clue to how he should proceed concealed on the mostly-bare wood panel walls. His mother's picture was the only personal item in the whole office, a video clip of the four of them—Mom, Dad, Terrin and him—together in one of the nature parks outside Argos, along with the German Shepherd they'd once had until it came out on the wrong side of a debate with a cougar. In the video, Mom was laughing, leaning into Dad's shoulder while he and Terrin wrestled in the dirt and the dog barked ceaselessly at the two of them as if scolding them to stop.

Be strong, Logan. He heard the words in her voice, the adjuration she'd given him before she'd gone out with her husband to do battle for their world with the Lambert usurpers. She'd been a scientist, a researcher, but there'd been no special mercy for civilians in that battle and she'd left them in a bunker with their nanny and gone off with a rifle in her hand.

She'd never returned. Logan had taken her last name when he joined the military, partially as a precaution to prevent special treatment by those seeking to curry favor with the Guardian, and partially to honor her sacrifice.

"It's the bandits, sir," he plunged into a murky pool with no idea how far down the bottom might be. "This Red Brotherhood we keep running into. We've got to do something about them. Something besides stumbling onto them by luck," he amended, just in case either of the men got it into their head to point out the battle from which he'd just returned. "Ramman, that base we raided, that was right on the edge of our settled territory and we didn't even know it was there."

"I agree in principle," General Constantine put in, "but we barely have enough ships to patrol the jump-points in our core worlds. How would you propose we monitor every barely-habitable rock between the Shang Directorate and Jeuta space?"

"I've been thinking about that," Logan said, pulling out the ideas he'd been kicking around in the long days of transit between jump-points. "I was thinking automated drones, like the kind our warships launch into systems to gather intelligence."

"That still doesn't solve the problem of not enough ships, Logan," his father objected. "Someone has to launch the drones and monitor them."

"Yes, Father," he went on, grinning at his own cleverness. "That's the thing; I was thinking we build a few automated ships, just a fusion reactor and a Kadish-Dean jump drive and some communications gear, and let them drift dark and cold in the border systems. We launch drones to all the mapped jump-points in the systems, and if they catch a bandit or a Jeuta raider, they transmit to the automated starships and then the ships jump to the next system over and transmit to the nearest Spartan warship."

Jaimie Brannigan shared a grin with Nicolai Constantine and Logan felt a sudden anger burning inside his chest. Were they dismissing his idea so easily?

"Son," Brannigan said, not with the mocking tone he'd expected but with a gentleness, "that's a very well thought out plan, but there's only one problem."

"Money," Constantine supplied, his voice laden down with cynicism. "You think you're the first bright boy to ever think that up? The problem is, building that many Kadish-Dean drives takes money." He shrugged. "Money we could spare, if it would work, but not money that would go unnoticed."

"Starkad has spies in our government, Logan," his father said.

"We try to root them out, but it's damn near impossible to find them all. If we were to divert funds to a project such as the one you suggested, it would be picked up on and Starkad would act against us, sending mercenaries to attack our production facilities, fomenting political unrest amidst our rivals, or simply waiting until we put the unmanned starships in place and then sabotaging them."

"So, we just give up?" Logan demanded, half-rising from his seat. "We let the Red Brotherhood rob and pillage and kill and rape unchecked? Why can't we farm this out, have every one of the Dominions except Starkad go along with it? If we isolate them like that, they'll be vulnerable to diplomatic pressure."

"Or they'll become even more openly aggressive," Constantine countered. "And in that case, this little cold war we've been dancing around between the Guardianship of Sparta and the Starkad Supremacy will become damn hot, damn quick."

"We aren't ignoring this problem," his father assured him. "It's just something without a simple solution. We keep putting pressure on the rest of the Dominions to crack down on the bandits using their own forces. It's not perfect, but it will, eventually, put the squeeze on the bandit armies without forcing Starkad into a corner." Logan was about to explode again at the idea, at how it wouldn't work fast enough and people would die, but his father forestalled it with a raised hand. "I know. I know it's not right, and it's not fair, and it's not fast enough. But these are the sorts of realities you'll have to deal with when you have this job."

Logan let his head hang for just a moment, the energy gone out of him.

"Yes, sir," was all he could think of to say that wouldn't get him in trouble. He pushed to his feet. "I need to get back to Laconia, sir. I'm supposed to report to Colonel Anders for the new training schedule rotation in an hour or so."

His father rose and grasped his shoulder, squeezing with what passed for gentleness from hands capable of crushing a man's skull.

"Don't lose heart, son. We'll get those bastards. It's just going to take some time."

Logan saluted and left the room, ears burning from the anger he couldn't show, blowing past Phillip, pausing only to grab his duffle bag before he stormed back out into the corridor... and nearly ran headlong into his younger brother.

"Whoa, what's the hurry, Logan?" Terrin stopped his blind bull-charge with a slender hand on his arm.

Terrin Brannigan was his opposite in many ways, thinner, slightly taller, with dark hair worn long and tied into a ponytail, but he knew you could see the clear resemblance in the cut of his chin, the high cheekbones they shared. The eyes, though, were the biggest difference. Terrin had a softness to his grey eyes, a reflection of a deeper softness Logan had once despised.

"I have to get back to base," he grunted realizing he was taking his frustration out on his brother but too pissed off to care. "If you're looking for Dad, he's in his office with General Constantine."

"I was looking for you," Terrin said, a tinge of hurt feelings in his tone. "I heard you were in, and one of Dad's aides told me you were coming to the palace."

"Sorry." He wasn't, but he also didn't have time for an argument with his brother. "What's up?"

"I'm going to be spending a few weeks up at the observatory with Dr. Kovalev," Terrin explained. "I thought you might want to get together for dinner tonight if you don't have duty."

Logan was ready to blow Terrin off automatically. He wasn't in the mood for small talk now and doubted he would be this evening. The two of them had very little in common. Terrin would drone on about astrophysics and wouldn't give a shit about Logan's war stories, and it would wind up being either boring or contentious… and then he thought about the message from Katy. She wanted to see the city, she wanted out of the hospital, and Terrin wanted to spend time with him for some damned reason.

"Sure," he said, and there might have been surprise in Terrin's smile. "As long as you wouldn't mind if I brought a friend along."

4

"I did say I wanted to see the city," Kathren Margolis admitted, laughing softly. He liked to hear her laugh. She'd managed to have some civilian clothes fabricated somewhere, a simple but tasteful white *chiton*, knee-length and sleeveless and it was difficult for Logan to take his eyes off of her.

She leaned forward in her chair, elbows on the table, and stared down at the lights of Argos spread out in the darkness of the Treska River Valley, a mirror of the starscape above, separated by a faint, glowing haze on the horizon. A chill wind tugged a strand of hair across her eyes, warring with the warming blast of the heaters beside their table for supremacy on the restaurant's covered patio.

"You get a really good view from up here," Logan Conner admitted, taking a sip of his drink. Just wine tonight; he didn't drink hard liquor on a date. He'd been told it brought out the asshole in him.

"I didn't even know there *was* a restaurant this far up Mt. Erebus," Terrin said a bit too loudly, just reminding Logan he was there. A mischievous grin curled the corner of his mouth, but he quickly hid the expression behind a water glass. "Then again, Logan has never taken me along on a date before."

"It's just dinner, *Terry*," he fired back, enjoying the way his brother's eyes bugged out when he called him by the hated nickname. "You said you wanted to hang out before you went to the observatory."

"Are you an astronomer, Terry?" Kathren asked him.

"I prefer Terrin and I'm an astrophysicist." He shrugged. "Among other things."

"Terrin Brannigan," Logan informed her in a tone of affected gravity, "has doctorates in astrophysics and nuclear physics, and is working on a third in hyper-dimensional physics. He's the brains of the family and he'll never let us forget it."

"Not everyone wants to spend their life bouncing around from one backwater to another, getting shot at." Terrin was trying to hold back a smirk and doing badly at it. "Some of us want to actually accomplish something."

"Did I mention I'm a Navy pilot?" Kathren asked, batting her eyes innocently.

Logan nearly spat out a mouthful of wine and Terrin began gabbling an awkward apology, rescued only by the arrival of the servers. In the cheaper places in downtown Argos, they might get away with using tabletop kiosks for ordering and server bots to bring your food, but in the *Estatorio Erebus*, they still used human waiters and servers and the manager still stopped by your table to ask how everything tasted.

That's why it costs so damn much to eat here. And why it takes three weeks' notice to get a reservation—unless you're the Guardian's son.

He didn't like trading on his father's name, but when he was trying to impress a girl…

"This is excellent," Kathren enthused after her first taste of the lamb. She had a sudden, stricken expression as if she were about to choke on the bite. "I don't know if my military pay account has been activated here yet."

"I got it," Logan assured her, waving it off, as if what was going to be a significant chunk of his next paycheck was no big deal. He grinned broadly. "You can pay for mine next time."

"Awesome!" Terrin enthused, leaning forward between them on the table. "When are the three of us getting together again?"

Now it was Kathren's turn to laugh around an extra-large bite of lamb, covering her mouth to keep it from spraying across the table, and Logan's ears began to heat up, whether with anger or embarrassment he wasn't sure.

"I thought you were heading up Bloodmark Mountain to the observatory for three fun weeks listening to interstellar radio signals or something," Logan reminded him, stabbing at his own meal with a bit more force than was required.

"It's a radio telescope?" Kathren asked him, brow scrunching in confusion. "In the mountains? Wouldn't that be a better place for an optical telescope?"

"Bloodmark *is* an optical telescope," he explained, casting an irritated glance at his brother for messing up the terminology, "but it's also got a link to the radio telescopes in orbit and on Hecate's far side." He shook both the irritation and the explanation off with a motion like a dog shaking water off its fur. "Anyway, we're cataloging man-made signals from the Dead Worlds, the old imperial center, in order to exclude them from future stellar surveys." He shrugged. "It's not sexy or ground-breaking, but it's necessary and everyone has to take their turn."

"You got a scientist girlfriend up there?" Logan asked him, a little bit teasing but also a little bit curious. His brother wasn't exactly a monk, but you could count the number of girlfriends he'd had on one hand and still have enough fingers to signal you were "okay." "Maybe one of those graduate students?"

"I'm researching a doctoral thesis," Terrin said, waving a hand dismissively. "I don't have time for a relationship."

"Hell, you've been working on one doctoral thesis or another since you were nineteen. You're about to turn twenty-five. By the time you manage to squeeze in a relationship, you'll be the weird, old professor all the kids hate to get for physics class at the university."

"Yeah and what about you? You going to give up being a mechjock to settle down, raise a family, get into politics?"

"Someday," he allowed, perhaps a little defensively, eyes flickering toward Katy. She was observing the interplay with what seemed like amused fascination. "I mean, you can't drive a mech forever. Even Colonel Anders is getting near the time-in-grade where Dad is going to force him to ride a desk."

"So, not forever, just for the next twenty years or so, then?" He was openly mocking now, reverting to an adolescent, nasal whine Logan hadn't heard from him since he'd left for the Academy. "And you think a warrior monk is any better than a scholar monk?"

"I think the scenery's better," he shot back, giving in to the anger and frustration of dealing with a smartass younger brother instead of rising above it the way the voice of reason in the back of his mind told him to. "I think one of these days, you're going to wake up and find out half your life is over and you haven't bothered to live it."

"And killing people is such a great way to live your life, Logan?" There was a flare behind Terrin's eyes, the same old sign that Logan had finally pushed a bit too far. "You think if you kill enough, it's going to be revenge for Mom?"

Red floated over Logan's vision and before he realized what he was doing, he was pushing up from his seat, the bottoms of the wooden chair legs scraping loudly against the hardwood floor.

"Food's getting cold, boys." Kathren's words were casual, but there was an edge to them, a gentle scolding not unlike the tone his mother had used when he and Terrin were at each other's throats.

He blinked, realized what he'd been about to do and settled back into his chair, still glaring at Terrin. He half-expected his brother to be smiling in satisfaction at pushing just the right button at just the right time; instead, Terrin's face was still screwed up in his own steaming funk.

And maybe he's right to be angry. I invited him along on what was basically a date just to avoid having to really talk to him. He hissed out a breath. *Shit. I really hate having to say…*

"I'm sorry," he said it anyway. He set down the fork he hadn't realized he was still holding, the metal clinking against the porcelain of his dish, an untouched morsel of lamb still speared on the tines. "I'm sorry I lost my temper in front of you, Kathren and…" This part was harder. "I'm sorry I was giving you shit, Terrin. Dad and I are both really proud of you and what you've accomplished. I know Mom would be, too. You've turned out exactly the way she hoped you would, Dad says it all the time."

Terrin nodded, pushing the hair back out of his face.

"I'm sorry, too," he said, voice and expression both calming. "I shouldn't have said what I did about Mom." He looked over at Kathren, guilt written across his face. "I'm sorry, Kathren. I hope we didn't ruin dinner for you."

She took another bite of lamb and chewed it well before answering.

"Terrin, my father is a cleric of the Old Way, a devout pacifist, and my mother is a medical missionary. And I have been wanting to fly military aerospacecraft since I was three, so if there's one thing I am used to, it's arguments at the dinner table…"

⊕

Kathren Margolis thrilled at the feel of flying.

Sure, it was just a hopper, a ducted-fan helicopter, and she'd only flown them back to the city from the restaurant parking area on Mt. Erebus, barely thirty kilometers. But it was still flying; she hadn't flown anything, not even a simulator in weeks, since before she'd made that last, ill-fated trip home.

She ignored the flashing warning about the altitude and the on-board computer imploring her to allow it to autopilot the craft the rest of the way down. She caressed the controls like the skin of a lover, guiding it to a soft and satisfying climax, the wheels touching down gently.

Wouldn't have spilled the copilot's coffee, she thought with a rush of satisfaction. If she'd had a copilot and if anyone in the hopper had been drinking coffee.

"Thank you for flying the Spartan Navy spacelines," she murmured the old joke, hitting the control to raise the canopy. "Be sure to use us for all your transportation needs."

She was feeling almost buoyant, not sure if it was the flying or the company. She cut power to the rotors, their lion's roar winding down to a gentle grumble and then a whisper. She let Terrin and Logan get out first, watched them speaking quietly to each other for nearly a minute before the younger man offered his brother a hand. Logan looked askance at the hand and pulled Terrin into a hug. The scientist seemed embarrassed and awkward, but eventually he returned the embrace for a few seconds before the warrior let him go.

When she saw Terrin walking across the public landing field to his little three-wheel runabout, she popped open the side hatch out of the cockpit and stepped down, taking Logan's proffered helping hand even though she didn't need it. It was warmer down here in the river valley and the evening wind tugged playfully at the hem of her dress like the gentle teasing of the angels.

"Thank you for the delightful evening," she said, holding on to his hand well after she was safely on the pavement. "Though if I'm treating next time, I'm afraid we'll have to find someplace a bit more reasonably priced and with no hopper rental involved, especially if your brother comes along."

"I promise," he said, raising the hand not holding hers as if he were taking an oath, "next time it'll just be the two of us."

"No, it's fine, I very much enjoyed meeting your brother. He's a genius, which I am used to at home but have not met quite so many of in the military."

He eyed her doubtfully.

"I'd ask if that's some sort of wise-ass crack about the military except you're *in* the military."

"I'm a pilot," she corrected him, grinning to take the sting out of the words. "We think of ourselves as separate from and, of course, superior to the rest of the military."

"Of course. But I would still rather it just be the two of us on our next date."

She let the corner of her mouth curl churlishly.

"Is that what this was? A date?"

"If it wasn't, I definitely want the next one to be."

He was direct, honest. She appreciated that. Too many men thought they could trick their way or talk their way into a woman's good graces. She was, despite her joke to the contrary, in the military and she appreciated a direct approach.

"Fine," she told him. "I accept your invitation to let me pay for our next, or perhaps first date. But only on two conditions."

They'd been walking—very slowly—toward his motorcycle, parked against the side of the hopper rental office, now long closed. He stopped and turned to face her, their fingers still intertwined.

"Anything," he vowed. "You name it."

"First, only my father and my superior officers call me 'Kathren.' My name is Katy."

"Katy." He seemed to be tasting the name, smiling when he evidently decided he liked it. "It fits better."

"I've always thought so, and while some people say it's lame to choose your own nickname, I'm exercising the right anyway."

"What's the other condition?"

Logan was close now, so close she could feel his breath teasing at her hair like the wind. His breath smelled like the after-dinner mint she'd seen him pick up from the table and she grinned. Just like a soldier: always prepared. She leaned up and kissed him, her arms slipping around his neck, his going around her waist.

It was just right, just as she'd imagined it and warmth flooded her in all the right places, washing away all thought and consideration. Luckily, she'd taken care of the thought and consideration ahead of time.

She pulled away, just slightly and their matching intake of breath merged into a single sigh of satisfaction.

"The other condition is that we get on your bike and you take me back to your apartment," she told him, her voice huskier than she thought it would be. "And our next date will be breakfast tomorrow morning."

"Katy," he said, something wild and ready in those grey eyes, "you drive a hard bargain."

5

The cold night air slapped Logan in the face, whipped through his hair as he guided his cycle up the winding mountain road. The hum of the machine's electric motor was barely audible above the roar of the wind, giving the whole experience a dreamlike quality. He could almost believe it was a dream on a night like this; a pale fog clung to the craggy sides of Bloodmark Mountain, backlit by Hecate and Circe, Sparta's twin moons, giving everything an eerie luminescence. His headlights barely cut through the fog enough for him to navigate the treacherous road, with dark forest on one side and steep cliff on the other.

I could have taken a hopper up to the observatory. But no...I thought it would be fun to ride up.

Well, hell, it was kind of fun. Taking risks was always fun. Otherwise he'd have been studying science like his brother, instead of becoming a warrior. He chuckled softly to himself, wondering what his father would have thought of his eldest becoming a scientist. He wasn't even thrilled about his younger son forsaking the warrior way, but he surely understood that it was just as important to design new ships and mecha as it was to pilot them. And Mithra knew, they had regressed enough from the Empire without neglecting scientific research.

What the hell is important enough for Terrin to call me up to the observatory at this time of night?

His brother had refused to tell him over his link—he'd insisted Logan come in person. So, much against his better judgement, he'd hauled himself out of bed, leaving Katy slightly disgruntled, and fired up his bike.

It wasn't too much longer before the observatory came into view, a white, domed building that housed not only a comparatively small optical telescope, but the hookups to an orbital radio/X-ray telescope and spectroanalyzer. It was, Logan thought ruefully, Terrin's personal toy. He'd pushed their father to expand the existing site and put up the orbital assembly. It now seemed he was spending all his time there.

Logan pulled his cycle up next to Terrin's flyer, kickstanded it and swung a leg off, his flying leathers creaking as he straightened. He adjusted his gunbelt, unzipped his jacket and headed inside. The reception office was dark and deserted, so he went ahead up the stairs to the monitoring bay, a huge upper room filled with the main body of the optical telescope and the readouts from the orbital assembly.

A small group of people were gathered around a bank of readouts; two of them he recognized. One was unabashedly old, tough and wrinkled as old leather, his hair white as the snow on the mountains, skeleton-thin under his worn and faded jacket. Dr. Damian Kovalev was the head of the Sparta Institute of Astronomy, and an old family friend. The other was his younger brother. Terrin had always been an introvert, shy and soft-spoken; the only things that excited him were physics and astronomy, and he poured every waking hour into them. At the moment, it appeared he'd had one too many hours awake. Dark circles couched his eyes, he looked too pale and his clothes looked to have been slept in. He looked up from the readouts at Logan's approach, his eyes brightening.

"Hey, bro," he said, nodding. "I'm glad you're here."

"Hope this is something big, Terrin." Logan shook his head, slapping his younger sibling on the shoulder. "You wouldn't believe what I left behind for you."

"Sorry." Terrin grinned, embarrassed. Logan wondered sometimes if his brother was still a virgin. "But this is big. Real big. I thought about calling Father, but I wanted to run it by you first."

"What happened? You rediscover the stardrive?"

"Just maybe." His brother's intensity surprised him. "You need to listen to this, Logan."

"We picked this up," Dr. Kovalev spoke for the first time, "from an isolated system about four hundred light years from here, on the other side of the Homeworld."

Logan thought it ironic that people still referred to Eurotas, the old Imperial capital, as the Homeworld, almost four centuries after it had fallen to the Jeuta. Nearly as ironic as the notion of an empire that spanned hundreds of light-years falling to the genetically-engineered slave race they'd created to do their grunt work.

"So, this signal originated three hundred years ago?" Logan cocked an eyebrow.

"Maybe more." Kovalev nodded, his manner just as serious as Terrin's, with an excitement tempered by age.

"There's not much," Terrin told him, "but with computer enhancement, we've salvaged a little."

"Let me replay what we've got," the older man hit a control on the console. There was a deafening silence for a few moments, then a burst of static from the speakers set in the low ceiling of the observatory control room...and a voice.

"...Colonel Walken Zeir..." The voice, though distorted by static, sounded tired and resigned, yet still with an underlying strength and dignity. "...of the 403rd Imperial Ordnance Battalion." Another burst of static obscured the next few words. "...stationed here on Terminus for the last..."

"Terminus!" Logan hissed, eyes widening.

"Listen," Terrin admonished.

"...years," Zeir's message continued. "When I came here, there seemed hope we could yet pull the fragments of the Empire back together. Now with the Jeuta invasion of the Homeworld, that hope is dead."

"Mithra," Logan muttered. That invasion had taken place more than four centuries ago.

"...send this message on a continuous loop as long as the generators hold out. I'm directing it..." More static. "...human worlds farthest away from the Jeuta incursions in the hopes rebuilding will begin there." A long burst of static erased the next few words. "If anyone hears this...if there's anyone left who can, and who can reach us...this system..."

The static-filled transmission ended with a touch of Terrin's finger on a control.

"It breaks up for a few minutes," he explained, "then repeats again."

Logan grabbed his brother by the shoulder and pulled him around to face him, his own pulse pounding in his ears.

"Tell me you have a location." The words seemed to come from someone else, too intense and focused for his own voice.

"We do," Kovalev answered for him, a tight smile breaking through his grey-shot beard.

He leaned over one of the control consoles and touched a button to activate the main monitor. It flickered to life with a star map, one Logan recognized immediately: it was a chart of all the known jump-points, the weak points in space time where the Kadish-Dean drive could penetrate through to the gravito-inertial pathways between stars. The jump roads were a cross-hatch of red on the map, a spider-web connecting the galaxy from one stepping stone to the next, and superimposed over the road map were the borders of the five Dominions.

Sparta was a blue globe running along the inner borders of the old Empire, toward the galactic center, encompassing dozens of stars and over a hundred habitable worlds, though there were only a half a dozen large enough to support more than a single city. Sparta was not at the exact center of the globe; instead, it hugged the far corner, only a few light years from Clan Modi. Modi sprawled in neon yellow, more jagged and irregular than the globular cluster of Spartan stars, sending rays of inhabited space into the gaps between the other Dominions, incursions not rich or important enough for the other governments to contest them militarily.

Off the shoulder of Modi's smoothest border was an elongated saddle shape outlined in green, the size and scope of the Dominion indicative of its political power. There were no political labels on the map, but there didn't need to be: the shape was iconic and every school-child knew it as the Imperium of Mbeki, the self-aggrandizing name their way of claiming to be the last remnants of the Old Empire. They weren't, not in any meaningful way, but they kept the trappings, the names, the offices and the pompous self-importance. They were not to be taken lightly, for all that; they also kept what they considered Imperial discipline.

Across the outer flank of Mbeki and Sparta was an orange disc shape, smaller than its fellows, though he knew the size was deceptive and the real story was the tangled weave of red gravito-inertial pathways intersecting in the star systems of the disc. The Shang Directorate controlled key star systems with connections leading all over the Five Dominions and out of them to enemy-held territory. The tolls they collected from those possessions were the source of enough wealth to build them an impressive military. They didn't use it for attempted conquest, happy to simply extend their commercial enterprises and shipping monopolies, but you didn't enter Shang space without permission… not even if you were the looming, menacing magenta sphere butting up against them.

The Starkad Supremacy occupied nearly half the territory of the former Empire of Hellas, the strongholds of the Outer Reaches where civilization had held on with a brutal, iron hand in the face of civil war, revolt and invasion. Tens of billions had died in the decades after the fall, entire star systems had been sterilized in a paroxysm of mindless violence, and he supposed he couldn't blame Lord Senator Starkad for seizing power and enforcing order to save what was left. At some point, though, the need for brutality and paranoia had passed and the practices had become tools to retain power.

Very effective tools, he admitted, with the sort of stark pragmatism he'd learned from General Constantine.

"The signal came from here," Kovalev explained.

He traced a line with his finger from Sparta through the Shang Directorate… and straight on into the Supremacy, out the other side and into an area with no designators for the planets and only strings of numbers to label the stars.

"In the Shadow Zone," Logan said, voice and mood suddenly swinging from hopeful to grim.

The Shadow Zone was a colloquialism, a sensationalistic label his Academy professors would have chewed him out for using. The technical designation for the area was long, boring, and academic, the Unrecovered Imperial Possessions. It wasn't adequate to describe the wasted, irradiated worlds littered with the wreckage of what had been a thriving galactic civilization, but military history professors weren't trying to write poetry.

"And the only way in," Terrin added, "is through Starkad-controlled space." He shouldered past Kovalev and pointed out the jump-points between Sparta and the projected source of the transmission. "But if it's *really* Terminus…"

Logan hissed out a breath, leaning back against a console behind him. One of Kovalev's assistants, a pinch-faced woman he'd never met before, shot him a dirty look, probably because he was sitting on something important, but he didn't get up. He couldn't. This was *Terminus Cut*. This was a bed-time story his mother had told him, a legend of a lost Imperial Navy research station, supposedly filled with advanced weapons and technology, things even the Empire had considered cutting-edge.

"If we can salvage anything," he mused, mostly to himself, "if anything's left…"

"I am not a weapons designer," Kovalev said softly, as if he were embarrassed to speculate, pressing his palms together, "nor have I ever been in the military, but as I understand it, the technology available in a place such as Terminus Cut would revolutionize the current military and technological relationship between Sparta and the other Dominions."

"You could say that, Doc," he agreed, running his hands through his hair. It was even longer now; he'd meant to have it trimmed when they'd returned from the patrol and the battle at Ramman, but Katy had told him she liked it longer. He speared Terrin with a glare. "We have to take this to Dad. I need you to go with me."

"You should bring Dr. Kovalev," Terrin told him, turning away but not quickly enough to hide the sullen expression on his face. "Dad would take him seriously."

Logan blinked, straightening up, noting out of the corner of his eye the relieved look on the assistant's face as he got his ass off of whatever instruments and controls he'd been sitting on.

"Where the hell is *that* coming from?" he wondered. "Of course Dad takes you seriously! He's always been proud of you." He shook his head, waving the subject away before Terrin could blather on about it anymore. "That's not important now, we *have* to take this to Dad and General Constantine."

He rounded on the two assistants present in the observatory control room. The woman still seemed irked with him, while the younger one, a man, seemed disinterested in the whole conversation. They both looked up at his stare.

"And *only* to them," he added. He turned to Kovalev. "All three of you need to keep your damn mouths shut about this." He'd seen the face Colonel Anders made when the man was dressing down a junior officer and he did his best to channel it as his eyes went back and forth from the two grad assistants to the astrophysicist. "If any word of this gets out, any chatter from our enemies, a rumor floating around the faculty lounges, a *fucking* drunken slip in the local bar, I *will* find out. The Guard Intelligence keeps an ear open for this kind of thing."

Which might or might not be true; he hadn't the slightest damned idea.

"And if any of it gets out, even a hint," and the Colonel's admonishing expression was exchanged for his own, more directly threatening one, "you're going to get an unpleasant personal visit from an Internal Security team, and you will *never* climb out of the hole they throw you into." A pause and he saw the two students blanche, although Kovalev didn't seem as alarmed by his words. "Am I clear?"

The assistants looked uncertainly at Kovalev and each other, but the astrophysicist nodded firmly.

"I understand completely, Lord Guardian," he said without hesitation. "Not a word will come from anyone here. I will make sure of it."

Logan nodded, his instincts telling him he could trust the man. He gestured at the control panel where they'd run the recording.

"Get me a copy of that message on a data crystal now," he directed Kovalev, "and an analysis of its source."

The astrophysicist gestured to the male assistant and the man nodded quickly, grabbing a blank crystal from a small cabinet mounted on the wall, then inserting the tiny, quartz-like spike into a socket in the control panel. The information was stored with a couple of strokes across a touch-screen and the young man pulled the storage spike free and handed it over to Logan with exaggerated care. He weighed the data crystal in his palm for a moment, gazing into the faceted depths of it, as if the secrets of Terminus Cut were visible there, then he stuffed it into his jacket pocket.

"I'm leaving my bike here," he said to Terrin, grabbing his brother by the arm, tugging him along. "We're taking your flyer back to the palace right now; I'll call ahead to have Dad and General Constantine there to meet us."

"This time of night?" Terrin objected, trying to pull away. Logan didn't let go; he didn't squeeze any tighter but he made it clear the course of action wasn't optional. "Dad is dead asleep right now!"

"And I would be, too," Logan reminded him, "if you hadn't thought this was important enough to get me up here in person." He held up a hand, palm-out to stop his brother's next objection. "And you were *right*. It was. And now it's important enough to wake up Dad."

Terrin was still squawking the whole time Logan pulled him down the stairs and out into the chill of the high-mountain night, but his voice seemed distant, his words indistinct. All Logan could think of was the balance of power tying the hands of the military, protecting bandits, pirates, and Jeuta raiding parties from retaliation just because they crossed an imaginary line in space, through a jump-point where Starkad or Shang let them pass because it suited their interests.

At its height, just before the fall, the Empire had perfected the star-drive, at least if the old histories were to be believed. No one now alive knew how it had worked, not a single record had survived in the worlds of man, but it had allowed them to travel faster than the speed of light through normal space, not restricted by the jump-points. If the Spartan Navy had the star-drive, their ships could bypass the central jump-points and the defenses clustered around them, could hunt bandits down wherever they tried to hide.

He thought of Katy and made her a silent promise. If Terminus still existed, he would be the one to find it.

"If this is real," Donnell Anders declared, "we have to find it, and as quickly as possible." He rubbed at the back of his head in what Logan recognized as a tic to hide his exhaustion. "Someone else is going to discover this message, Starkad or Shang or even the Jeuta. Right now, we might have a head-start, but eventually…"

Jaimie Brannigan nodded, pacing back and forth across his office, hands clasped behind his back. He was dressed in casual, civilian clothes, as were the others, adding to the surreal atmosphere in the room. In all the years he'd known General Constantine, Logan had never once seen him with one hair out of place, one stray wrinkle or misplaced crease even in his impeccable civilian clothes. Tonight—*this morning*, he corrected himself—Constantine was in what seemed very much like the T-shirt and sweatpants the man had worn to bed, and his hair was tousled and nearly as spiky as Lyta Randell's.

She was there too, arms crossed, back to the wall, watching the others silently. He didn't think she'd said a word since he and Terrin had arrived, leaving the questions and commentary to the senior officers.

"You're right, of course," Constantine said to Anders. "But need I remind you all of the elephant in the room here? Even if this is real, even if it *is* the Terminus Cut of legend, it's on the other side of the Supremacy. There's no way in hell we're going to sneak a military force through their lines, and I sure as hell wouldn't go into the Shadow Zone without some sort of warship."

"What about a Q ship?" Logan asked, daring to venture a suggestion, emboldened by the presence of his father, since it made his own involvement seem more in the execution of his duties as the possible heir to the office, rather than as a lowly Mobile Armor platoon leader. "You know, like the bait ships we send after pirates? Armed but with an exterior like a freighter or a passenger transport?"

"Not a bad thought," Jaimie Brannigan said, then dismissed it with a wave of his hand, "but even a Q ship wouldn't make it through the interior systems of the Supremacy."

"You need a backstoppable cover for that," Lyta Randell put in, and he was surprised she'd broken her silence. She was still leaning against the wall, her eyes alert but weariness seeming to drag her down like heavy gravity. "You need to have a legitimate reason for taking arms across the borders."

"You sound like you have something in mind, Captain," General Constantine said, managing to eye her shrewdly while simultaneously trying in vain to pat down the wild hairs standing up on the side of his head.

"I do, sir," she admitted, straightening and pushing away from the wall. "Something like this, if we want to do it right, it's going to take a long con. Weeks, maybe even months."

"Do we have that kind of time?" Jaimie Brannigan wondered, glancing over to Terrin.

Terrin seemed shocked that his father would bother to ask his opinion on the matter and it took him a moment to formulate an answer.

"I think we might have a few months," the young man said. "Someone might pick up the raw transmission, but it's broken and corrupted, and the only way we were able to decode it was with an algorithm Dr. Sandhurst came up with over at the University for cleaning up the data from deep imaging pictures from the radio telescopes. No one else has it yet outside the school."

"Nicolai," Jaimie said, jabbing a finger at the General, "get with the University President this morning and get that algorithm classified ASAP. I don't need it carrying off on some inter-school announcement web and spreading all the way to Starkad."

"I will do it now," Constantine said, pulling out his datalink and typing in a message.

"So," Colonel Anders interjected, bringing the conversation back to Lyta Randell, "say we have months. What's your idea?"

"We need a way to get armed troops and at least one, armed ship through Shang and into Starkad space without anyone twigging to our involvement," the Ranger officer outlined. "There's only one way to do that as far as I know." She cocked an eyebrow and Anders nodded slowly as he finally understood.

"Mercenaries." He nearly spat the word out, face screwed up in distaste.

"They're all over the Periphery, the non-aligned systems, the border systems with the Jeuta," she ticked them off on her fingers. "Anywhere not important enough to warrant the Dominions sending troops, anywhere they *can't* send troops because it's too close to a border and would destabilize relations with the other states." She smirked. "They tend to have colorful names and even more colorful personalities in charge of them. Goddard's Goddamned Cowboys, Mehta's Maulers, the Metal Fist of Vishnu..." She spread her hands. "They're mostly nuts, but with a legitimate commission from a local system, they can get through borders."

"It'll be tricky," Constantine warned, eyes still on his 'link, still tapping out a message. "You'll need someone we can trust, someone who can think on their feet."

"Donnell," Logan's father decided, snapping his fingers and pointing at Colonel Anders. "You can do this."

"No, he can't," Constantine corrected him, not even looking up at his ruler's annoyed glare. "Starkad Intelligence has files on our senior officers, and Shang's spies are even better, and we don't have time for reconstructive surgery." He finally glanced up. "Captain Randell could go, but we'll need a Mobile Armor contingent." He shrugged. "The mecha are the selling point for these hired guns. Usually the mech commander is the overall commander, simply for status."

"Then who the hell..." Jaimie Brannigan began, but Colonel Anders interrupted him, which surprised Logan nearly as much as what the officer said.

"I think you should send Lt. Conner."

"Me?" Logan blurted, wincing at the inanity of it.

"What the hell are you on about, Donnell?" Jaimie demanded, stopping his pacing, arms hanging at his sides as if he were about to leap across the room. He glanced between his son and the Colonel. "Why the hell would I send my son, a platoon leader, a Goddamned Lieutenant, on what could very well be a suicide mission?"

If Anders was intimidated, it didn't show on the straight, classic features of his recruiting-poster face. He clasped his hands behind his back in an at-ease stance, respectful but not backing down a centimeter. His words were clipped-off, precise.

"Sir, we have a dilemma: we need an officer we can trust implicitly, yet we can't send any senior officers because they'll be too well-known. We *have* to send someone the rank of Captain or below. Who else of that rank, of that age, would you be able to say you're sure is completely loyal to Sparta and to you?"

"And we need them *now*," Constantine interjected, finally looking up from his datalink, shoving it back into a pocket. "This is going to take months and we don't have months as it is, even if this," he gestured at where his 'link had been, "manages to shut down that algorithm before Shang or Starkad can get their hands on it. We sure as hell don't have weeks or months to pick someone for the job."

For once in his life, Jaimie Brannigan seemed at a loss for words. Logan couldn't recall him looking so nonplussed even when Mother had died.

"He's my son!" the Guardian of Sparta insisted, almost spluttering. "How will people not recognize him?"

"He's been making a concerted effort to *not* let anyone find out who he is since he got to the Academy," Anders reminded him. Logan was beginning to feel that the lot of them had forgotten he was even in the room. "People know, of course, but it hasn't been reported widely in the news nets and we've never allowed any unofficial news stories to get out. And General Constantine controls the official records."

Logan took a deep breath and finally spoke up.

"There'd be no way for them to connect my face to you, Father. And I could go by a fake name; Intelligence could build a history behind it, something that would match the story we'd be telling."

He trailed off, feeling he was talking too fast, like he had when he was a kid trying to convince Mom and Dad to let him do something against their better judgement. Constantine saved him, filling the awkward silence.

"There's are identities we have on file in Intelligence," he said, tapping his lower lip with a long, almost delicate finger. "We keep them up to date with full histories, personnel files, social media updates, the works. Just in case, you know?" He punctuated the words with a flicker of the same finger toward the others. "I think I remember one that would suit."

"You have them memorized?" Lyta raised an eyebrow, then seemed to remember who she was talking to. "Sir?"

The General shrugged diffidently. "Not *all* of them," he clarified. Knowing Constantine, Logan had the sense if he didn't have them all memorized, it was only because he hadn't bothered to read them all. "This one stood out when I audited the report. A young mech pilot, a Captain with a fairly good combat record but a bad temper, a sense of entitlement and a problem with authority." Another casual wave of his hand. "The file only stands out because it was being kept open to set up a possible double-agent to let Starkad think they'd turned one of our officers, so we could feed them bogus intelligence." He snorted a sharp laugh. "That and the name."

"The name?" Jaimie Brannigan repeated, still seemingly stunned by the concept of Logan going on this mission.

"It seemed on the nose for a mech pilot," Constantine explained. "Or for a traitor." The corner of his lip curled upward. "It was Jonathan Slaughter."

"Ha!" Jaimie barked the laugh, the irony apparently enough to clear the haze from his wits. "And what the hell would you call the mercenary company? The Slaughterhouse?"

"No," Logan said, feeling this was his chance.

He stepped forward into the center of the group, grinned broadly to hide the terror in his gut, arms folded across his chest.

"I'm going to call it Wholesale Slaughter."

6

Gateway was a city turned inside-out and sliced into a spiral, dizzying in the mind-bending curves of the horizon as it twisted around the distant hub, a grey cylinder colored a light enough grey to nearly blend into the clouds.

They have clouds, Logan thought, dazed and trying not to rubberneck like a tourist. *They have clouds inside a fucking space station.*

He bumped into a chair and forced himself to keep his eyes straight ahead lest he knock over someone's table in the tiny, open-air café and make a huge spectacle right in the middle of his first undercover assignment.

"How do they have clouds on a fucking space station?" he muttered aside to Lyta Randell, earning a baleful glare.

"Because it's a fucking *huge* space station," she explained just as quietly. "This thing used to be an asteroid, you know?"

He looked up again at the interior of the gigantic, hollow cylinder, inset with cities, parks, trees, even streams and lakes and then shot Lyta a look of utter disbelief.

"I've never heard of an asteroid shaped like this. And wouldn't it have taken years to hollow it out?"

"It did take years," the woman ground out, annoyed enough to actually stop in the middle of the café and face him, hands on her hips. "And no, it wasn't shaped like this, it was a damned sphere like most asteroids. They used fusion bombs to drill a hole down the center of it, filled the hole with water, set the asteroid spinning with *more* fusion bombs, then constructed mylar mirrors kilometers across to focus the sunlight from Olympia onto it. Can you guess the rest, or do I need to draw you a picture?"

He felt warmth rising in his cheeks and shut up. It was obvious when she put it like that. The reflected sunlight heated up the exterior of the asteroid, making it molten, at the same time as the water inside was heated to steam and expanded, hollowing out the rock. The fact it was spinning at the same time had elongated it into a giant, hollow tube, several kilometers long and then they'd just had to cap off the ends.

"That's pretty smart," he admitted, following Lyta as she led them deeper into the café, to a certain table in a certain corner. "But it had to cost them millions of credits... *tens* of millions. Why would they do that?"

She rolled her eyes. She looked so damned different in civilian clothes; still dangerous but more... criminal somehow, less military.

"*They* didn't do it, if you mean the people who run it now." She fell casually into a chair and waved for him to do the same. "Whoever the hell made it did it back before the Empire fell, and probably as a commercial operation. The Choe brothers stumbled across the place prospecting for water and turned it into the biggest pleasure station in the Five Dominions... and the biggest place to do business without having to worry about any particular government's laws applying to you."

"And how the hell do they manage that?" He sat down carefully, adjusting his jacket, not wanting the butt of his concealed pistol to bump against the back of the chair. "I mean, technically, we're still in Spartan space." It had only taken two jumps to get to the system, devoid of any habitable worlds but rich in jump-points.

"Because it's in everyone's best interest for them to manage it," she said. "Governments have to do deals under the table, just like corporations and criminals. Having this place as a giant magnet makes it easier to keep track of the latter two groups as well… better they do it here than somewhere we couldn't watch, like Shang or Starkad." She clucked at him, shaking her head. "For Mithra's sake, Logan…" She rolled her eyes. "*Jonathan*," she corrected herself, "stop sitting so damned straight and stiff. You look like you're carrying a concealed weapon for the first time."

"I *am* carrying a concealed weapon for the first time," he reminded her. And the bribe she'd had to give the Port Authority controllers to allow it had made his eyes bug out.

Every eye on every face seemed to have turned his way, every one of them an accusatory stare seeing through his leather jacket to the holster above his kidney. He ran a hand through his hair and scowled. He *still* hadn't had it cut, and according to Lyta, he shouldn't. Mercenaries, she'd told him, tended to be individual-istic and rebellious, which included non-regulation hair length. It was getting on his nerves; he'd worn it buzzed since he was twelve and he was starting to feel like a dirty civilian.

Just another thing I'll have to get used to. I asked for this.

He'd asked for it. But he'd been more surprised than anyone when his father had said yes. Oh, it hadn't happened immediately; there'd been ranting and raving and screaming and yelling, but Jaimie Brannigan hadn't spent twenty years as Guardian without figuring out when it was time to compromise. His closest advisors had badgered him until he'd finally given in, though he hadn't been happy about it.

He'd been even less happy once Constantine had explained to

him that not only could no senior officers be in charge, none could even go on the mission. Logan had insisted on choosing his own mech company, starting with Marc Langella and whoever from his platoon would come along, and Lyta Randell had declared she was going along with a hand-picked short company of Rangers and there wouldn't be any discussion.

Which had left just one thing to sort out.

"You'll need a warship," Constantine had pointed out. "Or at least a lighter, an armed freighter, something big enough to carry a mech company and the heavy-lift shuttles to take them down from orbit, at least well-armed enough to protect itself from pirates."

"We obviously can't just slap a new paint job on one of ours," Logan's father had snapped, probably the only one there who could have gotten away with being snarky. "What did you have in mind?"

"We'll have to find a privateer," Colonel Anders had suggested. He glanced at Constantine. "Do we have any already staffed by our Intelligence assets, sir?"

"Nothing large enough," the senior staff officer had admitted. "Our spy boats are small on purpose, trying not to attract attention."

"I think," Lyta Randell had put in, her expression thoughtful and perhaps just a touch reluctant, "I might have an idea."

Which brought us to this place.

He tried not to swivel his head around, and make it obvious he was looking for someone. He let his eyes scan back and forth casually, as if he were just people-watching in a new place, like any other tourist. It was easy enough to fake, particularly when the people here were so damned strange. He didn't think of himself as parochial, but he had to admit the colonies and outposts where he'd traveled for training and on operations were backwoods compared to this place. And Sparta, well... Sparta was Sparta, not severe or harsh but a bit pragmatic and utilitarian by heritage and tradition.

Gateway was *not* Sparta, and if any part of it was even close, it definitely wasn't the sector Lyta had called Bartertown, a cluster of bars, restaurants, coffee shops and various other gathering places where contacts could meet, deals could be made and money exchanged face to face for the sort of commerce neither party wanted recorded electronically. The tamest fashions walking through those twisted streets would have raised eyebrows in the wildest bars of downtown Argos, resplendent with leathers and furs and feathers in impossible colors, showing way more skin than he was used to and most of that skin tattooed. Even some of the *faces* were tattooed, which would have horrified any of the priests or matrons of the temples of Mithra at home.

And so many of the people here seemed unnaturally tall and skinny, most of them probably born on lower gravity worlds, moons or asteroid habitats, some of them towering over him and Lyta. Watching them walk even in the half-standard gravity on Gateway was like watching giraffes in a wildlife preserve, their gait long and stilted as if they were about to topple over with each step. One woman in particular seemed to have legs all the way from the floor to geostationary orbit, teasing through the broad central slit in her polychromatic skirt and he hadn't realized he was staring at her until he felt the smack on the back of his head. He turned with surprise to see Lyta smirking at him.

"Want me to tell Katy you were leering at some long-legged floosy?" she asked with what he hoped was affected anger, her right eyebrow rising. "She might decide to just leave your ass behind here."

A sting of lingering guilt reminded him one of his first command decisions had been to get his girlfriend returned to duty early enough to go on this mission so she could fly the civilian shuttle to Gateway from their ship. But she was certainly qualified and *really* wanted to get off Sparta for a few days after being cooped up for the last month, attending daily counselling sessions.

"How long before this guy's supposed to be here?" Logan wondered, eager to change the subject.

"He's not known for his punctuality," she told him, waving down a server. "Coffee," she told the pale, skinny man, who dutifully tapped the order into a flimsy tablet. "Black."

The hairless skeleton of a waiter eyed Logan expectantly, but he shook his head. Pale-face shrugged and headed off to the back.

"He'll be here when he gets here," Lyta expounded, settling back in her chair.

"How do you know this guy? Did you serve together?" She'd been less than forthcoming back on Sparta, simply insisting the man was suitable for their purposes, and curiosity had been eating at him the whole flight.

"Something like that."

An olive-skinned hand, thick-fingered and laced with old, white scars, set a coffee mug on the table in front of the woman, definitely not the hand of their skeletal server.

"Howdy, Lyta."

The voice was a boulder crashing on a field of gravel, and it hardly seemed possible it came out of the gaunt, raw-boned, singularly unimpressive man standing behind them. Maybe four centimeters taller than Logan, he must have weighed ten kilograms less, lean almost to the point of malnutrition, his faded T-shirt and age-worn leather jacket hanging off of him like a tent. His face was lean, leathery, sunbaked skin stretched over high cheekbones, all angles and sharp edges right down to the crook in his nose from a badly-set break, and he could have been anywhere between forty and a hundred and forty. Stringy dark hair hung loose and wild to his shoulders, strands of gray mixed in here and there.

His only prepossessing feature was his eyes; they were black, swirling storm clouds, perpetually angry despite the neutral expression on his face. They were eyes that seemed out of place in this man... until he leaned over and Logan noticed the big, black handgun dangling in a shoulder holster beneath his left armpit.

"Hello, Don." Lyta Randell rose slowly from her seat, uncoiling like a snake about to strike, not necessarily an *angry* motion as much as wary one. Her face, her stance, her eyes were guarded, as if she didn't trust herself around the man. "It's been a while."

Logan stood up, too, mostly because twisting around in his seat was making his gun dig into his back.

"It has," the tall mean agreed. "Years." A grin tugged the corner of his mouth upward. "They've been good to you, though." His accent was hard to place, but Logan thought maybe it was from Mbeki, or the borderlands near there.

"And you look like a hot mess, as always. How've you been?"

"Up and down," he replied with a philosophical shrug. "Over and out. Never over you, though."

Logan cleared his throat, beginning to feel invisible.

"Jonathan Slaughter," Lyta introduced him, and he swore he saw her eyes roll at the *nom de guerre*, "this is Captain Donner Osceola."

"Captain." Logan offered the man his hand, but the spacer eyed it as if his palm was smeared with cow-shit, looking the younger man up and down with a critical eye.

"Mithra's swinging cod," Osceola swore casually, "I think I have fucking underwear older than you, boy."

Anger and irritation welled up inside Logan's gut and he nearly gave way to them, but he tamped them down instead. This had the earmarks of the sort of tests the instructors threw at you in the Academy, and even if it wasn't one, he had the sense this Donner Osceola wouldn't be impressed by a temper tantrum.

"I believe it," he conceded instead, trying to keep his voice cold and calculating. "You look old as shit. The question is, did getting that old make you wise or just a wise-ass."

He wasn't sure if he'd managed cold and calculating, but at least he'd avoided spluttering rage. He thought he saw a barely-perceptible nod from the spacer, as if acknowledging the touch. Lyta hadn't said a word, and he wondered if it was because she approved or just didn't want to undercut him.

"I guess we'll find out," Osceola said. "The question is, what does a young smart-ass like you want with an old wise-ass like me?"

"We need a ship, Don," Lyta told him. "Your ship. And we're offering a long-term contract. Weeks, probably months. There's good money in it for you and yours."

"And a good chance at getting killed, I bet." He shrugged. "But what the hell, I'm here. Buy me a drink and make your pitch."

"Not here," Logan insisted, shaking his head.

"We'd rather discuss it on board the *Shakak*," Lyta explained.

Osceola seemed as if he was about to object, but she moved a step closer, hand going to his chest. He glanced from the hand to her face, an expression passing across that craggy, angular face with the fleeting transience of a breeze over a field of grain, a look that spoke of longing and memory and pain.

"Please, Don," she said, her voice husky with feeling. Logan wasn't sure if she actually cared about the spacer or if she was just as good at manipulating men as she was at killing them. "It's important, or I wouldn't be here."

"Oh, I'm sure of that, darlin'," he murmured. He closed his eyes, sighed out a breath. Something, perhaps resolve, seemed to run out of him apace with the breath. "All right," he conceded. "My shuttle's at the antipodal dock."

Osceola turned and headed toward the lift station, hands stuffed in his pockets, chin downward, as if he didn't care if they followed or not. Logan shot Lyta Randell a wide-eyed glance. Whatever he'd expected, this hadn't been it. She ignored his expression as she'd ignored his earlier questions and trailed after Osceola without a word. He realized she hadn't paid for her coffee and he hastily dug a few Tradenotes out of his pocket and fed them into the payment slot on the table; they didn't take the currency of the Dominions out here, though they offered exchange on the way into the station for an exorbitant fee.

Logan barely caught up with them before the doors to the lift car slid open. He tried not to get caught staring again, but it was difficult. The lifts ran up transparent, evacuated cylinders all the way to the central hub like the spokes of some world-sized bicycle wheel, changing direction when they reached it to head to the station's poles and the docking ports there. It was impressive enough even before his mind pushed the picture into perspective, realizing the hub was a kilometer away and adjusting everything else to scale.

He jogged to keep pace with Osceola and Lyta Randell, slipping into the lift as the door stated to close. There were two other riders in the car, both long-bodied belters with their characteristic mohawk haircuts and skin-tight clothing; he thought one was a female, but you could scarcely tell the difference. He thought for moment they'd be the only occupants of the car, but a gloved hand stopped the door only centimeters from closing, causing it to recoil open.

The leather glove ran into the leather sleeve of a flight jacket, a conservative brown with a corporate logo on the left breast. It was identical to the logo on the chests of the other three men with him and they seemed cut from the same mold: all of average height for natives of a world with near standard gravity, all medium build, all clean-shaven and wearing the short-ish hair of a typical corporate spacer crew. Only a slight difference in complexion, the smallest variation of bone structure in their faces separated one of them from another, but the first through seemed to be in charge.

He waited for the others to board before he moved his hand away from the sensor and stepped into the car, nodding a curt greeting to the other occupants before checking the control panel, seeing what destinations were already chosen and refraining from selecting anything different. Logan didn't pay them much attention except to squint at their logo patches to try to figure out who they worked for. It was some combination of stars and a ringed planet and stylized script he could barely parse without context. He thought it read "Logotech," but it could have been any one of hundreds of corporations who did business within and between the Dominions, their cargo ships and transports crossing borders unmolested.

Why didn't we try that? he wondered. He shrugged the question away. *Because we couldn't have taken anything we found back with us.*

The door hissed shut and the car jerked into motion, slowly at first as it climbed up the spoke toward the central hub. Once it got there, the perceived gravity of centripetal force would be gone and they'd be in free fall all the way to the docking bay. In anticipation, he began searching for the nearest unclaimed hand-hold.

"Kammy's missed you," Osceola told Lyta, his voice subdued. "He keeps asking me when we're going back to Sparta for a visit and I keep having to remind him we're still wanted there for that whole business with the customs inspector."

Logan heard the peel of laughter, knew it couldn't have come from anyone but Lyta, but still couldn't quite believe it was a sound she'd ever make. He glanced back at her with eyes wide. That was the only reason he saw one of the corporate freighter jocks sweep his jacket aside and wrap his hand around the butt of a compact pistol holstered at his waistline...

7

Logan acted without thinking, knowing instinctively he wouldn't have time to grab for his own weapon... or perhaps it was just that his instincts were more those of a brawler than a gunfighter. He lunged across the meter-and-change separating him from the closest of the corporate pilots and slammed the man into the wall of the elevator, jamming his gun-hand back behind him, trying not to let him have the room to draw his pistol.

He should be trying to warn the others, should be using the opportunity to grab for his gun, he knew it on some level, but he reverted to the most familiar training, unarmed self-defense. Knee strikes, elbow strikes, target the soft spots, stay close and don't give your opponent room to counter, room to escape. The gunman was strong and well-trained and managed to block the knee to his groin by twisting his hip around; Logan felt a flash of pain in his knee as it impacted bone but he couldn't afford to stop. Instead, he retargeted the thigh and slammed his knee into the common peroneal nerve. No matter how tough you were, getting hit in the nerve hurt like hell, he knew from personal experience.

The guy didn't cry out, but an involuntary gasp of pain betrayed how badly the strike had affected him and his guard slipped for just a fraction of a second. It was enough. Logan saw the opening and punched him in the throat. There was a sound he'd never forget, the sound a man made when you crushed his trachea, when he was fighting to breath but couldn't, when he was beginning to panic because he knew he was going to die. The man's eyes went wide, the whites so big the irises seemed lost, and his face began to turn red, all thoughts of drawing his gun forgotten.

Logan froze for just a heartbeat, not hardened enough to be inured to the sound and sight of a man choking to death on his own blood, until the deafening crash of a gunshot in an elevator brought him back to reality of the fight to the death going on just behind him. He spun around, finally drawing his gun and nearly putting a round into a man who was already dead. The leader of the four corporate crewmen who'd boarded together tumbled backward into one of the asteroid miners, missing the left side of his skull, his blood splashing across the face of the tall man—or woman, he still wasn't sure.

The asteroid miner screamed, the sound high-pitched enough for Logan to finally decide she was female, and tried to squeeze into a corner of the lift car as she wiped blood and brains from her eyes. The dead man crumpled to the floor, his pistol falling from nerveless hands.

That was two, some small part of Logan which was still thinking rationally and logically decided. Two down and two to go, and he needed to get a bead on them before one of them put a bullet in him. People were moving, muzzle flashes were doing their best to blind him, and the sound of the gunshots seemed muffled, as if he could barely hear them. Suddenly, everything came into focus, as if he were watching a video of all this happening to someone else.

One of the asteroid miners was down, clutching at his leg, blood welling from what looked to be a flesh wound in his outer thigh, his companion still screaming, though her cries and the man's painful moans were as muted as the shots had been. Lyta was nearly to the other side of the elevator, almost ten meters away, locked in a hand-to-gun struggle with another of the gunmen disguised as corporate spacers. The man had his sidearm in his right hand and he was trying to use his superior weight and upper body strength to power the muzzle toward her against the hand she had wrapped around his wrist.

He let his eyes slide off her fight, confident in two things: first, he had no clean shot, and second, Lyta Randell was the most dangerous and competent soldier he'd ever met. There was no way she was going to lose a one-on-one fight against this guy, whether he was a corporate freighter pilot or a bounty hunter or a hired gun. As it turned out, it was the right decision.

Catty-corner to the asteroid miners, Donner Osceola was on the ground, his gun centimeters from his hand on the floor of the car, a pressure cut above his eye already welling blood. The last of the crew of assassins stood over him, steadying himself, the muzzle of the gun he'd just used to club the spacer Captain to the floor coming up, ready to shoot.

The recoil of his handgun took Logan by surprise, just the way the instructors always said it should. He was only dimly aware of the muzzle flash, felt the report more than heard it, a pressure somewhere in his sinuses, but he saw clearly the gunman tumbling backward, the leather of the jacket over the left side of his chest charred and smoking, the dress shirt beneath it turning a dark crimson.

The dying man's gun slipped out of his grasp and Logan turned back to Lyta just in time to see her twist the pistol out of her opponent's grasp with a combination of leverage and technique executed nearly too fast for him to follow. The gun was in her left hand and her right was chopping into the man's temple. He staggered, stunned, and she jammed the muzzle under his chin and fired.

There was the sound of a balloon popping and brains exploded out of the top of the assassin's skull, painting the wall of the elevator in blood and cerebral fluid. She brought the gun to low ready and scanned around her, nodding to him when she saw the threats were down. She stepped over to Donner Osceola and grabbed him by the front of his jacket, pulling him to his feet...

And then they were in free-fall. It was hard for Logan to believe the gunfight had lasted only seconds, not even long enough for the lift car to make it to the hub, but the evidence was flying at him, micro-globules of blood suddenly spinning around the elevator in DNA spirals toward the air vent. He grabbed at one of the safety straps on the wall and pulled himself out of the way, hoping against hope the tiny, red meteors didn't impact on his exposed skin.

"Are you all right, Don?" Lyta asked the starship Captain, still holding onto his arm, somehow braced into a corner well enough to hold both of them stationary.

"My damned face hurts," Osceola complained, a palm pressed against his cheek.

"Who the hell were these guys?" Logan demanded.

He was frustrated and terrified at the idea their operation had been compromised before it began, sure the dead hitmen were Starkad Intelligence operatives, their notorious Committee for State Security or Com-Stat as they were known to their own people. Lyta didn't have the chance to answer; Osceola beat her to it.

"They're bounty hunters," he declared with sullen certainty, snatching his gun out of the air, where it had floated up from the floor. He shoved it into his shoulder holster, then grabbed at one of the hand-holds beside him on the wall and gave Lyta a significant glance. "And there'll probably be more of them."

The wounded Belter was still moaning in pain and now that he could hear again, the sound was starting to grate at Logan's nerves. So much so he nearly missed the connotations of what Osceola had said until Lyta brought it home for him.

"God damnit, Don," she sighed, closing her eyes for just a beat as she visibly brought herself under control. "What did you do?"

"It was the fucking New Saints," Osceola admitted, unable to meet her accusatory glare. "They caught me running illegal VIRware to the locals on Canaan." He shook his head, jerking against the hand-hold as it set him teetering in the microgravity. "You know how fanatical those assholes are."

Her expression was flat and unconvinced, and so was the tone of her voice.

"No matter how fanatical the New Congregation of Saints is," she said, "there's no way they're sending bounty hunters after you way out here just for peddling contraband porn to their teenagers."

"Well…" He stretched the word out as if he were putting off what had to come next. When it did, it was with a wince Logan sensed had nothing to do with the bruise on his cheek. "There was also the matter of one of the local militia who came after us and managed to get himself killed trying to stop us from getting to our shuttle. He… might have been the nephew of the Chief Deacon of the church…"

"I need a doctor…"

The wounded Belter said, a pleading note to his voice, desperation on his face. His companion was less than solicitous, curled up in a corner of the room, staring in horror at the whirlwind of blood and the grotesque, boneless dance of the corpses. There was an emergency call button on the lift's control panel, but she hadn't even made a move for it.

Logan sighed, holstered his weapon and pushed over to the lanky, impossibly tall man. He gently moved the Belter's hands away from the wound and looked it over with all the expertise a handful of first-aid classes could give you.

"Are there security cameras in here?" Logan asked, waving blood away from the ragged hole in the side of the Belter's leg. "Do we have to be worried about the station cops mobbing us the minute we get out at the port?"

"Bit late to be thinking about that, youngster," Osceola pointed out, snorting in dark amusement. "Maybe you shoulda considered that before you went after one of these guys in a damned elevator."

"He was going for his gun, asshole." Logan ground the words out through annoyance bordering on rage. He was a mech pilot; gunfights in elevators weren't in his job description. "You're welcome for saving your fucking life, by the way." He met the eyes of the Belter, trying to project confidence. "You're going to be fine. It didn't hit an artery; as long as you get to a medical center when we get to the docking bay, they'll fix you up fine, okay?"

"Answer his question, Don," Lyta snapped, apparently having lost patience with the man herself. "Are they going to be waiting for us when we get off this car?"

"The Enforcers?" Osceola shook his head. "No, they don't give a shit what you do to each other unless you're paying them for protection." He gestured at the dead bounty hunters. "The rest of these guys? Yeah, they'll probably be waiting."

"Get their guns, Jonathan."

It took Logan a second to remember she was talking to him.

I'm never going to get used to this, he thought ruefully.

The assassin's weapons were floating free, tumbling around

the car, ricocheting from one wall to another. Logan cringed as he waded through the rings of orbiting blood, trying to cover his face with a hand. Wet droplets splashed at his palm and teased the skin of his neck, but he gritted his teeth and grabbed the handguns anyway. They were all identical, chemical slug-shooters fabricated in a workshop somewhere, maybe right there on Gateway; it was probably easier to buy guns on the black market once you got there rather than trying to bribe your way past the Port Authority the way they had.

While he retrieved the guns, Lyta patted down the corpses and came up with spare magazines, distributing them among the three of them and then handing out the bounty hunter weapons, keeping the extra one for herself.

"Shoot with their guns first until you run out of ammo," she instructed as if she were running a class of Rangers through the training lanes he'd attended back on Sparta. "Then ditch them."

"They won't know you're with me," Osceola reminded her. "You two should use me as bait to draw them out."

"Thanks, I think I will," Logan assured him, wiping blood off of his neck and pushing across the car toward the elevator doors. He pulled his 'link off his belt and keyed it to the communications net for their shuttle. "Katy, this is..." He winced. "This is Jonathan."

A pause, but no reply.

"Katy, this is Jonathan, please respond. We have a situation." Again, only silence, and he shot a worried look at Lyta. "Could they be jamming us? I mean, they couldn't be because they don't know it's *us*, right, so they'd have to be shutting down all the 'links on the station."

"Or just this elevator, genius." Osceola's retort was dry and casual, as if this sort of thing happened to him all the time. And Logan didn't know, maybe it did. "I'd put my money on just this elevator; even the price the New Sainters have on my head, it'd cost them way too much to bribe enough people to shut down the whole damned station's comms."

"They're going to be posted at your shuttle," Lyta said to the spacer Captain. "We should head for ours, that'll make sure their forces are split up."

"Not a chance in hell," Osceola declared, making a slashing motion with his left hand, his right filled with a pistol appropriated from the dead bounty hunters. "I'm not hanging Kammy out to dry... once they twig to me not heading to the shuttle, they'll go after him."

Logan expected Lyta to dress him down with the same sort of cold anger she would have used on an argumentative Lieutenant, but instead she just sighed and nodded.

"All right." She nodded to Logan. "When this car arrives at the bay, Don's heading out and we'll move two seconds after him. These guys," she gestured at the corpses with the barrel of one of their pistols, "are groundpounders just like us, so they won't be thinking in three dimensions. They'll stick to the courtesy railings aligned with the shuttle docking berths horizontally and figure we will, too. I want you to go high, to the overhead bar."

He could picture what she meant; he'd noticed the peculiar arrangement of the port when they'd arrived. It was a cylinder ten meters across, flattened at the bulkheads to an octagon shape, with berths for passenger shuttles aligned on one axis along either side, while the crew access ports for the much larger cargo transports were on another, but only on one side. The reason for this was psychological: people raised in gravity liked having a surface they could designate "the floor" in their minds to help orient themselves.

In practice, this meant there was a line of handholds along the "ceiling," where the transport docking berths were spaced at broad intervals, but most people would never notice them.

"You stay even with Don," she told him, "and I'll come in

behind him." She craned her head around to the Belter woman, who was staring at them all wide-eyed, her head motions furtive like a cornered animal. "Hey, scream queen, you want to do us and your boyfriend here a favor and push the emergency button when the car stops so someone can haul him off to the medics?" The woman didn't respond, still curled up in the corner. "Are you tracking me, sugar? Do you read?" Lyta jabbed a finger toward the control panel. "Push the fucking button when the door opens!"

The Belter still couldn't speak, but she nodded. It seemed to be enough for Lyta, or least as much as she expected to get. Her eyes went back to the display above the door, to the flashing indicator showing them where the car was and how long until it reached its destination.

"Ten seconds. Get in position."

Osceola moved to the far end of the car, bracing himself against the wall, ready to push off, and Lyta squeezed in beside him after pushing one of the bodies out of the way. The man's clouded and unseeing eyes stared in silent accusation, blood still slipping from his slightly-open mouth, trailing away to join the spiral galaxy spinning through the center of the car.

Shit. Logan tried to get his breathing under control. He was coming dangerously close to hyperventilating from the adrenaline pulsing through his body. This was a different sort of experience from fighting in a mech cockpit, isolated from the reality of the violence. Even when he'd left his mech to kill the bandit pilot back on Ramman, it had all ended in seconds and the post-fight jitters hadn't been more than an inconvenience. This time, it could get him killed.

What was Colonel Anders thinking? What was I thinking? I'm just a Lieutenant, I don't belong on this mission.

The clock ran out and he shut out the counsel of his doubt, concentrating on doing his job. The doors slid aside and everything seemed to happen at once. Osceola shot past him as if rocket-propelled, nearly plowing through the crowd of people waiting for the car to arrive. He heard alarmed shouts, a single scream, and then Lyta was moving and so was he. She followed the spacer's trail, staying low, close to what had been the elevator's floor, still aligned as the "bottom" of the docking bay. Logan pulled himself through at the ceiling, slipping by over the heads of the crowd gathered at the doors, keeping his gun close to his chest and out of view.

Clouds of floating blood followed them out the door, drawn by the difference in air pressure, and more shouts echoed off the walls of the bay, some of them arcing upward in tone to panic. An alarm sounded, the call of the emergency alert the Belter woman had somehow found the fortitude to push, and then the clamor was behind him and all his attention was focused on what was in front... and below.

The docking bay assaulted his senses with a kaleidoscope of visual data, hundreds of people heading toward the lift banks and away to one or another of the dozens of occupied airlocks, each with their own trajectory and speed, each a potential threat to be watched. Light panels glowed at intervals along the walls, just bright enough to distract. Clear sections of transparent aluminum afforded views of the ships docked at each port, shielded from the cosmic radiation and micro-meteors of open space by a shroud of asteroid material stretching over the stationary hub, spinning in counterpoint, its rotation obvious from the gleam of the solar reflectors imbedded along its inner surface.

He tried to shut out the extraneous, pulling himself by feel along the padded length of one of the railings affixed to the "ceiling" of the octagonal tube of the docking bay and keeping his eyes scanning a ten-meter half-circle ahead of Donner Osceola, trusting Lyta to have the man's back. He didn't spot anything at first, and about thirty meters down from the lift car, he was beginning to wonder if Osceola was being paranoid in his conviction that the bounty hunters would be staking out the docking bay.

So intent was Logan on watching the action down below, he almost didn't notice the airlock hatch opening two meters ahead of him, one of the ports dedicated to cargo transports. He caught a vague blur of motion in his peripheral vision and tried to curve around the woman emerging from the airlock, nearly colliding with her and coming close enough to read the corporate logo on her leather flight jacket.

It said "Logotech." Logan felt a cold lump in the pit of his stomach and he grabbed at the railing. The momentum jerked painfully at his fingers, peeling skin off his palm and turning him away from the rugged-looking, short-haired woman as he tried to bring up his gun. Somewhere below, gunshots rang out and he knew he was too late.

Lyta Randell didn't second-guess herself, as a rule, but it wouldn't have been close to the first rule she'd broken for Donner Osceola.

This was a mistake. She heard the voice inside her head as if someone were whispering it into her ear, a conscience she hadn't heard from in a while. *I did this for the wrong reasons and it's going to get us all killed.*

What was it about this beat-up, ragged-out spacer that kept dragging her in when she should have run away?

She wanted to stare at him until she figured it out, but forced herself to look away and scan the crowd instead. If this had been any sort of civilized place under the constraints of a single government, if it had been the Gateway of Imperial days, all three of them would have already been in custody and her biggest worry would have been who to call to get them out of the local jail; on a place like Gateway, she knew if she'd seen the local

Enforcers, it would only have been because they'd they were working for the bounty hunters.

There was still panic behind her, raised voices calling for medics, calling for police who likely wouldn't come, but no one had tried to stop her or Osceola. She felt the stickiness of the blood still coating her hands, felt the dampness of her collar where it had splattered across her jacket, and she knew the people passing by her could see it. She felt their eyes settle on her and then quickly glance away, not wanting to get involved in someone else's trouble, or step into the path of someone else's bullet. She knew they weren't a threat by the studied lack of attention they were paying.

She knew the man with the close-cropped mustache, slicked-back hair, and corporate logo on his jumpsuit *was* a threat because he didn't look away. He stared, a rookie mistake, or maybe just a side-effect of dealing with amateurs for too long. He saw her looking at him, though, and made a play for his gun. Hers was already in her hand.

She fired by instinct, and her instinct betrayed her; most of her years of combat had been deep in gravity wells, and the weapons she'd used for her limited free fall combat training had been mission-suited, recoilless. The bounty hunter's slug-shooter wasn't. The first two rounds of caseless 10mm erased the mustached man's face, but the kick of the weapon also erased her forward momentum and left her drifting in mid-air, unable to reach the guide-rails.

The file of spacer crews and diplomats and spies and criminals all around her scattered like cockroaches from a light switch, leaving behind the echoes of shouted warnings and panicked cries and the floating body of the bounty hunter. And her, and Donner Osceola.

He'd brought himself to a stop against the guide-rail, yanking the gun she'd given him from the pocket of his jacket, trying to pull himself back toward her.

"Get out of here, you idiot!" she yelled. He was making himself a target and if he had any brains, he'd get to the shuttle, but she knew he couldn't hear her above the din of confusion and chaos and wouldn't have listened if he had.

She had to throw something away, get herself moving again and she began fishing in a pocket for a spare magazine while she kept an eye out for threats to Osceola. The volley of gunshots above her head interrupted the search and she snapped her handgun upward, caught a brief glimpse of another of the bounty hunters drifting away from him amidst a sea of amorphous red blobs… and then she realized the sudden motion of the pistol had sent her spinning backward.

"God damnit, I hate free fall!" she bellowed, trying to use the lessons she'd learned and twist herself around in a way to stop her spin.

Finally, she simply aimed the pistol over her head at a bare metal stretch of unoccupied bulkhead and fired off the entire magazine. She knew she was taking a huge risk the bounty hunters had been smart enough to load frangible ammo for use inside the station; if they hadn't, the ricochets could have killed or wounded innocents, including her.

Shit, how innocent can they be? They're here, right?

The recoil from the shots sent her downward to the lower guide-rails and she tossed the empty gun away, heading straight for Osceola, trying to grab her own weapon from the holster beneath her jacket. She was going to be too late, she could already see it. There were two of them, both dressed in the same freighter-crew disguise, and they were already firing.

Her ears were filled with the shrill whine of the gunshots she'd aimed at the overhead and she couldn't even hear the report from the guns, but she saw the results. Two civilians who hadn't been quick enough to get out of the way, both of them dressed in casual business wear, probably here to make an under-the-table deal, were between Osceola and the bounty hunters. He had his gun out but wouldn't take the shot with civilians in the way; the bounty hunters had no such scruples. Bullets ripped through the two bystanders on their way to Osceola and she saw him grunt as something struck him in the side, but she had no shot.

Gunfire rained down on the bounty hunters from above and she glanced up and spotted Logan secured to the upper guide-rail with one hand, firing with the other. She couldn't tell if he was hitting anything, but she also couldn't sit around waiting to find out. She pushed off, her own issue pistol at the ready, and passed right by Donner Osceola, tamping down a nearly irresistible impulse to check if he'd been wounded. Instead, she aimed herself like a missile at the enemy, firing the very second she made it past the wounded civilians.

At least one of the hunters was still kicking, reeling from a grazing wound to his neck but trying to bring his weapon up to target Logan. Her first round took him in the chest, and he tumbled backward but caught himself on the guide-rail; from the lack of blood, she intuited he was wearing body armor. Her second shot went to the head from only five meters away.

She transitioned to the other man, finally beginning to notice details. He was short, thick-necked, his hair dark and curled and curving down into long sideburns. He gasped for breath, the wind driven from him from two hits to his chest which hadn't penetrated the body armor beneath his jacket but probably hadn't been any fun at all. Blood welled from a wound in his arm, making him fumble with the spare magazine he'd retrieved, trying desperately to reload.

If the man had a moment to consider his situation, he would have been trying to run; like her and the others though, he was operating on training and instincts and the fight-or-flight part of his brain was already stuck on "fight." She'd seen it before and knew there'd be only one way out of this for the man. She aimed carefully and did the deed with a single round, only then pushing herself back toward Osceola.

The older man was doubled over, floating freely, hands clenching his stomach, but she couldn't see any blood. His mouth was twisted in a pained snarl and his gun was spinning in place next to him, forgotten. She secured it, tucking it into a pocket as she stopped herself beside him.

"Are you okay, Don?" She wondered if she'd actually asked the question, because she still couldn't hear her own voice, just a shrill whistle.

He nodded, unable to speak yet, which was just as well. He tugged at his jacket where the slug had hit and she saw the round hadn't penetrated. He wasn't wearing an armored vest, but his jacket was woven from bullet-resistant material, which had kept him alive if not comfortable; she was fairly sure he'd cracked a rib or three.

"Let's get you to the shuttle," she said, sure she was yelling the words out of tone. She was trying to scan visually, trying to make up for the lack of her ears and nearly put a round into Logan Conner's chest when he sailed down from the overhead and grabbed Osceola by the arm.

"We need to go!" Logan yelled so loud she heard it even with her abused hearing. "There's more of them coming from the lift banks!"

The younger officer pulled them both along by the guide-rail and Lyta followed, facing back toward the elevator station to try to catch a look at the threat Logan had noticed. It was hard through the flock of panicked tourists and crewmembers and assorted others heading away from them, but through those fleeing the echoes of gunfire, she saw the few rushing toward it. They might have been more bounty hunters or they might have been Enforcers finally deciding the gunfight was adversely affecting business, but she didn't want to wait around and find out which guess was correct.

"How far down is your shuttle?" she asked Osceola, trying to estimate how much of the four hundred meters of the docking bay they'd already traversed.

Before he could answer, she spotted the last of them just thirty meters down the docking hub, half-hidden behind the edge of an airlock attached to a shuttle. She knew it was one of the bounty hunters by the corporate spacer gear the man was wearing and the stamped-metal handgun he held uncertainly at his side as if he didn't know who to point it at. He'd seen his friends—*or his comrades, at least*, she amended—die in front of him and he'd had the time to think about it, and she saw the doubt in his eyes.

He probably would have run, but they were between him and his only way out. She hoped they wouldn't have to shoot him, but she was dolorously certain they would. Then a hand reached out from the airlock, as big as the bounty hunter's head, closing on the man's gun hand and breaking it with a relentless, crushing grip. The man who emerged from the airlock was proportionate to the hand, twice as broad across the chest as the bounty hunter, with arms as big as the smaller man's legs, and thighs the size of tree trunks.

His face seemed oddly peaceful, even amicable as he ripped the pistol from the bounty hunter's grasp and then picked him up by the neck and negligently tossed the smaller man further down the docking bay. The bounty hunter spun out of control, unable to grab onto a hand-hold to check himself before he slammed into the opposite wall with a meaty thud that easily carried the fifty meters. *My ears are clearing up*, she thought.

She wondered how the big man had done it, as even someone his size was still restricted by the lack of gravity and the difficulty in gaining leverage in free-fall, but then she saw the thickened, metallic soles on his massive boots and realized the soles were magnetic.

"Get us out of here, Kammy!" she yelled, nearly slamming into his chest as she let go of the guide-rail, aimed at the air lock. The big man caught her with surprising gentleness for someone of his strength, giving her a brief hug before he pushed her ahead of him through the lock into the shuttle.

"And a pleasure seeing you again, too, *ho'onani*," he said in a cheerful baritone. It meant "beautiful" in some obscure, ancient dialect he'd learned from his grandmother, who'd learned it from her grandmother all the way back to when Earth had been a living world.

The big man shook his head as he followed Logan and Osceola through the lock, slapping the control to close it. Lyta helped Logan strap the older man into an acceleration couch before she dropped into one herself, still fastening her restraints when Kammy hit the controls to cut loose from the docking umbilical.

"Can I assume we're in trouble?" Kammy wondered, still seemingly untroubled.

"It's the fucking New Saints again," Osceola grunted through a haze of pain.

"Running for our lives from bounty hunters," Kammy mused, nudging the shuttle's steering yoke, "with Lyta dragging your ass out of the fire just in time."

Maneuvering rockets banged against the hull and the shuttle began to drift outward, into open space. Kammy looked back at Lyta and grinned so broadly it nearly split his chubby, cheerful face in two.

"Seems like old times."

8

"How the hell," Kathren Margolis murmured aloud, "did I get stuck waiting here?"

Well, you asked *for it, didn't you?* she reminded herself, silently this time. The shuttle was empty except for her, but talking to herself was likely to be another sign for the trauma psychology board that she wasn't yet ready to report back for duty. And as much as she appreciated the time she'd been able to spend with Logan back in Argos, she just couldn't spend one more minute sitting around on her ass while he got to do actual work.

She'd run every single meter of the city and several kilometers outside of it in the nature parks and told herself she was training for a marathon even if she had no idea when the next marathon was going to be held. She'd spent hours in the gym, some of it with Lyta Randell getting in-depth training in hand-to-hand combat, and more hours with the Ranger captain on the tactical range, determined to never, ever be captured alive again. And then Dr. Saito had the nerve to declare all her preparation as "symptoms of post-traumatic stress" instead of the sensible reaction she was sure it was.

"She can kiss my ass," Katy muttered. Then she punched the armrest of her acceleration couch. "Shit, I'm talking to myself again."

She pulled off the seat restraints and kicked out of the cockpit, determined to *something* beside sitting in the pilot's seat waiting for a status report and feeling sorry for herself. She knew she should be grateful for the chance to fly again, even if it was a milk run like this. Logan had gone out on a limb to get her on this mission and one of the concessions he'd had to make to the intractable Dr. Saito was that Katy wouldn't leave the shuttle.

But it's Gateway, she thought, a pout passing across her face as she rummaged through the shuttle's supply cabinet for something to eat. *Every kid has read about Gateway, seen movies about it, played games set in it, with all the spies and underworld wheeler-dealers, and here I am and all I get to do is eat freeze-dried noodles and check the weapons' calibration.*

She shrugged. The noodles weren't that bad. She'd grown used to them on her shake-down cruise after flight training. Logan hated them, even after three years in the service; he was a bit of a food snob, which she could understand given his upbringing.

And I'm, what... in a relationship? In love? With the son of the Guardian, who's about to go incognito as a mercenary on a suicide mission? When did my life get so damned complicated? Maybe my parents were right...

The ship's communications board lit up yellow, flashing an incoming signal, and she touched a control at the 'link on her belt and transferred the call to her earpiece.

"Margolis here," she said automatically, the way she'd been trained to answer a 'link call when she was in the Academy. She threw what was left of the noodles in a recycler and pushed back up into the cockpit.

"It's me." Logan's voice, strained, as if he were exerting

himself or maybe... under acceleration? "We're in Osceola's shuttle, on the way out of the dock. There's been trouble, he has a whole crew of bounty hunters on his tail and they might have a ship out there. We need aerospace cover to get back to his ship."

"On my way," she told him, pushing down from the overhead fuselage and sliding into the pilot's seat.

Her hands fastened the boost restraints with rote motions and she didn't feel excitement, not the way she thought she might on her first actual combat mission. Instead she simply felt... right. Complete. This was what she'd been trained for, and all the shooting and running and martial arts were distractions from the goals she'd set for herself, reactions to the derailment of her life.

This was her life. She sent out an automated undocking notice to the station's traffic control computer, ignoring the warning in return telling her she was not next in line and she'd face a heavy fine against the credit account set up when they'd docked if she didn't wait her turn.

"I love spending government money," she said, smirking at the thought of all those zeros disappearing from the Military Intelligence black-book spending account with just a nudge of the thrusters.

Thank you, taxpayers. She felt their wrath in the hammer-blow of the maneuvering jets kicking her free from the berth. *Thank you so very much.*

Logan Conner had never been in a space battle before, and he decided he didn't like it much. It had mostly involved being squashed under the hobnailed boot of eight or nine gravities of acceleration and not knowing what the hell was going on.

"Kammy," Lyta Randell gritted out past clenched teeth from somewhere to his right, too far out of his line of sight for him to risk turning his head, since it weighed about fifteen kilos at the moment, "how many of them are there?"

"Two." The big man's voice didn't sound as strained as Lyta's, perhaps because he was more used to dealing with the heavy boost. "Not military-grade, just cargo transports with armor strapped on and weapons pods rigged up in the freight bays."

Logan could see the big man; his acceleration couch was directly behind the pilot's station. Somehow Kammy managed a shrug, which was more than Logan could have done.

"They're enough to blow us into little, glowing chunks though, if they can get close enough."

The bounty hunter ships had been on them since about two minutes after they'd boosted out of Gateway's docking collar. While Logan wasn't sure exactly where Osceola's ship was, he was pretty certain it was too far away. He would have asked the captain, but the man had passed out a few seconds into the initial boost. Combat acceleration and cracked ribs really didn't go together.

"Shouldn't we be in suits?" He'd tried to yell the question, but it came out as a pained grunt.

"Sure," Kammy agreed with his unflagging good cheer. "I'll just call time-out and cut thrust for a bit so we can all go change. I'm sure these dudes won't mind."

A warning light began flashing red in a corner of the main viewscreen with the musical accompaniment of an annoying, whining alert.

"What's that?" he asked.

"Mining laser they got rigged up as an anti-ship weapon."

The boost cut out for the space of two seconds and maneuvering jets pushed his abused body into whole new sections of the acceleration couch, shaking him back and forth like a bone in a dog's teeth before the main engines kicked in again with their steady, crushing torture.

"Okay, we're good for a minute," Kammy announced. "The other guy is gonna flank us though. He's riding the angle to cut us off and ain't no way we can take him out without cutting boost and changing course, which'd make us a sitting duck for this guy."

"They aren't using missiles?" Lyta wondered. Logan understood the question. If the bounty hunters had radar-guided missiles like the ones military assault shuttles used, this bird was toast.

"Gateway don't like no one using missiles or cannon in their shipping lanes," Kammy assured her. "They don't care if we take potshots at each other, but if we start sending shit downrange that could just keep going and hit one of their customers, that could be bad for business, and they got some bad-ass defense systems to enforce those rules. These assholes won't be using anything except lasers if they know what's good for them."

Logan forced his right arm to move, despite the crushing weight piled atop it, touched a control on his 'link. He'd put his earpiece in place before he'd strapped in, so at least he didn't have to try to do anything that delicate under this sort of acceleration.

"Katy," he grunted the words out, "need you to take down one of these birds. You are cleared hot."

Her voice was calm and measured and professional and exactly what he needed to hear.

"Roger that, Captain Slaughter. Give me two mikes."

$\oplus$

The enemy bird was tubby and ungainly, a bulbous lifting-body meant for delivering heavy payloads from orbit. In any sort of atmosphere, it would have been nearly helpless; but out here in the vacuum, its outsized drive gave it plenty of thrust to haul around extra tons of armor and weapons. It was pretty much untouchable by the weapons a civilian or even a crew of bounty hunters could afford.

Luckily, Katy wasn't flying a civilian shuttle, even if it was dressed up like one and wearing a civvie registration number. Nine gravities of boost flattened her into the gel cushioning of the acceleration couch, the tight, familiar embrace of an old friend, and the closest of the two cargo transports seemed to leap toward her in the view screens. It gleamed silver-grey against the darker hues of Gateway looming behind it as big as a world, the station's radiator vanes nearly outshining the system's primary in their race to cool it down.

What the hell was the name of that star, anyway?

She couldn't remember, so she concentrated on centering the targeting reticle on the cargo transport's weapons pod, a grey tumor protruding from the open loading doors on the craft's belly. They could armor up the rest of the boat, but they couldn't put much armor on the laser or it would overheat, which was the weakness of a civilian ship retrofitted for a fight. *Her* shuttle was built for combat, and the cooling systems for the laser were twisted vanes of liquid nitrogen deep inside the armored belly. The reticle went from a flashing red to a steady, confident green and she pushed the firing stud.

They were in a hard vacuum; there was no sound, no visible beam. But the tactical computer supplied the imagery of a broken red line between her shuttle and the enemy ship, a representation of the second-long burst of laser pulses from the flower-petal emitter lens which had unfolded just beneath the cockpit. It didn't have to simulate the flash of sublimating metal and boron when the pulses struck. Those were lit up from the flare of their own burning gasses, an expanding white globe nearly as big as the shuttle.

She couldn't see anything through the ball of gas, not even on thermal, but the radar was reporting bits of the fuselage flaking off and the cargo transport was going off course, its vector altered by the thrust from the directional blast. The miniature star-burst of the drive flickered and then died and the transport ceased accelerating, still heading off in a skewed vector from its momentum. They might still be alive in there, but they were out of this fight and they'd need help if they didn't want to drift off into interstellar space and die of anoxia in a few days.

My first shots fired in anger, she mused. It had felt like nothing, like a simulator. People could have died and she felt nothing. Should that worry her?

"Splash one," she transmitted to Logan on Osceola's shuttle, her voice flat and unemotional. "Targeting the second boat now."

She shoved the control yoke to her left and downward and throttled back the thrust during the course adjustment, changing her shuttle's vector to intercept the second bounty hunter cargo bird. As it turned out, she needn't have bothered. The pilot of the second transport had broken off and changed course, decelerating and turning to go after the wounded craft.

Guess she has friends on board.

Katy killed the drive and took a deep breath for the first time in nearly a half an hour, then hit the 'link control again.

"Second boat has broken off," she informed Logan. "Awaiting instructions."

There was a long pause and she wondered if he was puking. A lot of groundpounders puked after their first taste of high-g maneuvering. His voice was hoarse and rasping when he finally spoke.

"Follow us in, Katy. We're heading for the *Shakak*."

"Roger that," she acknowledged.

She fixed the shuttle's radar and lidar lock on Osceola's bird and let the computer match velocities with it. Suddenly, her mouth was dry and her hands were beginning to shake. It took her a few minutes to get her breathing back under control and her heart rate down. Then it was past.

Just a bit of post-adrenaline withdrawal. Nothing emotional. I'm good. Dr. Saito can go to hell.

If she kept saying it long enough, she might even believe it.

"There she is."

Logan saw Kammy smiling at the image on the shuttle's main view screen, though he didn't see much to smile about. The ship was nestled behind a smallish rock, hidden from the view of Gateway in an oppositional orbit, and if he was being brutally honest...

"That looks like a big pile of scrap metal."

Osceola glared at him, but Lyta couldn't quite contain a snorting laugh.

"Welcome to the *Shakak*, Captain Slaughter," she said, waving at the ship. "Despite her looks, I think she'll suit us just fine."

Logan shook his head. He hadn't been exaggerating. The *Shakak* had the lines of a converted cargo hauler, one of the older models from early in the Reconstruction, all bulbous and rounded at the nose, cylindrical and tubby behind, with ungainly protrusions at the waist to shelter heavy-lift cargo shuttles beneath heavy shielding while under way. A separate bay for passenger shuttles was set along the belly just behind the nose armor like the mouth of a sperm whale, growing brighter and looming larger as they approached.

The ship was all slapped-together, the armor plating layered in scales, the welds ugly and obvious, the weapons pods cancerous growths extruding from the flanks of the great beast, out of place and awkward. It looked very much as he would expect the ship of a crew of shoestring mercenaries to look, and he'd been hoping for something more.

"Shuttle Two," a female voice blared harsh and grating over the cockpit speakers, "I'm picking up a trail behind you. You want I should light them up?"

"Negative, Tara," Osceola told the woman, the scowl he shot at Logan indicating he'd had to consider the answer. "They're a friendly. Stand down weapons and tell the docking crews to prepare for two incoming birds."

"Got it, boss."

At least they asked.

"How are your ribs doing, Don?" Lyta asked the master of the junk heap.

He winced, rubbing his side gingerly.

"They hurt like hell," he admitted. "But I guess it beats the alternative. I owe you one, Lyta."

Logan cleared his throat and earned another dirty look.

"Okay, I owe *both* of you." Osceola granted him. "But that's just me. I have to think about my whole crew, so I'm not committing to anything until I hear the full risk assessment."

The pilot, the big slab of marbled beef called Kammy, had flipped the shuttle end for end and was firing the main engine in short bursts for deceleration, the jolting bangs of thrust making conversation impossible for a few minutes until he'd matched velocities with the *Shakak*. A few more hammer blows to the hull, softer this time but still obnoxious, and the shuttle was floating backward relative to the big ship, slipping into the open berth with practiced ease. There was a shudder and then a sharp jerk as the bird was pulled into the magnetic grapples. Then they were still.

Relatively, he reminded himself. The whole ship, them included, was still moving thousands of meters per second around the asteroid, which was orbiting some gravitational center at thousands of meters per second, which was, in turn, orbiting the primary star, which was orbiting the galactic center, etc.... Nothing was ever "still" in space, but this was close enough for government work.

Osceola leaned forward in his seat and hit a control to switch the view from the dull grey of the interior of the docking berth to an exterior camera showing Katy's approach in the Sparta-made assault shuttle. The bird was angular and deadly, not fooling anyone with its civilian markings.

"Let's see how your girlfriend does bringing her bird home," Osceola said, leering back at him.

"How did you know..." Logan tripped over the words, shut his mouth. "I mean, what makes you think she's my girlfriend?"

Osceola barked a laugh, cutting loose of his restraints.

"Kid, you are as transparent as the observation bubble on a star cruiser. Even half-conscious, I could hear the way you talked to her when you were asking for help."

Logan tried to maintain a poker face, but he'd always been horrible at poker and he could feel his ears warming. He tried to avoid Osceola's eyes and concentrate on watching Katy's approach. Pride surged in his chest as she brought the assault shuttle in smoothly, without a hesitation or last-minute burst of maneuvering jets, sliding into the docking berth as if she'd been stationed on the *Shakak* for years and docked with her a thousand times.

"Sweet," Kammy commented, drawing the word out a few extra syllables and nodding his appreciation. "She got some smooth moves there, brother."

"Well, let's not keep the lady waiting." Osceola yanked down the red-painted lever to release the airlock and pulled the door inward, bracing himself against the fuselage. "Damn!" he hissed, clutching his side again.

"Oh, Mithra's horns, Don," Lyta sighed, pushing across the cockpit and pulled the door the rest of the way open, before going through and undogged the outer door. "How the hell have you kept your head on straight without me?"

"It ain't been easy, love." He hissed out a breath, letting Kammy squeeze past him, offering a comforting pat on the arm.

Logan glanced between Osceola and Lyta Randell, wondering again just how close the two of them had been and if their relationship was the reason she'd wanted him for the mission. But he couldn't imagine the Ranger captain ever putting her personal feelings ahead of the mission, and he suspected the only reason he was even having the thought was his own guilt at bringing Katy along.

But she proved herself. All he's done so far is fuck up.

The docking umbilical led them out into a narrow corridor, just wide enough for crew, without even a viewscreen to show the docked shuttles much less a window like the station. It would be claustrophobic, if Logan had been given to that sort of thing, though the microgravity helped to ameliorate the feeling; but he didn't know how the hell Kammy could stand it, since the man's shoulders were nearly as wide as the tunnel.

The corridor curved around to meet the outlets from the other docking berths, and Katy was already heading out of the central one, still dressed in her grey Navy flight suit, a sidearm holstered at her waist. She never went anywhere without a gun, which he'd noticed but hadn't mentioned. Whatever she needed to do to cope, she'd earned it.

"Lieutenant Kathren Margolis," Lyta introduced, "meet

Captain Donner Osceola and his First Mate Kamehameha-Nui Johannsen."

"That was some nifty flying, ma'am," Kammy told her with a nod of appreciation. "Thanks for pulling our butts out of the fire."

"It was my job," Katy told the big man. "If things work out here, then it'll have been my pleasure."

"Whoo, she's a cool one, isn't she?" Osceola laughed. "You got your hands full, boy."

"Boss, you guys okay?"

Logan recognized the voice from the transmission to the shuttle, female but sounding as if she gargled with broken glass. The face matched the voice, rough and weathered and scarred, her hair cut short and spiky, brown with just a touch of grey. Osceola and Kammy had come to Gateway in civilian spacer's clothes, but this woman wore what appeared to be some sort of ship uniform, brown fatigues with *Shakak* emblazoned across a patch on the left breast.

She pushed herself out of an access hub, a tube running down the core of the crewed part of any large ship, the fastest way to get around in free-fall. And clambering out behind her was...

"Shit!" Logan blurted, clawing at his holster, forgetting to hold onto the guide-rail on the side of the passageway and floating off, shoulders impacting the bulkhead behind him.

Behind Tara was a Jeuta. There was no mistaking them. The thing's skin was thick and dark and rubbery, like a sea lion's, where it emerged from his brown, sleeveless shirt, nearly as big as Kammy's. Its ears were concave recesses in the side of its smooth, almost featureless head, and twin slits lay flush where a nose would be on a human. The eyes were shark-black and sheltered under bony ridges, but the most alien thing about a Jeuta was the mouth. Slitted and broad, snakelike, with teeth to match, always hanging open for cooling.

They were The Enemy with huge capital letters and Logan

had trained to fight them every day of four years in the Academy. His gun was millimeters from clearing leather when Lyta Randell's hand closed over his, pinning the weapon in place.

"It's okay," she insisted, her voice low and commanding. "He's not a threat, *Captain Slaughter*." The use of his nom de guerre shocked him out of his conditioned response and he met her dark eyes, saw the reassurance in them. "He's part of the crew."

Logan glanced back and forth between her, Osceola, and the Jeuta, his eyes wide. The Jeuta was staring back, but he couldn't read the thing's eyes, couldn't tell if it was angry or scared or simply bored. He finally saw the ship logo on its vest and he let a deep breath from between his teeth.

"Meet Tara Gerard, my Tactical Officer," Osceola said, a wry smile playing across his face, obviously amused at Logan's reaction, "and Wihtgar, one of my Engineering techs." He shrugged, smiled more broadly. "Well, he also doubles as ship's security, 'cause, you know…" He waved at the size of the Jeuta, the taloned vice grips it had for hands.

"Tara, Wihtgar, this is Captain Jonathan Slaughter, the man who wants to hire us. Say hello to the nice man."

"Pleased to make your acquaintance." The Jeuta *spoke*.

He knew they *could* speak, of course. They couldn't have had a technological civilization otherwise—well, they couldn't have maintained what passed for a technological civilization, anyway. But all the intelligence reports on them said they only conversed in their own tongue, never deigning to speak Basic, only using computer translators when they dealt with humans. Something about how they didn't care to use what they still called their "slave language." He'd never heard one speak in the human language before.

"You must have one hell of a story, Wihtgar," Logan said,

fingers still clutching unconsciously, as if they longed for the butt of his gun, or the controls of his mech.

"Come on," Osceola urged them. "Let's get to the bridge and get this bucket moving at a reasonable acceleration." He chuckled, leading them into the access hub. "Then we can all tell our stories."

9

"Hold on just a damn minute." Donner Osceola held up his left hand, his right still wrapped around the glass.

The ship's doctor—well, *medic*, anyway, "doctor" being too prestigious a title for someone whose only medical experience was as a Navy corpsman—had warned him against drinking alcohol with the painkillers she'd given him for his ribs, but what the hell did she know? Besides, you didn't greet guests with water or juice or any such kiddie shit. And you didn't waste good vodka.

"You're telling me you want us to *pretend* to be mercenaries?" His gaze darted back and forth between Lyta and this Jonathan Slaughter character. He was sure it was a fake name, and a fairly new one to the kid, since he seemed to take an extra half-second to respond to it. "And actually take jobs and fight, just so we can get through Starkad territory?"

"We're not going to pretend," Lyta corrected him, taking a sip from her own glass. She'd always appreciated a good vodka. It was one of the things he loved about her. "We're going to take jobs *and* take money." She cocked an eyebrow. "And the money, by the way, is one hundred percent *yours*, on top of what we'll be paying you, which will not be inconsiderable."

Osceola came up short at that, leaning heavily against the table they'd commandeered in the ship's galley after they'd chased out the crew who'd been grabbing a bite between shifts. Kammy was weighing down a chair not nearly sturdy enough for his bulk at one gravity of acceleration, and his eyes lit up at the mention of the money.

"All of it?" he repeated, calculations running through his head of how much a mercenary company might make, gross, for a job. And it *would* be the gross, since all their expenses would be paid by Sparta.

"So," Captain Osceola prompted, suspicion overcoming greed for a moment, "what's the catch?"

"Besides the part where we all might get killed," Kammy added with a casual wave of his hand, the one with the beer bottle in it. Wussy didn't drink the hard stuff. "We're kind of used to that, by now."

"The catch is," Lyta told them, using her empty glass as a pointer, "absolute and uncompromising secrecy. You *can't* tell anyone who we really are, not in a drunken stupor on liberty, not baring your soul among other things to some local joy-girl." She shrugged. "Or boy."

"Lyta, baby," Osceola insisted, not sure if he was actually hurt by the implication or simply acting hurt out of old habit, "would I ever…"

"Save it, Don," she cut him off with a slash of her hand in the air. "If *anyone* talks, there will be consequences, and I don't mean hurt feelings or a bruised ego." She looked to the kid, as if reminding him he was in charge, and he nodded.

"We're going to be out on the edge," Slaughter told them, voice firm and commanding, if perhaps a bit self-conscious. The kid wasn't a fuck-up, Osceola decided, he just had very little experience. "We're not going to be able to count on any backup, any sort of support. If anyone gives us up, we're all most likely dead."

The fingers of the kid's right hand flexed unconsciously, like he was working a control.

"Anyone who you think can't keep their mouth shut, cut them loose now or we'll find another ride. If it happens during the mission, we won't have a trial, we won't have a prison... we'll just have an execution."

Kammy whistled softly, face pinched and thoughtful, but Osceola tried not to let on it bothered him.

"I trust my people," he declared, then downed the last of his vodka and set the glass on the table beside him. "I wouldn't have hired them in the first place if I didn't."

"Even the Jeuta?"

Osceola glared at the kid, his own face taking the stubborn set usually a close precedent to the start of a fight.

"Wihtgar," Lyta answered the question since he wasn't about to, "was just a teenager when the crew found him out on the Periphery. His father and older brother were part of a raiding mission into Starkad territory and they brought him along to get 'blooded.' But it was a trap, and Starkad destroyed their ship."

"Good."

Well, he couldn't blame the kid for his reaction. Jeuta raiders were the bane of most Periphery colonies, merciless and unrelenting, killing man, woman and child and burning human settlements to the ground wherever they found them.

"Wihtgar," Lyta went on as if Slaughter hadn't spoken, "was the last survivor. He'd been stuck into a life-pod by his father and some of the colonists found him."

"That place was rough, dude," Kammy put in, sympathy in his smooth baritone. "They put the boy in a cage and made him fight the local animals."

Even Slaughter had to wince slightly, then. Osceola's gut still roiled at the memory of the Jeuta youth covered in blood, much of it his own, his clothes shredded rags, his only bathroom a bucket at the corner of his cage.

"Wihtgar has never been anything but a loyal member of this crew," he said, his tone flat and final. "He goes where we go."

The kid shared a look with Lyta and she shrugged.

"All right, then," young "Captain Slaughter" said, a sigh going out of him as if the load of making the decision had slipped off his shoulders. Something of the cocky mech jock returned, replacing the grave weight of command. "I guess that means you're hired. How about showing me what I'm paying for?"

Osceola snorted without humor.

"Shit," he drawled, "I don't remember saying I wanted the job."

"Don," Lyta sighed, pressing her fingers together as if in a prayer, "for once in your life, do something smart."

Somewhere in those dark eyes, Osceola made his choice.

"All right." He pushed away from the table, and the cheap plastic creaked beneath him, threatening to break. "Guess I can give you the three-credit tour."

He still wasn't sure about this, but Lyta had never set him on the wrong course. When it came to her, he'd always been the one who had trouble navigating.

Logan drifted somewhere in the twilight zone between sleep and wakefulness, the warmth of bare skin against his, the feel of the smoothness beneath his right hand almost dreamlike. Katy's breath teased at his chest hairs and he smiled.

"These sheets are scratchy," she said, her tone playful.

"Really?" he mumbled. "I hadn't noticed."

He rolled over to face her, the highlights of her blond hair glinting in the pale glow of the chemical striplights along the floor. He couldn't quite see her eyes, but he thought she was smiling when he kissed her. She purred somewhere in her chest as his lips traveled to her ear, then the juncture of her neck, and any thoughts of sleep were forgotten.

"I'll have to bring my own for the mission," she said, a bit breathlessly.

His head snapped upward, his eyes suddenly wide-open.

"What?" he blurted.

Now he could see her eyes, noticed a flash of irritation in them.

"I'm coming with you," she said, in a tone she might have used with a slow child. "On the mission." She shrugged. "You're going to need a good assault shuttle pilot." She cocked her head to the side, resting it on the heel of her hand. "Actually, you'll probably need two, along with a couple heavy-lift lander drivers who can double as backup shuttle pilots."

"Whoa, hold on," he said, raising a palm to slow her down and sitting up in bed.

The bed was surprisingly big, as was the cabin. Navy ships were typically over-crewed and space was always at a premium. He supposed things were different when you had to pay everyone in the crew out of your profits instead of from the pockets of the taxpayers.

"Look, Katy, it was one thing to bring you along on a short run to Gateway to recruit Osceola, but there's no way in hell I can get away with assigning you to the mission!"

Now he wished he *couldn't* see her eyes very clearly, because there were storms brewing behind them.

"Are you saying," she asked in a tone much like the warning rattle of a diamondback, "I am not qualified for this mission?"

"Of course you're qualified!" he blurted. "But I'm the

commander!" The word came out a squeak and he cursed himself. "What's it going to look like if I abuse my position by bringing my..."

"Your *what?*" she interrupted. "Your *girlfriend?* Is that what I am, Logan? Your girlfriend?" He could feel warmth again, but this was a totally different kind, the sort where you needed protective gear if you didn't want to get burned.

He spluttered helplessly but finally just decided to be honest.

"Well, yeah! I mean, aren't you? Aren't we... ?" He gestured wordlessly, even though he wasn't sure she could see it.

"You'd better get your shit sorted, Mister!" she snapped, poking a finger into his chest. "Just because we're... whatever we are..." She lost her train of thought, frowning deeply. "What the hell are we anyway? Am I some stray you decided to take in because you felt guilty? Some lost soul you thought you could fix?"

Logan's head was spinning as what had previously been a very nice evening had somehow turned into his worst nightmare and he desperately tried to slug his brain into gear. Unfortunately, it wouldn't do anything but sit there grinding and smoking, so he spoke with his heart instead.

"You're the woman I'm in love with," he told her.

He thought, for one, endlessly long moment he'd said the wrong thing, because her mouth seemed frozen in mid-sentence, her eyes narrowed and suspicious. He was about to apologize because that was the only other thing he could think to do, but she grabbed him by the back of his head and kissed him fiercely. He hadn't had time to take a breath, and the lack of oxygen along with the sudden rush of blood to other places in his body made him light-headed, but she came up for air a few seconds before the blackness closed in.

"Damn it, Logan," she said softly, "just when I was getting a good mad going, you manage to get me all soft and gooey again."

She smiled. "I love you, too." Then she arched an eyebrow and her face became stern for just a second. "But I'm going, and that's final."

He opened his mouth, closed it, thought hard for several seconds and finally managed to say something coherent.

"I have to be able to justify this to my father and General Constantine," he said, what he thought was a well-reasoned point. "If they think I'm bringing along my girlfriend so I won't get lonely, they'll yank this thing out of my hands quicker than shit through a goose."

"Where the hell did you hear that?" she asked him, laughing, a sound like water pouring over crystal.

"From Lyta." He grinned. "I've known her since before she went to the Academy, back when she was an NCO. She was like my big sister when I was a kid."

"Tell her you want me along," Katy suggested. "If she's known your father that long, she'll know how to convince him."

"All right," he said, throwing up his hands in surrender. If he was being honest with himself, he was glad of it. Mithra alone knew how long they'd be gone, and he hadn't been looking forward to saying goodbye, but he would have felt guilty asking her to come along. He wondered if she'd known that... "But if you come along, you have to promise me one thing."

"You *better* not tell me I shouldn't take any unnecessary risks," she warned him. "Not the way you throw your ass around into every dangerous situation."

"I'd like to," he admitted, "but no. Though you do have to take my orders, whether or not you like them," he cautioned her. "That's not negotiable. We can't make this work otherwise."

"I understand," she said, with what he knew was false meekness. "When we're around anyone else, I will treat you as my commander and superior officer. But what was the one thing you wanted me to promise you?"

"You can't call me 'Logan' anymore," he insisted. "Not even in private. If anyone finds out who I really am, we are done. I'm 'Captain Slaughter' in public, and 'Jonathan' in private, no exceptions."

"No exceptions?" She tilted her head and looked at him side-long. "Even when I yell out your name?"

He ran his hand down her shoulder, smiling broadly.

"Especially then," he teased. "You're really loud and these bulkheads are pretty thin."

She put a hand against his chest and pushed him backward. He went with the push and laid back against the pillow.

"Is that so?" she demanded, straddling his hips. "Why don't we see how loudly you can make me shout 'Jonathan,' then?"

She leaned over and kissed him, her breath starting to come in short gasps.

"I don't know." His hands went to her hips, pulling her into him. "Maybe I can make you yell 'Captain Slaughter' instead."

She paused in her motion to smack him lightly and playfully in the side of the head.

"Don't make me break something I might have a use for later," she warned him, laughing breathlessly. "Wholesale Slaughter my ass…"

10

"**M**an, where the hell have you been?" Marc Langella didn't look up from folding his laundry, just threw a wadded-up sock at Logan as he stepped through the open door of the Bachelor Officer's Quarters room. "You been MIA for three-fucking-weeks!"

Logan ducked the sock, letting it bounce off the wall out in the hallway behind him. Langella scowled, pausing in his chore to grab a slice of pizza from a plate perched perilously close to the edge of the bed.

"You could have caught the sock, at least," he remonstrated around a mouthful.

"No thanks," Logan said, pushing the door shut behind him. "I know where your feet have been."

The BOQ at Laconia headquarters on Sparta had a biweekly cleaning service and Marc Langella made those poor bastards earn every credit of their pay.

"Seriously dude," Langella got up from his bed, wiping his right hand on the front of his T-shirt before offering it to Logan to shake, "where the hell you been? You missed company training and I had to take your damned platoon!"

"That's what I'm here to talk to you about, Marc." Logan leaned against the dresser across from the bed, motioning for his friend to sit back down. He paused for a breath, trying to organize his thoughts. He'd been rehearsing this for days and it still sounded lame and unbelievable. "How would you like to have your own platoon permanently?"

"Well, of course I want my own platoon." Langella shrugged, then caught the dish with the rest of the pizza before it could tumble off the bed and onto the carpeting. He set it on the nightstand instead. "Another six months in grade and I'll be eligible…"

"I mean right now," Logan clarified. "You could have your own platoon starting immediately, get an instant promotion to full Lieutenant. Be on the fast track to captain."

Langella ran long fingers through tightly-curled dark hair and regarded Logan with what might have been a mix of skepticism and keen interest.

"Seriously? What's the catch, Log?"

Logan winced. Marc Langella was the only one who he let get away with calling him "Log," though he supposed it wouldn't matter much longer.

"It's a deep-cover operation, Marc. Indefinite duration, high risk." He raised a hand palm-up to stop what he assumed was the younger man about to trip over himself to say yes. "*Very* high risk, Marc. No support, no backup. We'll be on our own. And you won't be able to tell your family, your friends where you're going or when you'll be back." He didn't bother to mention a girlfriend. Langella hadn't been able to keep a relationship going for more than a month since he'd known him and he didn't think the last three weeks had changed that.

Langella stared at him, arms crossed, waiting.

"You done trying to scare me off?"

"I guess I am." Logan rubbed his eyes with thumb and forefinger. He trusted Langella and wanted him along, but he also didn't want to be the reason his friend got killed, and the cognitive dissonance was giving him a headache. "Did it work?"

Langella smirked all the way to his closet, grabbed a duffel bag and tossed it on the bed.

"When do we leave?"

"Langella's coming along?" Lyta asked him.

He nearly had to jog to keep up with her pace, but at least it was keeping him warm. Winter was closing in on Argos, and while it wouldn't ever be as cold here as it was on Ramman, he still had his jacket's hood thrown up. The weather didn't seem to bother Lyta Randell, but nothing ever did, not the dimly-lit streets, nor the vacant, foreboding towers of downtown looming over them in the midnight hours.

"Not just him," he said, raising his voice to be heard over the automated cargo truck rumbling by on the other side of the street, kicking up a spray of salt and melted ice. "The whole platoon. Marc's going to work on the maintenance techs, too." He picked up a step to catch up to her. "What about the Rangers?"

"One hundred percent participation." She might have been reading off an official military report, but he thought he could hear just a hint of the pride she felt in her tightly-reined voice. "The whole company and support staff."

"Nice."

He was nodding even though she couldn't see him under his hood. Keeping unit cohesion was going to be tricky in a mission like this, and recruiting them intact would make it easier. Now came the hard part, the part he'd been dreading since they'd arrived back on Sparta only forty hours ago.

"What about the drop-ship and assault shuttle crews?" He

tried to keep his tone casual, as if his was merely a professional interest. "Have they been selected? Who's going to be running point on that?"

He was grateful he hadn't had to raise the question with General Constantine. It had been relayed to him via secure radio transmission up in orbit that he should stay away from the palace altogether during his visit for security reasons. All the official connections between him and his father had been scrubbed from the paperwork when he'd entered the Academy, at his request, to avoid special treatment, and he'd managed to stay out of the press. It helped that General Constantine had agents planted deeply in the official media agencies and a team of hackers to scrub the unofficial ones. But people knew him by sight at the palace and it would be better if he just weren't around for a few months before the mission went down.

Lyta hadn't answered him for a long moment and he was beginning to wonder if the wind whipping down the canyon formed by Athinas Boulevard cutting through the center of the city had carried away his words.

"I am," she said, finally, her eyes hidden by the fall of her fur-trimmed hat across her cheek.

He let out a sigh. *That* was the best news he'd heard in days.

"Okay, then there's something I wanted to ask you, kind of a personal favor." His stomach roiled a bit at what felt like a betrayal, though he knew it was the right thing to do. "Katy has it in her head she wants to go on this mission and she's not taking no for an answer, not from *me* anyway. But I *know* it's totally inappropriate and there is no way in hell I would ever ask for my girlfriend..." Mithra's teeth, that word sounded inadequate to describe their relationship. He pushed on anyway. "...to come along on a military mission, so I was wondering if I might be able to get you to play the bad cop and tell her you won't allow it."

There. It was out. He'd done it and if Katy found out and

dropped him like a hot rock, at least he could console himself that he'd done the right thing, and maybe he'd kept her alive, which was more important to him than her being with him. Maybe she'd even understand that...

"Wait, what?" He'd been so embroiled in his own thoughts, he'd misheard Lyta's reply.

He *must* have misheard it.

"I said," Lyta repeated, matter-of-factly, "Lt. Margolis is already assigned to the mission as an assault shuttle pilot."

"Since when?" He hadn't meant the words to carry quite as much invective as they did, but he couldn't pull them back in, so he doubled down. "I thought we just agreed that was a horrible idea!"

"This may come as a shock to you, Logan," she said, turning her head just enough for him to see her eyebrow cocked upward, "but strategic and tactical military decisions often occur with no regard whatsoever to whom you happen to be dating."

"But I'm going to be in her chain of command," he protested, exposing his hands to the cold just so he could spread them expressively. "I'm going to be at the *top* of the chain! That's against regulations, isn't it? Oh, shit," he realized, the breath going out of him, "I'm going to have to break up with her, aren't I?"

Lyta stopped so suddenly he nearly slid on a patch of ice trying to turn back toward her. She was staring at him the way she had when he'd asked a series of progressively stupider questions as a young teenager and she'd still been "Aunt Lyta."

"Do you think," she asked him, slowly and carefully, as if he were that dull-witted thirteen-year-old again, "I would make the decision to bring her along if I thought either of you would be stupid enough to put your relationship over the mission?"

"Well, no, of course not," he agreed readily, now that she put it in terms of her own reliability instead of his. "But even if you think I won't do something stupid, how can you be sure Katy won't? I mean, you've known me my whole life, but you've only known her a few months."

She sniffed at the question and started walking again. Not knowing what else to do, he followed.

"Part of my job is knowing what makes people tick, junior. It's how I know which way a guard is going to move, whether he's going to look up at the wrong time before one of my Rangers guts him. It's how I know who to send on a long-range foot patrol alone, how I know who to send through the door first. When push comes to shove, Katy is the type of woman who'll do her duty even if it hurts." Her shoulders shrugged, barely visible through her thick, winter jacket. "If you want to know why *her,* it's the same reason we're here trying to pick up a company's worth of mech jocks instead of sitting in Colonel Anders' office and asking for volunteers to report there. No one knows her. She hasn't even reported to her first duty station yet. And she's already proven to me she can keep her head in a sticky situation, which is why I let you get away with bringing her along to Gateway in the first place."

"And you don't think I'd do something to compromise the mission to protect her?" He wasn't so much asking for confirmation of her faith in him as a leader, as he was honestly wanting to know the answer. Because he wasn't so sure.

"What makes you think I'd *let* you do that?"

That's a gut punch, he thought, feeling properly cut down to size. *How much*, he wondered not for the first time, *am I actually in charge of this mission, and how much am I just a figurehead?*

"Here it is." Lyta nodded toward what looked like nothing else so much as a hole in the wall. It didn't even have an illuminated sign, just hand-worked metal bent into the crude shape of a Sentinel strike mech.

"Why the hell have I never heard of this place?" he wondered, stepping up beside her on the sidewalk, hearing a murmur of voices through the thick, varnished wood of the door.

"This isn't the kind of place you want to go if you're aiming to be Guardian someday." Her mouth twisted into a half-smile. "I believe it would be on the proscribed list if anyone above the rank of Major knew it existed." The smile hardened. "This is a hard crowd and they won't know who you are, so keep your head on a swivel."

"Can't be harder than Gateway," he said, snorting humorlessly.

She shrugged at that and pulled open the door. Music blasted through it, distorted by a blown speaker and a bad digital conversion on whatever system they were using, twenty years out of style. The warm air was more welcome than the music, and he squeezed through the door before Lyta yanked it shut.

The place was decorated in a style he'd mostly seen out in the more primitive colony worlds, no fancy, holographic art or video walls, as little electronics as possible. The bar was real wood, hand-polished, as were the tables, while the walls were decorated with memorabilia and bits of armor from various model mecha, some of it decades out of date.

The customers were mech-jocks and technicians, he could tell by a quick scan of the place, by the way they walked or their haircuts or the way they dressed. He might be just a Lieutenant, but he'd grown up around mecha and their pilots and the mannerisms were hard to miss. But no, this was no place for staff officers or battalion commanders. Hell, he'd be willing to bet not even a company commander had ever set foot in the bar. Warrant officers mostly, and younger platoon leaders who didn't know any better.

Which describes me, too, and I still wonder how I didn't know about this place. Marc must know... bastard has been holding out.

He followed Lyta to the bar and let her order something for him so he could keep his eyes on the clientele. There *were* other people here besides the mech-jocks and techs. He'd never seen them in such numbers, but he still knew what they were: Gun Bunnies, they were called. Men and women both, though more women than men for some sociological reason he'd never bothered to look up. Their outfits were tight and of a style and date with the hard-driving music, replete with leather and metal studs and a lot of skin. Hair flowed in meters of bleached blond and red, and even green and purple while oversized sunglasses were nearly *de rigueur*, along with outsized leather, brimmed hats.

They were here for the mech-jocks, though they'd probably settle for the techs if there weren't enough pilots to go around. He shoved down the visceral disdain and contempt he felt for them and took his dark ale from the bartender when it was offered. The bartender stood, waiting, and Lyta gave him the eye.

"Oh." He pulled out a handful of paper Tradenotes and laid them on the bar. It was wet and he could see the moisture soaking into them. The bartender took them as if it were no matter, and didn't offer change.

"You ain't a jock."

The words were slurred, and the glaze in the big guy's eyes spoke to just how much he'd already had to drink, but he was nearly two meters and probably two hundred kilograms of very little fat. And he'd been talking to Lyta.

"You ain't a jock," he repeated, more clearly this time, as if the first iteration had been practice. "I can tell." And he probably could. He was in his thirties, maybe forties, and probably a tech, since you didn't find too many people his size who wanted to squeeze into the cockpit of a mech. "You ain't a tech either."

"She's with me," Logan told the man, hoping to avoid a scene.

The big man had bushy, auburn eyebrows with no hair above them, and they rose in obvious skepticism.

"And who the fuck are you?" he demanded. He looked Logan

up and down. "You look like a jock," he acknowledged grudgingly, "but I ain't never seen you in here before."

"Benjie," the bartender snapped at the man, his voice like ten kilometers of gravel road and a face to match, "no one fucking appointed you the fucking bouncer, so stop harassing the fucking customers."

Benjie burped a response, then flipped the bartender a bird and went back to whatever was in the glass in front of him. The glass was shaped like the lower leg of a Scorpion strike mech, which seemed infinitely kitschy to Logan but it held a hell of a lot of something alcoholic.

"There." Lyta was looking across the room, through a scrum of tables and a cluster of pay-to-play VIR games based on mech simulators to the rear area of the bar.

Nearly lost in the shadows back there were a half a dozen men and women, all wearing leather jackets festooned with unit insignias and campaign badges, huddled around a single, large table, nursing what might have been their first pitcher of beer or maybe their tenth. He thought he recognized one or two, though he'd never served with any of them.

Lyta received some curious glances as they crossed the room, a few sets of eyes widening with what he thought was recognition, but no one else challenged her. Even the Gun Bunnies turned their noses up at what they probably thought of as a "crunchie," an infantry soldier, though a few seemed to perk up when he passed, probably intrigued by the new guy.

The jocks at the table in the back, though, they paid attention. He thought they knew who Lyta was from the respectfully fearful sideways glances they were giving each other. One of them was going to be the first, the one to risk speaking up, and he'd already made up his mind it would be that person he'd wind up trusting.

"You looking for someone, Captain Randell?"

He was about Logan's age, maybe a bit older or maybe it was

just the weathered lines on his face making him seem older. He had the look of a man raised in the outdoors, probably on one of the smaller, more backward colonies from his accent. His dirty blond hair was shorter than regulation, a buzz a couple of centimeters long, and his eyes were narrow, careful, watchful.

"I'm looking for you, Lt. Kurtz," she told him. "We're looking for all of you." She shrugged. "More or less. Four of you at least."

"We've read your files," Logan put in. "We know your service records. And we know none of you is all that happy with your current assignments."

"And you are?" This one was the taller of the two women at the table, tall enough and thin enough she might have been raised on a lower-gravity world. Her features were narrow and sharp and quite striking, amber skinned and hazel-eyed, with brown hair pulled into a tight ponytail. Ford, he thought her name was.

"Jonathan Slaughter." One of them opened their mouth as if they were about to say "no, you're not," and Logan interrupted her. "As far as *anyone* here knows, I am Jonathan Slaughter. And I'm looking for volunteers for a mercenary crew to head out to the Periphery and fight bandits and pirates."

"What the fuck?" This guy was short and squat, his head shaved shiny, and was definitely the oldest of the bunch. Paskowski. From the smell of his breath, he'd had more than his fair share of the beer. "Mercenaries?" He almost spat the word out. "Why the hell would we want to be fucking mercenaries?"

"Shut up," Lyta said with a flat, toneless danger to her voice, her eyes going hard. Paskowski bristled and she slammed a hand down on the table hard enough to nearly topple the empty pitcher. "Keep. Your. Mouth. Shut."

Paskowski swallowed hard, as if he'd suddenly sensed he was messing with the wrong person, and Kurtz edged away from Lyta ever so slightly.

"This is an op," she told them, voice low without whispering. "You'll be gone as long as you need to be gone, doing whatever we tell you to do, and we'll be all on our own without any support or backup. And if you die out there, you'll be officially registered as having resigned your commissions as of today."

Logan stepped in, sensing this was his time to be "good cop."

"But you'll be piloting mecha in combat, killing bandits and traveling to systems you'd never have seen otherwise. And if we succeed, probably achieving the biggest strategic coup in the history of the Dominions." He grinned. "And getting combat pay the whole time… accruable when you get back, of course."

Which had never meant anything to him, but Langella droned on and on about it constantly, so he assumed it would be just as important to these guys.

"And what if we decide we don't want to volunteer?" Rougher around the edges, less respectful, shirt-tail hanging out, hair edging pretty far over regulation cut. This guy was a Warrant Officer, not commissioned, didn't go to the Academy, just straight from enlisted to mech training.

He let Lyta answer, because this was the sort of thing she was better at than him.

"If you don't want to volunteer, Warrant Officer Darren Aventura," she said in the same muted tones, "Service Number 345H6389, mother Sharon, father David, current girlfriend Camilla Watson…" Her lips skinned back from her teeth in half a smile, half a snarl. "Then I think no one should *ever* hear about this from you. If you'd like to enjoy a nice, long career and a fruitful life."

Aventura nodded slowly, then began chuckling, not as if he didn't take the implied threat seriously, but more like he appreciated the art of putting it together.

"I like her," the Warrant said, wagging a finger at Lyta. "Oh, yeah. I'm definitely in."

Kurtz looked around the table at the rest of them and there were nods all around.

"You folks sure do know how to sell a feller on a pig in a poke," Kurtz said, offering Jonathan a hand. "I assume we'll find out what's really going on once we get there, huh?"

"I assume so," he agreed, shaking the hand.

"You'll all be getting very vague orders through your chain of command," Lyta told them, not offering to shake anyone's hand nor receiving any such invitations. "Pack light but... comprehensively."

He barely saw her turn out of the corner of his eye, had just enough time to follow her without looking like an idiot who'd been left behind.

"You know," he told her as she fitted her cap back onto her head and pushed the door open, "I sometimes wonder what you'd do to someone if you weren't bluffing."

"Logan," she said into the chill wind of the night street, "I never bluff."

11

"I don't like this," Logan—*no, damn it, I'm Jonathan now. Can't even think of myself as Logan anymore*—muttered, watching the bulbous cargo pods drifting across the sullen face of the gas giant. The freighter they'd launched from was nearly invisible at the planet's terminator, an intruder crouching in the shadows.

"What?" Marc Langella wondered, not looking up from the tablet as he checked off another delivery. "Everything's come through okay so far, and Fourth Platoon should be coming over with the next shuttle."

Langella was a beanpole at the best of times; anchored to the deck of the *Shakak's* cargo bay by magnetic boots, he swayed and flapped like a ribbon in the wind, the tight curls of his jet-black hair shifting with the air currents from the vent in the overhead.

"I don't like not being able to say goodbye," Jonathan confessed. He leaned against the bulkhead as if it were an actual window rather than simply a view screen connected to the external cameras. "I thought I'd be able to go home one last time, but they wouldn't even let me talk to Dad or Terrin."

"Would have been risky," Langella allowed, shaking his head, his body tottering precipitously with the motion. "Hell, they barely told us volunteers anything before we shipped out. Didn't say where we were going or how long we'd be gone, just that it was an indefinite assignment and we'd be getting hazard pay for the duration."

"You didn't even get to tell your family you were leaving?" Jonathan wondered. *Shit. Should I call myself "Jon?" I never had to come up with a nickname for "Logan." Is Jonathan Slaughter the type of guy who'd want to be called "Jon?"*

"I didn't even get to pet my damn dog," Langella told him, laughing sharply. "After you made your visit, I had about two hours to pack and get to the spaceport. Anyway," he went on, shrugging, "the whole damned platoon came, didn't they? Along with a bunch of the best drivers in the battalion and I don't know how they talked Anders into letting them go." He frowned, waving a hand at the view screen as if motioning all the way back to Sparta. "I thought you said the… ," Langella hesitated and corrected himself from saying something like "the Guardian" to, "…I mean, your *dad* sent you a goodbye message."

"Yeah," Jonathan—*not "Jon," that sounds too generic*— grunted. Dad had sent him a text-only message, vague and name-less for security. And yet he still remembered every word:

Son,

I know this is something you have to do, and I know your mother would be proud of you for following your heart. I confess to having my doubts, not of your ability but of the danger inherent in the path you've chosen. I am, above all else that I am, a parent, and I share the fears of every parent.

I trust you to take care of your people and do your job, but I implore you to take care for yourself as well. You may think we here at home can get along without you, but I assure you, we cannot.

Love,

Your father

PS: Your brother has not answered my messages. I think he feels betrayed that you have left him behind. I will make sure he knows the choice was not yours. I can't take the chance of losing both my children.

Great. Not only would he not get the chance to say goodbye to Terrin, but his brother hadn't even sent a message and was blaming him for not bringing him along. He'd felt like they were beginning to get along before he'd left, but now he might never get to see him again.

I might never see anyone *again. I could die out here.*

The thought hit him low in the gut, a sudden realization of his own mortality not even being shot at on Gateway had brought home. Even though he was surrounded by his former platoon-mates, as well as a hundred other Guard and Navy personnel, he felt alone. Before, even with just him and Lyta and Katy, he'd still been cognizant of the trip back home he'd expected to take before embarking on the mission. Then the message had come through the relay to stay with the *Shakak*, to wait there for the cargo ship bringing mechs and shuttles and crew and suddenly, there was no trip home, no chance for final words.

What was the last thing I said to Terrin? Something like "see you when I get back?" Did I even shake Dad's hand?

He felt a shudder go through the hull of the ship as a transfer pod locked with the magnetic seals of the cargo bay at her belly, the first of the mech shipping over from the Spartan transport.

"I should go supervise the unloading," he told Langella, slapping the man on the shoulder, next to his brand-spanking-new Lieutenant's rank.

Everyone had gotten a bump up for this mission, including Lyta, who was now a Major. It fit with their back-story. Mercenaries usually promoted themselves from their last official rank. But he'd also been assured it would be official if and when they got back.

Walking with the magnetic boots was awkward, like plodding through mud. You had to work to pull your foot up from the deck plates, and it seemed to suck you down when you planted it again. The clomp-clomp sound it made was gratingly annoying, not just from his own footsteps but the other personnel working in the cargo bay. Most were *Shakak* crew, but there were already a dozen or so Navy technicians on board, helping to set up the cradles for the incoming mechs. They wore the same ship uniform as the others, but theirs were cleaner, their hair shorter, their general demeanor more professional.

He hoped by the time they had to interact with a potential client the differences would have smoothed out a bit. Right now, he would have been happy if he could have just bought the ship off Osceola outright and taken it over, but Lyta had assured him the Captain's reputation was half of what they were hiring.

The cargo lock was by far the most impressive section of the ship as well as the largest, a gigantic, spherical compartment two hundred meters across, now fitted with magnetic cradles for a company's worth of mecha as well as enough ammo and spare parts to supply and service them. At the center of the compartment, a fifty-meter-wide mechanical iris hatch was slowly and laboriously grinding open, already mated with the pressurized cargo pod, while freight-handling arms craned inward from mounts on the bulkhead like monstrous claws ready to strike.

The metallic scraping of the centimeters-thick iris vibrated through the deck, through the magnetic boots and into his marrow. Just when he thought it couldn't get any more irritating, the chugging, grumble rumble of a huge freight elevator joined the chorus, pushing a pallet of cargo fifty meters across through the hatchway and into the bay. Most of the space was taken by up by mecha, and he spotted his own machine almost immediately, a humanoid shape with massive legs resting on heavy, rounded pads.

Colonel Anders had offered him the Scorpion he'd taken down; it had been salvaged mostly intact. It was heavier and better-armed, but his Vindicator seemed like an old friend and he hadn't even considered parting with it. It rose from the shadows of the cargo pod, surrounded by an honor guard of shorter, squatter Golems, and as it ascended the spotlights from the bay bathed it in a golden glow. The glare lit up the cockpit at just the right angle for him to notice the human-shaped figure sprawled in the mech's easy chair, motionless and lifeless.

"What the *fuck?*" he blurted.

He started to run, abruptly remembered the magnetic boots and paused to unstrap and pull them off, leaving them affixed to the deck and pushed away, sailing across to meet the pallet even before it had risen all the way into place.

"Medic!" he bellowed in mid-flight, pitching his voice to carry across the bay. "Somebody get a damn medic in here!"

He could feel the eyes on him, hear the exclamations of surprise, but he was focused on the cockpit. How the hell would someone wind up in there? The freight had been sealed in place for the duration of the voyage; except in case of emergency, no crewmembers on the cargo ship would have had any business screwing around inside the pods. And if someone had been trapped in there all the way from Sparta, with no air, no water, no heat... well, a medic wasn't going to do them any good.

He slammed into the chest of the Vindicator shoulder-first, the breath whooshing out of him with a dull pain spreading down into his lower back. He knew it would hurt even worse in a few hours, but he shoved it aside for the moment, grabbing at the emergency external access panel and yanking the quick-release lever. The cockpit canopy swung upward with a pneumatic hiss and he was pulling himself inside before it was halfway open, already noticing the bulky, oversized outline of the occupant, understanding on a gut level before he'd even processed the information.

The man wore a vacuum suit, and there was an external feeder conduit plugged from the chest panel into a jack in the side of the cockpit to provide air from the mech's on-board recyclers and heat from the batteries. This wasn't some idiot cargo handler who'd tried to sneak a ride in the easy chair and died for his stupidity; this was a stowaway, someone with a plan to be here. The helmet was turned away from him, shielding the face inside from view until he grabbed the yoke and jerked the shoulder toward him, turning the head of the man inside.

It was a familiar face, soft-lined and thin with dark hair spilling out over his face, his eyes closed, but breath fogging the interior of the faceplate just slightly. It was his brother, Terrin, and he was alive.

"Oh, you fucking idiot," he murmured. Then yelling, back out to the cargo crew, leaning out of the cockpit. "Get me a Goddamned medic!"

Light and darkness swam across Terrin's vision in nightmare shapes and a silent terror built up inside his chest like steam pressure in a boiler, threatening to explode if it wasn't relieved. He was sure he was dead, stuck in a nebulous afterlife so unlike the one the religion of his parents had described, with no heaven or hell, just endless, weary planes of shadow.

"Are you awake?"

Light and shadow solidified into the face of his brother.

"Holy shit," he rasped, his throat filled with cotton. "Log…"

"Yeah," his brother interrupted, leaning over him, eyes narrowing. "It's me, *Jonathan*. Remember?"

Terrin blinked, squeezing his eyes shut, trying to piece

together scattered bits of memory into a coherent thought. When he opened them, he saw Logan holding a cup of water, waiting for him to sit up and take it.

No, not Logan. Can't call him Logan. It's Jonathan Slaughter for as long as this mission lasts.

"Thanks," he said, sitting up in the bunk and taking the water.

Wait… sitting up? An open cup of water?

"Where *are* we?" he tried to ask, but this time his voice failed, his throat simply too dry. He gulped the water down, feeling it soothe on the way down, feeling his throat open up. He sighed in relief and tried again. "Where are we?"

"Two days' burn out of our entry point in some system no one's bothered to name," Logan… no, *Jonathan* told him. *Damn, this is going to take some getting used to.* "Twelve hours out from the next jump-point toward the Periphery." He fixed Terrin with a glare. "Now tell me why the hell you're here."

"Thanks for not sticking me on the freighter back to Sparta," Terrin said, letting his head fall back against the pillow, setting the empty cup on a table next to the bed. Fear so palpable and intense it had formed a solid shape in his gut began to slowly melt away. "Mithra, I didn't know if I was going to make it."

"You very nearly didn't, damn it!" Jonathan snapped. "The shit you took to put yourself out for the trip might have let you survive, but it also put you into a coma. You were so dehydrated, your organs were shutting down by the time they got you to the sick bay. You could have fucking *died*. Now tell me what was so fucking important you had to do this."

"You're going to need me," Terrin said. It might have sounded a bit more egotistical and condescending than he'd intended, but he couldn't think of any other way to say it. At Jonathan's skeptical glare, he went on quickly. "How big is your science team for this mission?"

His big brother's eyes went thoughtful at the question, and

Terrin knew it wasn't because he didn't remember; it was because he hadn't thought of it previously.

"We have the technical team to maintain our mechs," he replied, the anger and intensity gone from his voice. "I think Lyta said two of them have physics degrees…"

"And she and Dad and General…" He caught himself. "And the others were afraid of putting an actual research team on the mission because they wouldn't have military training and they might blab. Not to mention, it would look weird, a mercenary company hauling around a bunch of scientists. That's why you need me." He ticked his points off on his fingers, suddenly feeling energized. "I have a degree in astrophysics, a degree in hyperdimensional physics, a degree in fusion engineering, and I've been tinkering around the Spartan research laboratories since I was old enough for Mom to take to work with her. I *am* your science team, and since there's just one of me, I won't attract that much attention."

He pounded a fist into the lumpy hospital mattress, anger surging through him.

"Dad doesn't understand how badly we *need* this." He fixed his brother with a stare born from years of pent-up frustration. "Do you know why we use mecha?"

His brother blinked at the non sequitur, stuttering out an answer.

"Because they're the best, most versatile ground assault weapon we have?"

It was a line from the Academy; Terrin hadn't even gone there and he still recognized it.

"I've seen some of the old records most people don't get access to." He shrugged his indifference. "The brass thinks some of the Empire's military history would be destabilizing to the general public, but the government researchers can access it… Mom could." An old twist of pain in his gut at the thought of her, of how she'd died. "Mechs are about the most inefficient, impractical and useless piece of military technology ever invented."

"What the fuck?" This new "Jonathan" looked a lot more like the old Logan in that instant, full of righteous indignation and thoughts of honor and nobility.

"The only reason mecha work for us is we're *frozen* technologically." He was winding up now, like five minutes into a guest lecture at one of Dr. Kovalev's university classes. "If we had the targeting AI the Empire did at one point, if we had the hyperexplosive warheads for man-portable missile launchers, if we had the autonomous weapons systems and smart mines, mecha would be useless. They'd be nothing but huge targets, a walking coffin."

Terrin waved a hand expansively. "But."

"But the Empire fell," he went on, "and the mix of technology we've been left with has made them practical. We have Electronic Counter Measures sophisticated enough to take down self-guided missiles, so the only practical missile systems have to use laser line-of-sight guidance, with all the limitations that brings with it.

"We have fusion reactors small enough to fit inside a mech, but we barely understand how they work, we just build them according to old specs, on machines we built according to those same specs, and it's more like chanting a spell than understanding the engineering.

"We lack the AI computer systems that could automate weapons like mecha and obviate the need for pilots, and some people believe it's no accident, that the Empire banned them. So we have mecha and they work for our sorts of wars because of our level of technology, but that level is *unnatural*. It's imposed on us by our politics, by the whole system of the Five Dominions."

"You say that like it's a bad thing," his brother countered, perhaps a bit defensively. "Mecha force us to keep war human, to keep it from being impersonal and automated. Maybe it's not such a good idea to change that."

"But it *will* change. If not by us now, then by someone like Starkad or Shang. Things *can't* last as long as something like Terminus is out there, waiting for someone to find. You and I," Terrin motioned between them with a finger, "if we find it, we can make sure it isn't misused, doesn't just turn into a tool for destruction. I wouldn't count on Starkad sharing the sentiment."

"Why didn't you put it to Dad like that?" Jonathan demanded, throwing up his arms in frustration.

"I *did*," Terrin replied. "And he told me he wasn't going to risk seeing both his sons dead on this mission."

Jonathan sighed, hands rubbing at his eyes as if he'd had little sleep lately.

"So damned glad he has such confidence in me." He let his arms fall to his side, giving up on the argument. "All right, you're staying. There's no safe way to get you back now without diverting a significant portion of our people and resources and blowing security all to hell in the process." A final glare, one remnant of his brother's lingering anger. "And *that's* why I didn't send you back on the cargo ship. They're running a long circuit before they hit Sparta again, to throw off anyone trying to trace the shipment of weapons and crew. We can't be connected to Sparta or we'll never get clearance through Starkad space."

Terrin's gut felt empty, and he wasn't sure it was from the lack of solid food. He was totally cut off from home. It was what he thought he'd wanted, but it suddenly seemed like he hadn't thought this through at all. He stared at the bulkhead of the *Shakak's* medical bay, bare white stained a faded yellow with age and use, but didn't see it so much as he saw his own bleak, hopeless future.

"I guess it turns out," his brother said quietly, stepping over to the bed and putting a hand on his shoulder, "Jonathan Slaughter has a cousin named..." He shrugged, a mischievous grin taking years off his face. "...*Terry*. Terry Conner"

Terrin groaned, covering his face with the bedsheet. He found out he was wearing a hospital gown and it was cold in the compartment, but he was more disturbed by the choice of names. People *always* tried to shorten his name to "Terry," and he'd spent most of his life fighting against the idea. Now, he had no choice. Not only would he have to live with other people calling him "Terry," he'd have to start thinking of himself that way.

"Oh, shit," he sighed, letting the sheet fall off of his head.

"You're not a scientist here, though, *Terry*," Jonathan warned him. "We're a mercenary company, we don't *need* scientists, remember?" He raised a finger in revelation, as if he'd just had a thought. "But I bet you Captain Osceola's engineering team could always use another reactor tech." He cocked an eyebrow in challenge. "Is that degree in fusion whatever actually good for anything practical?"

Terrin... *Terry* threw off the sheets and swung his bare legs off the bed.

"Give me some clothes and let's find out."

12

"What a shithole," Donner Osceola murmured. "Why the hell would anyone want to live here?"

Jonathan couldn't argue with the assessment, though he felt as if he should have. The planetary government here on Arachne was their employer, after all; as the commanding officer and President of Wholesale Slaughter LLC, he should be defending their very first client, even if it was just an anonymous listing on the Merc-Work user network.

But you couldn't pay me enough money to live on this damned planet.

They'd passed over the eastern hemisphere during atmospheric entry and even cloaked in darkness, it was clearly a barren, wind-swept desert, nearly devoid of life and totally unsuitable for human habitation. Maybe the Empire at its height could have made something of it, but planetary engineering on so great a scale was beyond the star-nations of the Five Dominions and not even an outpost broke the sameness of the wastes.

Past the terminator, over a vast, green ocean and into the dawn light of Minerva, the system's primary star, the western hemisphere blocked in moisture with towering, sharp-edged mountains. It was probably fairly nice and temperate near the foot of the mountains, but no one would ever know because the whole region was rocked by landslides; he'd seen one just flying over and the reports he'd read had said they were endemic.

The only habitable region of the whole planet was farther east, hundreds of kilometers past the savage peaks in a river valley stretching over half the continent. And habitable did not mean comfortable. Temperatures hovered at a miserable thirty-five degrees Celsius for the length of the valley, the humidity running near eighty percent when the whole region wasn't being flogged by torrential rains. Everything unpaved was impassable mud and the cities were built on concrete platforms to keep them above the flooding.

"Not everyone can afford to pack up and move their life to another system, Don," Lyta Randell's words were barely audible over the roar of the shuttle's jets and the buffeting of the thick atmosphere.

Jonathan craned his head around to his right; he was in the first row of seats behind the pilot and copilot's stations, even with Terrin—*No, Terry now*—while Lyta was seated across from the *Shakak's* captain.

"Maybe in the old days, it wasn't so bad here," now-Major Lyta Randell went on, still peering at the projection on the main view screen. "Maybe the Empire had the technology to alter the weather patterns here and after the fall, the people left here were just stuck."

Jonathan couldn't see Osceola's shrug, but somehow, he felt it, heard it in the man's words.

"I'll take your word for it, love. I still don't know why you dragged me along on the price negotiation. You've known me long enough to figure out I'm not much of a businessman, and God knows I don't want to be drinking the soup that passes for an atmosphere down there."

Jonathan answered that one, having had it explained to him in detail by Lyta just a few hours ago when he'd asked the same question about bringing Osceola along.

"We're an unknown quantity. These people couldn't even afford to hire us if we weren't, and they might not bother if we didn't have someone whose background they could check to prove we're legit."

Osceola barked a laugh, sharp and harsh.

"By God, this must be the first time anyone has accused me of being legitimate!"

"We're coming up on Piraeus," Katy announced, her voice clear and pitched to carry, as if she'd been ignoring the conversation going on behind her. "We should be touching down at the port in ten mikes."

"Ten mikes," Osceola scoffed. "Leave it to the Navy to complicate something as simple as a minute."

"Weren't you in the Navy?" Terry asked him, frowning.

"Doesn't mean they aren't full of shit, kid. You ain't never been in the military, or you'd know they're full of shit most of the time."

Jonathan tuned the man out, watching the morning light bleach the buildings of Piraeus white. The city was strangely fascinating, built on platforms of concrete, with pilings sunken deep into the muddy ground in a heroic effort to brute-force itself out of nature's tenacious grasp. It seemed to him the embodiment of the human refusal to surrender in the face of the chaos and violence of the fall and the Reconstruction, and he began to feel an affinity for the people who forced this inhospitable place into something homelike.

As they circled around to the west side of Piraeus, the affinity turned to pangs of sympathy. A block of what might have once been factories or warehouses were charred and blackened and partially collapsed, whatever might have once been produced inside or stored behind their walls now just ash under piles of rubble. They'd been hit by raiders, and fairly recently.

He shaped a low whistle at the damage.

"They didn't bring us here to have a parade through downtown," Lyta reminded him, her voice grim. "We wouldn't be here if they weren't desperate."

The spaceport was grandly named for what it was, a square of flat concrete on a raised platform, connected to the city by a causeway broad enough to haul loads of freight from heavy cargo shuttles. A flyer waited for them already, parked only ten meters or so from the edge of the pad, a demonstration of confidence in Katy's ability as a pilot, which was, of course, warranted though the people down on Arachne couldn't know that.

She justified their confidence and his own, bringing the bird down in a narrowing spiral until the airspeed was slow enough to switch thrust to the belly jets. Most Navy pilots, in his experience, liked to show off during a landing, hitting the jets at the last second, kicking the passengers in the ass and touching down hard enough to send the bird pogo-sticking on the landing gear hydraulics. She set them down as gently as a step off a curb, as expertly as a civilian passenger flight, barely a jolt.

"Welcome to Arachne," Katy announced with the casual, bantering tone of one of those commercial pilots. "It's a comfortable thirty-three degrees outside and skies are sunny. We know you have many choices for your transportation needs and we thank you for choosing Wholesale Slaughter."

"Do we have to stay in the shuttle?" the copilot asked, a whining undertone to the question. His name was Acosta and he was a Sub-Lieutenant just out of the Academy; he'd been sent by Colonel Anders as one of the support crew. None of them had worked with Acosta before, and Katy had already told him she didn't like him. "It's gonna be hot as hell in here with the engines shut down."

Katy rolled her eyes at the man, but Jonathan controlled himself; he was a captain now, and a commanding officer, and he had to be an example.

"Someone has to stay with the shuttle," he reminded the man, "and Lt. Margolis outranks you."

"I'll stay with you, Francis," Katy assured the man. "We can take turns patrolling outside the bird to get some air."

She shot Jonathan a look and he knew her well enough now to know she was staying because she didn't trust Acosta not to do something stupid. Lyta powered her acceleration couch around and led the others out of the cockpit, slapping the control for the belly ramp while Katy began shutting down the turbines. The fading whine of the engines nearly drowned out the grinding motors of the ramp, but there was no mistaking the blast of heat washing up from the opening. It was wet and suffocating, a waterfall of steaming humidity slamming into him with an almost physical blow, staggering him as he took a step down the ramp.

"Holy shit," Osceola muttered from behind him. "Let's get in the damned flyer and hope they have air conditioning."

The side door of the ducted-fan helicopter was open and waiting for them, the interior seats arranged facing each other limousine-style. The pilot didn't look around, didn't acknowledge their existence; but as he ducked under the clamshell hatch, Jonathan saw a petite, dark-haired woman sitting in the center of the rear couch, legs crossed. She wasn't beyond middle-aged, if he was any judge, though she was probably somewhere north of sixty, and had the air of a professional politician. He'd met enough of them in the palace at Argos to know the type. The suit told the story, not expensive or well-tailored enough for a corporate executive but still tasteful and attractive.

He recognized the expression on her face as well; he'd seen it on his father's closest advisors just after the coup. Stressed, overworked, the weight of the world on her shoulders. He decided to go with his instincts and take the chance of looking foolish for the reward of being taken seriously.

"Prime Councilor Garrett," he said, bowing slightly and offering a hand. "I'm Captain Jonathan Slaughter."

He saw the slightest twitch of the older woman's eyebrow and he knew he'd scored the point. She took his hand, nodding in return.

"Captain," she said. She eyed the others as they climbed into the flyer, blinking at Osceola, as if in recognition. "Jenkins," she said to the pilot, "close the doors and get us in the air. Let's go somewhere we can talk."

"We are not a weak people." Samantha Garrett stared at the pale, amber liquid in her wine glass as if the answers to her problems lurked under the surface. "Arachne is not a world for weak people. We drill oil from the depths of the jungle, collect duerte-fruit from the sides of steep, jagged mountains, raise aurochs in the grasslands in the face of a dozen species of predators. People die for this each year, but the work continues because it is all that keeps our colony alive. We live close to the edge out here in the non-aligned systems."

"At least you get a nice view out of it," Osceola said, masking a dry smile behind a sip of his wine.

It *was* a nice view from the balcony of the *Palacio de Gobierno,* overlooking the river valley. The palms and cypress choking the banks seemed picturesque from here, far above the clouds of mosquitoes and biting flies, away from the stalking jaguars and *Titanis* terror birds. A riverboat chugged along, chopping through underwater growth with a wheel at its bow, while on the banks, massive aurochs grazed in a scene that might have come from the earliest days of pre-Imperial colonization.

It was less humid up here, the spinning blades of a ceiling fan stirring the air beneath the shadow of an overhanging section of roof.

"When Captain Magnus first came here," Garrett went on, ignoring Osceola's barb, "he sent down a representative to demand we pay him tribute or his forces would destroy our crops and drilling rigs, kill our livestock, and slaughter our militia, then sell the rest of our people into slavery." Her brown eyes flickered upward to meet Jonathan's, glancing aside to Lyta's before she shielded them with a sip of wine. "Because we live so close to the edge, with so little surplus from our paltry share of trade to Sparta and Clan Modi, we agreed. The Council decided it would be easier and cheaper to push production, to work the people harder, than to take the risk of trying to fight them." She sniffed at the thought, her lip twisting in what might have been disdain.

"We paid them and, three months later, they were back." Her eyes came up and locked with his. "This time, the tribute demands were doubled."

"Predictable," Lyta commented, the first words she'd said since they'd exited the flyer just outside the *Palacio.*

"Indeed," Garrett agreed. "And I had predicted it." Her shoulders shifted with uncomfortable memory. "We tried to buy time, tried to tell Magnus' emissary we hadn't built up the surplus to meet his demands, asked them for another six months." A hissed-out breath. "Three days later, Magnus landed a platoon of mechs and destroyed a city block with most of the fabrication facilities we were using to try to produce weapons to arm our militia, killing over two hundred people in the attack. He sent us this message."

She reached out to the center of the table, to a small display screen mounted there, and touched a control beneath it. The face filling the screen was as much metal as flesh and Jonathan sucked in a sharp breath almost involuntarily. Cyborgs weren't exactly shunned in Spartan society, not the way they were in other places in the Dominions; after all, soldiers badly injured in battle often needed cybernetic replacement of lost limbs or eyes. But it was common practice to make the replacements as lifelike as possible, so as not to offend Mithra, who had designed humans in His own image. Those who purposefully flaunted their bionics with bare, silvery metal were usually trying to make some sort of religious or social statement... or simply to look intimidating. He had a sense this was the latter.

"I am," the cyborg said with a voice gravelly and hoarse, probably from the same injury that had cost him half his face, "Captain Magnus Heinarson of the Red Brotherhood, and I wait for no one. You have one month to meet my demands to the last credit, or the death and destruction you just experienced will be visited upon every part of your capital, upon every one of the pitiful cities on your pitiful world." The half of his mouth on the cybernetic side of his face seemed frozen in place by nerve damage, but the biological half curled in a sneer. "You say you don't have the 'surplus' to give me what I ask, as if I care about your trade deficits or your economic stability. I don't give a shit if your children starve! You will give me what's mine, or the ones of you who aren't already dead will fucking wish they were!"

The recording froze again on the scarred, bifurcated face and Garrett punched the button again with a fierce, violent motion, as if she wished she could do the same to the man in the video.

"That was two weeks ago."

"Do you have any intelligence about where the pirates are based?" Jonathan asked her.

"We do." Her voice deepened with what might have been bitterness. "It's not exactly a secret, since there are no governments willing to ferret him out in the non-aligned systems; none of them consider it their problem since there's nothing out here worth exploiting."

She fished a dataspike from the pocket of her suit jacket and inserted it into a receptacle on the table beside the screen. A star map snapped to life on the viewer, with the Minerva system haloed in green and another, only one jump away, highlighted in a deep and angry red.

"There's no official name for it on the Imperial maps, but we've taken to calling it Clew Bay, for historical reasons."

Jonathan had no idea what those historical reasons might be, but the question didn't seem relevant, so he didn't ask it. Garrett enlarged the system in the image, showing them an F-class star with a rocky planet far too close for life, an asteroid belt and two gas giants. The closer-in of the giants had ten satellites, two of them nearly the size of a planet; one of the two was fringed in red.

"This moon is habitable, barely. It's mostly water." She zoomed in again with a spread of her fingers, showing the blue surface of the satellite. "But there are a couple large islands where you can grow food. It's not worth a colony; not enough land and nothing worth exporting. The old maps say the Empire terraformed it, probably just because they could. It's a damn fine place to put a pirate base, though."

Her fingers tapped on the table, the nails clicking like the night calls of some mating insect. She pursed her lips as if she were carefully considering her next words.

"If you weren't new to the business and willing to work cheap, we couldn't afford you. Some members of the Council think we still can't afford to hire you."

"Our fee is going to be a lot cheaper than what you'd have to pay this Red Brotherhood," Lyta pointed out.

"Not the money," Garrett explained, shaking her head. "They think it's too big of a risk. If you screw this up, Magnus and his people will kill us all, leave this place a ruin as a warning to his other victims." She held a hand out, palm up, as if weighing their options. "Or, if you are good enough to do the job, you might just decide you should be the ones to demand tribute, and we are still, if you'll pardon my language, fucked. That's the problem with living in the cracks between the Dominions, in the systems no one else wants. Everyone's happy about the freedom and self-determination until you need to call a cop. No one's military is willing to risk a war to help some dead-end squatter colony deal with pirates or bandits."

"I understand," Jonathan said, leaning back in his seat, regarding the woman.

He wasn't sure he did, not to the extent he should have, wasn't sure what the point of bringing them here had been if the Council was afraid to hire them, but he had the feeling this was some sort of test, and one he'd have to pass without help from the others.

"Do you know why I resigned my commission from the Spartan military, Prime Councilor Garrett?" he said. "Why I sold everything my parents had left me and invested it in this company?"

"I'd assumed," she ventured carefully, "that there'd been some trouble. That's usually how people wind up starting your sort of business, a court-martial or some such disciplinary problem." She frowned, forehead curling in thought. "Of course, usually the officers who become contractors are a bit older…"

"Usually," he agreed. "I was one of the most highly-decorated officers of my rank in the history of the Spartan military. I'd been on a dozen combat operations since graduating the Academy and had commendations for every single one of them."

The words were flowing naturally now, without filter. He was quoting his cover back-story for Jonathan Slaughter, but he could just as easily been talking about Logan Conner… which was why it was the perfect cover identity for him.

"Our patrol ship received a distress call from a civilian passenger ship taking colonists from Nike to one of the border settlements, one of the newer ones set up in just the past few years. The ship had been hit by pirates and, by the time we caught up with them, they'd already hauled the survivors back to their base on some worthless planet with a couple of degrees of habitable area in an ocean of ice and snow."

The ice filled his veins, set the hair on the back of his neck standing on end and he was back in the snows of Ramman, with the Scorpion pilot shooting at him.

"They were working their way through the crew, torturing them to death one at a time. They intended to sell the passengers on the slave markets... after they'd gotten some use out of them." The words seemed to be coming from someone else, someone standing behind him, narrating while he shivered in a cold so unlike the warmth on Arachne. "It ended about as well as it could have for those people: we showed up and most of them lived. They'd be scarred for life, nothing would ever be the same, and it would take them years to recover, those who ever would."

His lip twisted into a snarl.

"And everyone seemed to consider it a win, something to be celebrated, a good enough reason for promotions and medals and slapping each other on the back for a job well done." He saw Katy's face the way it had been in the infirmary, swollen and bloody, her eyes dead and full of hate and he thumped his clenched fist against his thigh so he wouldn't slam it against the table. "When I didn't, when I wouldn't keep my mouth shut about it, when I said the wrong things to the wrong people, I was given a choice: get out with my record clean, or face a court-martial."

He shrugged, not so much a motion of indifference to his fate as one of a weight coming off his shoulders.

"I was lost, didn't know what I was going to do, when Lyta..." He nodded toward her. "...Major Randell here, came to me and told me she felt the same way about the bandits, the pirates, the outlaw trash. And she knew a lot of other people like her, people who'd be willing to give up everything to go do something about it. So, you don't have to worry about us turning bandit and taking your livelihood; we'd likely do it for free if you couldn't afford to pay us."

He leaned forward, hands clasped in front of him on the table, grinning without humor.

"As for us fucking things up and losing to those pirate trash, well… losing implies you're playing a game, fighting a battle. We are not here to play games and we're not here to fight battles. We are going to exterminate these bastards like the vermin they are."

Samantha Garrett didn't reply for a moment, and Jonathan wondered if he'd overplayed his hand, bought too far into his new, bloodthirsty mercenary persona and left too much of Logan behind. He had to suppress a sigh of relief when Arachne's Chief Councilor leaned forward and offered him a hand.

"In that case, Captain Slaughter," she said, "I believe we have a deal."

13

"We need to hit them where they live," Jonathan declared. "We need to get to them before they head back here to finish the job."

Terrin—*damn it, it's Terry now, I keep slipping up*—watched his brother—*No! Cousin by Mithra's horns!*—Jonathan, with an odd fascination. Back home, he'd only ever been around him away from the Academy, away from his military assignments, in a family atmosphere where what his father called "shop talk" was not allowed. He'd never thought of him as a leader, though he knew he was considered so by his military peers. He'd just been family.

Pacing back and forth in the *Palacio's* second-largest conference room, Jonathan Slaughter seemed a man possessed, consumed with the task of getting this job done. Terry wondered if it was just to further the aims of their mission or maybe it had more to do with the woman sitting at the table two seats down from him.

She was pretty, from just a pure external, physical point of view. Not his type, too tall and athletic and intimidating, but he could see the attraction. Sometimes she seemed an engaging, pleasant, good-humored person and sometimes there was a hardened edge to her personality, though he didn't know her well enough to tell if it had been there all along or had grown like a shell after what had happened to her on Ramman. Was it the engaging, pretty woman who attracted Logan—*Jonathan!*—or was it the hard edge, the raw anger?

"I'm not so sure," Lyta Randell said, shaking her head.

She was someone else he'd known forever but rarely saw in action. She'd been the fun-loving aunt who would take him and his—he rolled his eyes this time and forced the word into his thoughts—*cousin* for ice cream or out to chase the dogs around the park when things were bad at home, when his father was in a dark mood, especially just after Mother had died. He'd entertained the notion, just recently, that perhaps she and Father had been involved back then, that he'd turned to her for warmth and a shoulder to cry on. He couldn't quite make himself believe it. About her. Father, yes.

"You don't trust that intelligence 'everybody knows' about the pirate base?" Osceola asked. The captain was lounging across a hand-carved wooden chair, his leg hanging over the arm rest, casual and irreverent no matter what the setting. Terry couldn't help but like the man, for all he was a bit oily and shady, with the vibe of a used-flyer salesman.

"The intel is probably accurate," Lyta acknowledged, shrugging. She wasn't pacing, but Terry thought she seemed as agitated as Jonathan, in her own way. "You saw the video—this Captain Magnus character doesn't seem the type to go in for counter-intelligence. Besides, he doesn't think he has anything to worry about. The planetary government here doesn't have so much as an armed shuttle to throw at him."

"Then what is it?" Jonathan wanted to know. "You think we should just sit here and wait for him?"

"He's coming here anyway, isn't he?" Terry pointed out. Five sets of eyes turned to him and he shrank in on himself a bit. He felt as out of place here as he had the one year he'd tried out for the baseball team. "I mean, that's what he told them."

"He's got a point," Katy said, technically the most junior officer present, but not shy at all about speaking out. "We'd have more time to set up a defense."

"Wouldn't work," Osceola stated, likely more direct than the others would have been. "Guys like this Magnus, they're not smart, but they're clever. They have a sense for threats, it's how they keep from getting skragged by their own people. They're slippery, and they can feel a trap. We build up defenses around Piraeus, they'll spot it, no matter how careful we are."

"If they run," Terry asked, frowning in confusion, "isn't that just as good?"

Jonathan sighed in obvious frustration and Terry wasn't sure if it was with him or with the argument. He moved to his chair—well, theoretically his, he hadn't sat in it once the whole meeting—and grabbed the back of it with a grip so tight, Terry thought he wanted to break it into pieces.

"No," he ground out, not a patient type at the best of times. "If he runs, he can wait us out. He knows mercenaries won't stay here indefinitely, that it's too expensive. He'll go hit someone else and come back here at his leisure, and he'll kill everyone when he does come back, just to make a fucking point." He spun on Lyta, his glare almost accusatory. "But doesn't that mean we *have* to take the fight to him?"

"You're in command," she said, and her words seemed to Terry to be chosen very carefully, "and I'll support whatever decision you make. But if you want my opinion, our best bet is to get him so riled up, he makes a mistake and comes in here blind with rage."

"What?" Osceola asked, laughing sharply. "You gonna give him a bad review on the Online Bandit Registry?"

Lyta didn't crack a smile.

"I'm afraid it's a bit more drastic than that." Her face was grim, her voice doubly so. "None of you are going to like it." She met Terry's eyes, almost seeming apologetic. "Especially you."

"I don't see the point," Acosta said again. "Their anti-missile defenses are going to shoot this thing down before it gets within twenty kilometers of their base."

Katy rolled her eyes and tried not to lose her temper. She found herself doing it a lot around Acosta and she wondered if maybe she could convince the other shuttle crew to trade co-pilots with her before she killed the man.

"That *is* the point," Terry said from behind them, his voice sullen and resentful. *And yet he came along. He could have stayed on the* Shakak.

It was easier for her to think of him as Terry than it was to think of Logan as "Jonathan." Maybe because she hadn't known him as well, or maybe because he seemed more of a "Terry."

Jonathan had tried to argue him into staying on the ship, back at the jump-point where it was fairly safe, but Terry had insisted he needed to be on the shuttle in case there was a problem with the delivery vehicle. "Delivery vehicle" was an obscenely workaday euphemism for a missile, something a civilian would come up with to assuage his guilt for designing it.

I don't know why he should feel guilty. "Jonathan" or Logan or whatever you wanted to call him, had it right. Bandits were vermin and they should be exterminated, not treated like lawful combatants in an honorable war.

She chuckled at how the term would horrify her parents: "honorable war." She could hear her father's dismayed clucking, his face pinched in righteous indignation as he lectured her about how no war was honorable, it was just useless, pointless slaughter. She wondered if he would have said the same thing if he'd been on the *Atlas*, if he'd seen the depths to which humanity could sink.

She imagined a targeting reticle floating over the pearl-blue world ahead of them and tried to feel guilty. She couldn't.

"Two minutes to firing range," Acosta said, finally making himself useful. "They'll have spotted us by now," he added, as if in an effort to make up for it. "Hope they don't have patrol shuttles out here."

"I hope they do," she contradicted him, eyes still fixed on the moon. "Then I get to kill them."

She could feel Terry's stare; his face horrified the way her father's would have been.

"Anyway, there's nothing coming," she elaborated, waving a hand at the sensors. It felt strange burning along at one gravity as if it were a leisurely stroll instead of a combat patrol. "We're just one shuttle. We can't be carrying anything that would hurt them."

The gas giant was behind them, over the starboard wing of the shuttle, and the forward view made the water moon of Clew Bay seem so isolated and vulnerable, so harmless. It was an illusion. There were spy satellites, little black spots against the blue oceans, warning drones scattered in various orbits around the gas giant and its other moons, and, somewhere out there, the bandit's ship. They'd keep it hidden, powered down as much as possible and stuck in some hard-to-detect orbit probably around one of the other large satellites.

She wondered if the bandits would bother to hail them or just wait for them to get close enough for a railgun shot. No legitimate military would use railguns in an inhabited system, but these bastards were pretty far from legitimate. She waited, one eye on the tactical display, one on the main screen, but only silence greeted her.

"Prep the missile," she told Acosta.

She'd let him do it, but she watched from the corner of her eye, just to be sure. The process was nearly fool-proof, but fools were so ingenious…

"This is a living planet," Terry reminded her, pain and doubt in his voice. "Even if this works just the way we think, we're still committing a war crime."

"This isn't a war."

She saw the range display counter reach zero and her hand went to the physical switch Terry and the shuttle techs had rigged up on the central weapons console, large and awkward and obvious, a silver lever covered by a red, plastic flip cover. She tried to think of something momentous to say, but nothing came to mind. She thumbed the cover open and snapped the lever forward.

"Launching."

A bang vibrated through the shuttle's fuselage, the concussion of explosive bolts blowing along the bird's belly, kicking free a missile as long as the shuttle itself. It would drift away a few hundred meters before the main engine ignited but they should see it within ten seconds or so.

"There it is," Acosta pointed at the drive flare lighting up on the main view screen, as if they couldn't all already see it.

They were still accelerating at one gravity, but it left them behind as if they were already braking, boosting at twenty g's, streaking out against the darkness. She cut thrust to the shuttle's engine and free-fall left them drifting against their harnesses.

Terry made a quiet retching sound behind her; she hoped to hell he'd remembered to take his motion-sickness meds, because there was nothing worse than globules of vomit floating around a cockpit.

She gently nudged the control yoke, a steady push instead of the jerky, hesitant maneuvers a lot of even well-trained Navy pilots resorted to in space flight on small birds like this. Instead of jolts and banging hammer blows, the steering jets were a faint rumble, a gentle push until she let up and gave a slight correction to keep them aligned one-hundred-eighty degrees from their course of travel.

"Secure for heavy boost," she warned, pausing for a beat before she opened the throttle.

Now *this* was a combat maneuver. Six gravities, burning for endless minutes until you thought you'd always weighed five hundred plus kilograms and always would. The main screen was showing the view from the nose camera, since the rear would be washed out by the plasma flare of the drive, but she was watching the tactical display. It had a laser link to the missile's telemetry, guiding it in via the sensor readings from the warhead, and a corner of the display showed the view from the nosecone camera. The ocean moon filled the screen, the island chains stretching across the southern hemisphere visible now, green and lush.

Clew Bay was pretty, from a distance, though she didn't imagine it would be a pleasant place to live, long-term. The files Arachne had shown them said the background radiation from the gas giant wouldn't be lethal immediately, but it would eventually start causing cancer without energy shielding, which bandits wouldn't have, and all that beautiful blue water was filled with radioactive minerals. More cancer. The sea life had been engineered to survive the exposure, and the Jeuta could probably live there—maybe it had been intended for their use when the Empire had terraformed it, but if so, they hadn't stuck around after their uprising.

Maybe the Jeuta just don't go for surfing.

She couldn't feel the difference in the thrust, but a quick glimpse at the displays showed they'd burned off their momentum and were accelerating back toward the jump-point. You couldn't trust your body in microgravity, which was why even veteran pilots preferred flying in atmosphere. She dialed back the thrust, bringing the acceleration down to a more-comfortable one gravity. Breath rushed out in sighs of relief from Acosta and Terry and she fought back a sneer. Boost had never bothered her, but she tried to have sympathy for other people less gifted. It was hard.

"They'll be firing anti-missile defenses soon," Acosta said.

"It's got enough shielding and enough maneuvering fuel to get through the first wave," she told him.

Her words might have been prophetic, or maybe she'd just been timing the flight instinctively; fireflies swarmed upward from the island, rockets from the anti-missile battery rising into the upper atmosphere. They'd be radar guided, but they'd planned for that. The space in front of the missile seemed to shimmer as clouds of electromagnetically-charged chaff erupted from canisters strapped to the warhead, scattering the radar signal and sending the rockets pinwheeling off out of control.

The view from the camera began to shake, thickening atmosphere buffeting the warhead. The readouts showed her the boost stage of the missile had fallen away and it was running on gravity and maneuvering thrusters now, coming down directly over the spot where thermal sensors had pinpointed the bandit's settlement.

Not too much longer now.

Prescience again, or was it just training?

The first coil-gun round missed, fooled by the radar jamming, but it wasn't alone. Nickel-iron slugs were cheap and easily-fabricated, and fusion energy was just as cheaply obtained and they sprayed the anti-missile turret fire in negligent waves of metal like an arrow-storm in a battle from ancient Earth. The warhead was only a few kilometers up now, but it would be destroyed long before it reached the ground.

It didn't need to.

The picture from the missile's camera disappeared, as did the telemetry, long before the bandit jamming should have killed it. The view from one of the shuttle's rear-facing external cameras replaced it, showing a second star rising on the day side of the moon, a pinpoint of brightness spreading slightly like a flower blooming.

She tried to picture the detonation from the ground, the way the bandits would have seen it. Those who'd been looking straight at it would likely never see anything again unless they found a good medical lab somewhere—there surely wouldn't be one there. The blast itself wouldn't do much to the base, would barely cause the background radiation to rise in the long run when measured across the whole planet. On that island chain though, there would be a noticeable rise in radiation levels, as well as an electromagnetic pulse which could fry unshielded electronics.

It wasn't the electronics they'd been aiming to disrupt, though.

"Do you think anyone died?" Terry's voice sounded agonized.

She turned in her seat, almost ready to snap at him but tamped down the impulse at the expression on his face. He was a scientist, not a soldier. They'd made him build them a nuclear warhead and delivery vehicle from spare parts, since nukes weren't something even a civilian ship would be allowed to have, even one carrying around a mercenary unit. He'd probably spent his whole life being taught of the evils of nuclear weapons, how they'd been used by the Jeuta to sterilize Imperial worlds in revenge, how they'd ended the Golden Age and ravaged Earth.

"No," she said, voice soft and carefully neutral. He was smart; if he thought she was just trying to comfort him, he wouldn't believe her. "The detonation was too high. All it'll do is make them very, very angry." She grinned, lips skinning back from her teeth in a feral expression. "And angry people make mistakes."

14

Magnus Heinarson didn't sweat. Getting burned over sixty percent of your body would do that to you. Some nights he woke up gasping for air, reliving the unspeakable agony over and over, watching the timbers of the rough-hewn house collapse around him and his wife and their little girl. He'd scream the way she'd screamed, and thrash about, but he wouldn't sweat. He couldn't.

He never knew if it was a Starkad or a Spartan missile that ended the night in fire, but it was Spartan troops who found him, Spartan field medics who'd treated him... Spartan surgeons who'd cut away what couldn't be saved and replaced it with bionics. Theirs had been cheap plastic, nothing more than prosthetics; he'd paid for the overpowered metalwork himself, later, after he'd begun to exact his revenge in lives and treasure. He'd paid for the reinforcement of his spine and shoulders and hips he needed to ensure the new cybernetic limbs wouldn't rip themselves right out of his body the first time he used them, paid for the isotope pack to be installed to power them, paid for the security to watch over him while he was in recovery, to make sure none of his new enemies took advantage of his weakened state.

And after, he'd never paid again. He'd made *them* pay, Starkad, Sparta, Shang, Modi, and Mbeki, all of them for bringing their fights to his world, to all the fringe worlds and all the colonists who had the bad luck to make their homes in disputed systems. He'd never looked back, never regretted an instant of it. Oh, sometimes things got too hot and you had to pull back from raiding the Dominions, and then, well, what was a man to do? His people had to eat. It wasn't as if he *enjoyed* stealing from independent worlds, which was why he always gave them the chance to pay up without getting hurt.

And this was the thanks he got. The sky of Clew Bay still glowed a raw, angry violet, as if the world itself had been bruised in the thermonuclear assault. The reminder hung over their crude tent city, stoking the anger and fear of his people... and firing their resentment. True, most of their military gear was shielded against the EMP, but the damned lights wouldn't work inside the tents, because who thinks to buy EMP-shielded lights? The darkness had scared people, and here and there, bonfires crackled, fed with scrap paper and cardboard.

It was a damn good thing he couldn't sweat, though, because he would have been sweating now.

"We can't let them get away with this," Sungurlu said, standing at the forefront of the group of sub-leaders he'd called to what he called, with a bit of admitted vainglory, the "command post," a canvas roof slung over a foldable metal frame. You couldn't use wood here on Clew Bay; what passed for trees here were useless for building anything, with a thorny bark as tough and hard to work as iron. "We could tell one of the Dominions... Modi, maybe, or Shang. If they found out some non-aligned colony was using nuclear weapons, they'd stomp the shit out of them."

Magnus scowled at the ugly, bearded troll of a man, and not because of his looks. Mehmet Sungurlu was one of Magnus' most reliable allies, but he was hesitant, tentative in the face of hard decisions. He wanted to label Sungurlu an old woman, but that would have been an insult to the old women he'd known.

"And once Shang 'stomps the shit out of them,' what then?" he demanded, taking a lumbering step forward from the raised hump of dirt he used as a stand to look down on his troops when he addressed them. "What will be left for us? Remember, Mehmet, we chose Arachne because we *need* what they have. Have you forgotten what happened to Cai Quian on Ramman? We needed his tribute and we received nothing, because he was stupid enough to let Sparta find him. If Shang or Modi strips Arachne of anything useful, this was all a waste of time and resources."

If it had been anyone but Sungurlu, he wouldn't have tried to explain, would have simply mocked the other man's weakness. Or taught them all a lesson about doubting him to his face. Because when you gave a centimeter to ruthless bastards like this...

"If we'd just killed them all and taken their shit when we first landed," Reyes snarled, shoving Sungurlu aside, "we wouldn't be in this position, would we, Captain?" He gave the title a sardonic twist and Magnus barely restrained himself from smashing the man's face.

Reyes was a big man, nearly as large with natural muscle as Magnus was with bulky metal, and it was easy for a big man to forget he might not be the strongest or most dangerous around. It might be time to remind him, as well as the others. If this was going to be a theater, he'd have to set the stage.

"Yes, Jessie," he growled low in his chest, taking another step forward, less than a meter from Reyes. Close enough to catch the musty odor of the wolf-skin cloak he wore as if he were some sort of sword-wielding barbarian out of Old Earth legends. "If we'd killed their leaders and burned their factories and destroyed their machines, we could have taken what was there. But you know what dead people can't do, Jessie?" He was bellowing now, leaning forward, the force of his breath blowing Reyes' bleached blond hair out of the big idiot's face. "They can't make *more* shit we can steal! How many worlds do you think are out there, you fucking moron? Do you think if we burn every single one of them down that we won't fucking starve to death, drifting through space with no fucking fuel because we were fucking stupid enough to listen to your advice?"

Reyes' normally corpse-pale skin was beet red now, his teeth bared as if he were emulating the poor animal whose pelt he wore over his shoulders.

Damn dog was probably smarter than he is. There should be a wolf on some colony world wearing Reyes' skin for a cape.

"Maybe if you'd listened to my advice about Ramman," Reyes snapped back at him, "Cai Quian wouldn't be dead! I told you months ago that place was too close to the Spartan shipping lanes for his people to put a damned base there! They were bound to be found out and you let them sit there and get slaughtered!"

The others had stepped back now, giving the two of them room. Sungurlu watched intently, always ready to hang back and watch for an opportunity to advance himself. So far, Magnus had been able to channel the man's instinct for self-preservation into support for him, though that could change at any moment. But there were more people to think about than just the half-dozen gathered beneath this pitiful overhang.

"Do you want to challenge me, Jessie?" he asked, not backing up; he was determined he'd force Reyes to back away first. "We got eight people with their eyes burned out, we got radioactivity about to fall down around our ears the next time it rains, and we got about enough food to last us all another three weeks, maybe four if we shoot the blinded ones. If you think it's my fault, if you think you can do better, let's go out there..." He pointed with a shining, segmented metal finger at the crowd of maybe a hundred people gathered in their "town square," the courtyard between the canvas and nylon tents where their food and water were stored. "…and decide this right now."

Reyes's right hand twitched, and Magnus thought the big man might go for the gun he carried in a crossdraw holster at his waist. That could complicate things. Magnus had a lot of metal, and hitting the parts that weren't would be tough, even at close range. But bullets were democratic little fuckers, and they'd take down a leader with a lucky shot just as well as a follower.

He was hoping he could goad Reyes into facing him unarmed, work the man's monstrous ego. You had to be able to see people's weaknesses to lead them, to bring them to heel like the dogs they were, and you couldn't show them the fear you were feeling. Reyes was vacillating between a healthy respect for Magnus' raw, physical power and the rage he felt for the insults Magnus had so carefully hurled at him. He'd have to tip the balance.

Magnus strode past him, shoving him carelessly out of the way and walking into the center of the courtyard. Clay crunched under his boots, dried and desiccated from weeks with no rain. Angry red clouds gathering in the dawn light told him the rain would come soon, bringing radiation poisoning and death with it. He had to work fast.

Dozens upon dozens of eyes followed him, men and women but more men than women by a factor of two, and some of the women were pillage, or had started out that way. No children though. It was his rule. He'd allow children when they had a world of their own to rule, someplace nicer than this fetid shit-hole, where it was always too hot, or too cold, or too wet, or too dry. At least he didn't have to worry about one of them getting up the balls to shoot him in the back; he didn't allow anyone except his sub-leaders to have guns in the camp. Even his foot soldiers only got issued the weapons in the drop-ship.

He stood in the center of the courtyard and turned in a slow circle so that they could all see him, all meet his gaze.

"Red Brotherhood!" he yelled, hands raised to the glowing sky. "We have been attacked by our enemies, by the ungrateful bastards on Arachne, who mistook our mercy for weakness! I won't put up with this shit! I am going to lead you back to their miserable swamp of a world and march into their city with our mecha, with our foot soldiers, and burn it to the fucking ground!"

There were cheers and blood-thirsty whooping from the audience, some of them raising their hands to imitate his stance. *Fucking cattle.*

"But before we board our landers, before we call our ship and begin the journey of vengeance, it seems as if there are some here who blame what has happened on my leadership."

His hands drifted downward until both forefingers were pointed at Jessie Reyes, just emerging from beneath the command center awning.

"My lieutenant here, Jessie Reyes, a man I thought was my friend and ally, has decided you would all be better off if *he* was the leader of the Red Brotherhood!"

There were boos and catcalls at that, but not as many as he would have liked. Some of the onlookers appeared thoughtful, which was bad. None of them were smart enough to be thoughtful or *they'd* be the leader and he'd already be dead.

"So, I am going to challenge Jessie for the leadership of our little band!" he roared. "I am going to make him *prove* in front of Ahriman, the Dark Lord, that he is the man who should be leading us!"

That Dark Lord shit had been Sungurlu's idea. He came from some cult of devil-worshippers on some backwoods colony, morons who bought into bullshit myths and even bigger morons because they bought into the *losing* side of a bullshit myth. At least the sheep who worshipped Mithra figured He was going to win the struggle in the end. But whatever got the cattle moving...

Reyes started to say something, something that seemed way

too close to an attempt to defuse the situation, and he couldn't have that. Reyes was an asset, but he needed to deal with the unrest the nuke had caused before he took his people into battle.

"And since I am the challenger," Magnus went on, shouting over Reyes' dithering, "I will allow Jessie to choose the weapons we use. I think he'd have to agree, though, that neither of us should use a gun, seeing as how all of you good people are so closely gathered around."

Well, he'd have to agree *now*, anyway. Magnus could tell by his sour look that Reyes would have chosen a gun if given the choice.

"And," Magnus went on, knowing he had to sell this hard, "since some people might say I already have an advantage..." He flexed his bionic hands tightly and there were a few chuckles and grunts of appreciation. "...whatever weapon Jessie chooses, I will only use the weapons Ahriman and a well-paid team of surgeons gave me."

Laughter. Maybe a bit nervous. Hooded eyes flickered back and forth between Magnus Heinarson and Jessie Reyes, waiting for the response, and probably waiting to see if he'd play by his own rules.

Reyes' expression had gone from doubtful through fearful and circled back around to rage. Magnus had thermal vision built into his bionic eye, but he didn't need it to see the heat building up inside the big man's head.

"I accept your challenge, Magnus," he growled. And he smiled, the sort of smile you saw on an incredibly stupid person when they think they've finally had a great idea. "And for my weapon, I choose a power breacher!"

Well, shit. That is *a pretty good idea.*

Wilhelm Krieger brought the tool up for him through the gathered crowd. Krieger was a snot-nosed little pissant who followed Reyes around like a lost puppy and Magnus could see in his face who he was pulling for in this fight. The breacher was a heavy weapon... well, a tool, really. He'd heard from the old-timers it had started life as a rescue tool for freeing crew trapped in sealed compartments after battles, but for much longer than he'd been alive, it had been used by boarding parties to breach spaceship airlocks after their drives had been disabled... and for breaching body armor once you got through the lock.

It looked like half a fire axe had a mutant baby with a wrecking bar, and it was wielded two-handed on a pair of insulated grips—insulated because it also had a powerful electromagnet built into the business ends, which you could trigger from the grips to repel metal. Metal like him. Using the meter-long breacher, the dumb bastard actually had a chance against him.

Well, if it wasn't close, no one would be convinced, he reasoned.

"This thing'll peel you like a fucking grape," Reyes said, holding the weapon up across his body, feet squared.

"I'm gonna' stick that toy up your ass sideways, Jessie," Magnus assured the man, falling into a ready stance at the center of the courtyard. Usually, in matters such as these, the spectators would form a ring around the opponents; but no one wanted to be too close to Reyes while he was swinging around a power breacher.

There was no referee like he'd seen in the cage matches they put on in the pleasure stations, no signal when to start. One second, they were standing there, watching each other jockey for position and the next everything was in frantic, violent motion. Magnus was faster than people usually figured, and he knew it; he was counting on a wild swing, on the chance to duck inside and lock Reyes up. Once he had his hands on the man, the fight was over.

But Reyes knew it, too, and the wild swing with the axe head was a feint; he speared backward with the prybar end, his fingers jammed down on the electromagnet trigger. Magnus felt the brush of the field, felt it twisting his hands, pulling them inward, and he threw himself backward with all his weight. Outside the pull of the field, his arms flopped to his sides and he pushed down with them, throwing himself backward into a barrel roll.

Back on his feet, he set his stance and waited for the rush he sensed was coming, but again Reyes surprised him by holding back, circling around to the left, closer to the center again. There was a low cunning in the set of the big man's eyes, and it worried Magnus. He didn't like surprises, particularly in a fight.

Maybe I shouldn't have been so quick to give up on a weapon of my own.

He'd let Reyes take the first swing last round, but this time he played it aggressively and faked a punch before lashing out with a low kick at the other man's ankle. It was close; the edge of his left boot brushed the back of Reyes' calf as he hopped backward, barely a touch yet the big man seemed to be favoring the leg slightly. When he took his fighting stance again, it was with renewed caution, the power breaker held like a shield.

Magnus came out of his ready crouch and smirked at the man.

"You were full of big talk a few seconds ago, Jessie. You already losing your balls? Maybe I'll rip them off and let the boys have you as a new toy, give the pillage-girls a rest, huh?"

That got him. There was red behind his eyes and he advanced quickly, passing his weapon through an intricate figure eight. It took some strength to handle a breaker that way, he had to admit —the man had skill, and technique. When it came, the shot was lightning-fast, an uppercut with the prybar, the field activated for the space of a second, just long enough to force Magnus to acknowledge it and step away from it. The axe head followed through nearly too quickly to follow, slicing through the air and scoring a white scrape across the metal of Magnus' left arm. The metal-on-metal skritch set Magnus' teeth on edge and he fought an urge to shake the arm out, as if it were still biological. If Reyes had kept the field activated on the cut, it might have torn the arm right off, but he'd drained the capacitor with his upswing... and left himself open.

Reyes was still holding the shaft of the breaker ahead of him to block anything Magnus could throw, but he had to *hold* the thing and physics were still physics. Magnus slammed his massive right fist directly into the shaft. Had Reyes been able to trigger the magnetic field at that exact moment, it would have been suicide: Magnus' arm would have been torn from his shoulder and likely taken his spine along with it. But he was a fraction of a second too slow, and the punch to the bar tore it out of his hands and smashed the heavy weapon into his face.

It wasn't a fatal blow, wasn't even enough to incapacitate an experienced fighter like Reyes, a man used to the feel of taking a hit. If he'd had a second, a *half* a second, he could have recovered, grabbed the bar before it fell and been ready to hold off any follow-up attack. Magnus didn't give him the half-second. The cyborg was feeling the flux; the flow of the battle had fallen into a rhythm and he was moving with the beat, running just a half-step ahead of his opponent.

Reyes's face was a mask of rage and pain and desperation, blood flowing across his white-blond beard from his smashed nose, his eyes focused on the shaft of the breaker, every ounce of concentration spent on trying to get his hands back around the weapon. Magnus' first instinct had been to smack the bar out of the way, get it out of the equation, but his gut had rejected the idea without bothering to ask his head, knowing without thinking it would have cost him too much time, too much leverage. Instead, he chose the shortest distance between two points, straight into Reyes' chest.

It was a huge gamble. One touch on the electromagnet's trigger and the breaker could have ripped the metal right out of

Magnus' torso, and stopped his heart. Somehow, he just knew it wouldn't happen, knew Reyes couldn't reach the switch in time. Sometimes, when he thought about it, he wondered if he *actually* intuited what would happen during a fight or he'd just been lucky so far and had only assumed it was because he was so smart. There was an old saying among pirates though: "better a lucky captain than a good one."

This time he was lucky *and* good. Reyes' fingers didn't close on the breaching bar, just clutched at air, and Magnus' palms struck his opponent square in the chest, launching him backward as if he'd been shot out of a cannon. The breaking bar fell straight down to the clay at Magnus' feet with a massive thud, as if it had been laid down in surrender. Reyes' landing was less graceful, though no less of a surrender. He hit flat on his shoulders, his scapulae breaking with a snap like a tree limb giving way in a storm, then rolled twice before winding up on his back.

The wolf cloak had fallen away, a shapeless lump on the ground meters away. Without it, Reyes looked almost normal, unremarkable in work pants padded and reinforced at the knees, and an insulated vest. The outer garment concealed the damage to Reyes' chest, but Magnus had felt the ribs giving way under the sledgehammer blows of his hands. Reyes coughed fitfully and red droplets sprayed with the expelled breath. His feet kicked as he tried to roll over, tried to get up, but the shattered ribs and broken shoulder blades left him immobile.

Magnus breathed in deeply, savoring the chill in the air. Air, water, food, liquor, sex… it was all better after you lived through a fight. He bent over at the waist and picked up the breacher, careful not to touch the triggers. He couldn't feel weight, not the way he'd used to be able to before the bionics. There was a pressure, a sense connected to his surviving nerve endings, but the experience was qualitatively different. He wished he could feel the weight; it would be more satisfying.

He stood over Reyes, grinning broadly. The man glared up at him, still able to summon the energy for rage despite his injuries, tried to kick at Magnus' legs.

"Oh, Jessie," Magnus said, shaking his head in affected sadness. "You were a good man in a fight, but you never learned to keep your head."

He slammed the prybar end of the breaker through Reyes' face and the kicking and coughing and thrashing all ceased. The crowd had gone silent, but when he raised the bar over his head, dripping with the blood of the vanquished, the cheering began again, more fervent this time.

Sungurlu came forward, screaming his name over and over, fists pumping in the air, and Magnus tossed the breacher at him. Sungurlu wasn't a weak man, but he stumbled back a step at the weight of the massive weapon, finally cradling it across his chest while Magnus stepped into the center of the courtyard. Bloodlust was strong in the faces of the crowd, fevered by the ferocity of the combat, but fear warred for a close second place, and he sensed a desperation behind the fervor of the cheers and the chants.

"We have wasted enough time here!" he yelled, drowning out the clamor. The noise stopped as if he'd flipped a switch, though some of the fists stayed raised in the air, as if they were afraid to lower their hands, afraid of being seen as unsupportive. "Get the drop-ships loaded! We take off in two hours and anyone who isn't on board gets left behind!"

He met each of the stares, scanning across their faces with one biological eye still afire with adrenaline and one cybernetic ocular, always cold, always neutral.

"If you're with me," he roared at them, "then kill our enemies with me! Take what they have and leave nothing behind!"

This time, the enthusiasm was real, and universal.

It had damned well better be.

15

"You risked using the nuke in the first place, so why not go all the way and just kill them with it?"

Lyta Randell suppressed a sigh, then had to suppress the yawn running hard on its heels. She hadn't slept much on the trip back from Clew Bay, and while part of that had been Osceola's fault, mostly it was because every time she closed her eyes, all she could see was an Omni-Alert posting in every military outpost across the Five Dominions with all their faces on it and the notice "Wanted for War Crimes."

"We risked it because it was the only way to guarantee they'd go through with the attack on Piraeus even if they noticed our preparations," she explained, grabbing for patience with both hands. "But if we had actually managed a ground burst, well, I'm not sure we could guarantee even our own crew might not have reported it to the military. Still, we might have risked it except there was no way in hell it was going to work."

Arachne's Chief Councilor was a lion in a cage, pacing restlessly in the tiny, ten-meter room and making Lyta feel even more tired sitting hunched over on a well-padded chair at the central table. It was dimly-lit and stuffy in here despite the air conditioning, but Garrett had insisted on it, said the room was the only place in the whole *Palacio* she could be sure they wouldn't be overheard or bugged.

And isn't that all reassuring?

By all rights, Jonathan should have been here with her, explaining everything to one very agitated head of state, but he was supervising the unloading of the heavy-lift cargo shuttles and the outfitting of the mecha, which left the task to her and one sullen and conflicted Terry.

Is it daylight outside? she wondered. *Did we land at dawn or dusk, local time? I can't even remember, if I even knew.*

"Why wouldn't it have worked?" Garrett demanded. Lyta wanted to label her as petulant, but she knew she was being unfair; the woman was terrified. "It was a nuke. They can destroy whole cities!"

"Fusion weapons aren't magic, Councilor," Terry snapped, sitting on a small sofa wedged into a corner of the room. "Their yield is determined by the quantity of deuterium and tritium you pack into them, and they can only propagate their blast wave so far."

"And it's not really possible to get them closer with current technology," Lyta explained. She couldn't really blame the woman for not knowing. Out here, nuclear weapons were about as mythological as unicorns. "The ECM—Electronic Counter Measures—even someone like Magnus has access to is enough to shut down the best guidance systems most military weapons have. Fusion weapons or, hell," she shrugged, "*any* munitions not guided by a human operating a laser designator are only good against unprepared targets, which makes them useless militarily except as weapons of terror."

"Which is why all of the Five Dominions proscribe them," Terry put in, the words raw and bitter. "Using nuclear weapons is a war crime."

"No one is going to bring in a cross-border military intervention into the non-aligned systems over an airburst over a semi-habitable moon being used as a pirate base," Lyta assured Chief Councilor Garrett. "Particularly when it didn't even kill anyone. We're not going to tell anyone about it, you're the only one in your government who knows about it." Which was a backhanded way of telling her "if it gets out, we'll know it was you."

"The only one we have to worry might talk is Magnus," she concluded, "and he won't be telling anyone anything after we kill him."

"Assuming it worked, and he does what you think he'll do," Garrett interjected, "and comes after you here."

"We could see his ship heading back in to Clew Bay before we jumped," Lyta told the older woman. "He's going somewhere, in a hurry. And given we just did something I found distasteful and personally abhorrent, and put ourselves at risk of becoming fugitives all the way across human space, I certainly hope it was worth it."

It felt good to be back inside a mech. Even if the cockpit was dark and dripping with humidity and oppressively, mind-numbingly hot. At least the mosquitos couldn't get in through the transparent aluminum canopy. Logan could see them in the dim, green-tinted glow of the few instruments he'd left active, running on battery power. They bounced off the canopy with bloodthirsty persistence, more determined than any soldier he'd ever met, showing him exactly what would happen if he gave in to the almost manic desire to crack open the cockpit and let in some fresh air.

This was your idea, genius.

And it had seemed like a good one, at the time. Their biggest worry was Magnus catching sight of their defensive posture and taking off, living to pillage another day. He'd done the sensible, tactical thing and arrayed his company of mecha under the tree canopy, along the riverbanks, powered down and waiting. The *Shakak* was hiding out as well, tucked behind Arachne's small moon, biding her time until the bandit ship had moved into orbit and launched her shuttles and landers.

They were taking a risk there, as Chief Councilor Garrett had repeatedly pointed out; the bandit ship might open fire on the city from orbit, and she could cause a lot of damage before the *Shakak* could intercept her. But he, Lyta, and Osceola all believed someone like Magnus wouldn't be able to resist the lure of plunder. He'd send his people down first, to take what they could get before he blew it up. And once his forces were on-planet, he wouldn't chance orbital strikes.

But they had to be in place before the bandit ship was in visual range, which meant spending hours inside a closed mech with no air conditioning, nothing more than the fan you could run from the battery backups and an occasional hit from the on-board oxygen line. He couldn't even use the radio. They didn't want to chance any thermal, microwave, even laser signal from the hidden mecha. All he could do was wait for the incoming transmission from the command bunker in town.

And sweat. He'd been doing a lot of that, and the padding of his easy chair was soaked with it. The smell was the worst part: the cockpit was starting to remind him of the locker room at his High School gym.

Gonna have to get the crew to hose it out, assuming I survive.

"All Slaughter units, this is the Slaughterhouse."

The transmission made him jump, even though he'd been waiting hours for it. It was Lyta's voice—she and her Rangers were staying at the *Palacio*, ready to deploy anywhere in the city if needed, and she had been monitoring the sensor data from there.

"We have drop. I say again, we have drop. All Slaughter units power up."

"Oh, thank Mithra," he muttered, smacking his palm against the control to ignite the fusion reactor. A cold startup took a few minutes, which meant still more heat as the charged capacitors powered ignition lasers and magnetic fields instead of the air conditioning, but at least the end was in sight.

"Enemy drop-ships inbound," Lyta announced. "ETA fifteen minutes. *Shakak* is moving to engage."

Once Osceola moved in on the bandit ship, Magnus wouldn't have the option of aborting the landing and returning to orbit. He'd have to dig in and try to establish a beachhead on the planet, make it too difficult for them to dig him out. It was a simple plan, but the best ones usually were.

Indicators began to light up red across his board, moving to yellow before finally flashing green as systems came online and *finally* cold air began to rush out of the vents like the sweet breath of the *Spenta Mainyu* spirits, washing across the exposed parts of his face. He grabbed at an already-soaked towel hanging off a support strut and wiped the sweat away from his matted hair before he settled his helmet on and fastened the chin strap. It wasn't just for comfort: the neural halo had to have a clean connection. Trying to operate a mech through manual controls would have been next to impossible. He'd read once there had been experiments with haptic skinsuits, but the problem with those had turned out to be a very practical one. The suit required freedom of motion, and safety concerns required the pilot to be strapped in securely.

The whole board was green and the sensor display was active. He grinned, activating the company's communications network.

"All Slaughter units, this is Slaughter One. Arbalest Platoon, move to launching positions and target their drop-ships. Fire as you bear. All other platoons, move into attack positions and prepare to engage enemy forces. Sound off by platoon."

"Arbalest Platoon, roger." Lt. Mandy Ford's voice was steady and clear, though he knew this would be her first actual combat. Colonel Anders had thought she'd be a good selection, though, and he knew soldiers.

"First Platoon, roger." Langella. Sub-Lieutenant no longer, he had his own platoon and the thought made Jonathan nervous. Marc Langella was a great mech pilot and the best friend and wingman a guy could have, but unproven as a leader.

And you're not? He shrugged admission to himself.

"Second Platoon, roger." Lt. Valentine Kurtz drawled. The man was reserved, soft-spoken, intelligent, at least when it came to technical stuff, textbook tactics. He was from the backwoods, some colony Jonathan had never heard of, and usually the backwoods rednecks took to combat well.

"Third Platoon, roger." Lt. Alliyah Hernandez. He knew her, casually, someone he'd drunk coffee with in the Battalion ready room before briefings. Confident, even as a Sub-Lieutenant, always ready for a fight. He remembered she had family back on Sparta and wondered how they'd take her being away this long.

"Fourth Platoon, roger." The last, and the oldest. Gerald Paskowski was a lieutenant who would have been promoted to captain in another month if he'd stayed, but he had his heart set on leading a strike mech platoon, and none were coming open. Except in Wholesale Slaughter. He was piloting the Scorpion one Lieutenant Logan Conner had captured on Ramman, before that particular officer had been sent off on a long patrol and gone incommunicado… officially.

"Arbalests moving into firing position," Ford added.

The HUD in a company commander's cockpit was considerably larger than the one in a platoon leader's mech. It had to be to have room for the IFF displays from twenty-five separate mecha in five different platoons. It had taken him weeks of practice in the simulator before he could make heads or tails of the damned thing in battlefield situations, but he thought he had a handle on it. He recognized Ford's machines trudging slowly and steadily up the bank of the river, out into the open where the twin missile launch pods mounted on their hunched shoulders could have a clear view of the night sky.

The other platoons were marching upriver, still under the tree cover, Paskowski walking his strike mecha straight up the center of the waterway, mud be damned, counting on the sheer power of the huge machines to keep them from getting stuck. It was a bold move, and the water could help alleviate overheating in a fight, but it could get them killed if he was wrong about the depth and consistency of the mud.

He watched them moving past his position, fighting an urge to run out in front of them. A platoon leader could get away with that, but not a company commander. He waited until the strike mecha and Langella's platoon had passed, then took a cautious, probing step forward, making sure he had solid ground to stand on.

"Slaughter One, this is Cover One, over." Katy's transmission rang in his helmet's headphones, nearly sending him off balance.

"Go," he snapped, too caught up in trying to move his own mech and coordinate all the others to observe proper radio procedure.

"They have four converted passenger landers, armed up and armored, configured for air support. They're not military craft, but they have numbers and it's going to take us a while to get rid of them. I don't think we can hit the drop-ships before they land. Over."

He sighed. It had been a long-shot, anyway, but it would have saved them a ground fight. Their first ground fight as a unit, his first as a company commander. Maybe it was better to rip the bandage off quickly.

"Roger that, Cover One," he said, trying to keep the disappointment out of his voice. "Go take down their birds, we'll handle the rest. Slaughter One out."

"Arbalests in position," Lt. Ford announced, and he double-checked on the HUD to make sure she was, not because he didn't trust her but because he knew the final responsibility for every shot they fired was his. Colonel Anders had pounded the truth into his head when he'd taken over as platoon leader and it was a hundred times more relevant now. "We have a radar lock on the drop-ships through the *Palacio* headquarters feed and I estimate they will enter firing range in thirty seconds. Over."

"Roger that, Arbalest One. Fire as you bear. Out."

He watched the feed from the headquarters bunker, enjoying it while he could. The bandits would jam it as soon as they reached the ground, if they had the sense Mithra gave a newborn. The drop-ships descended on pillars of fire, not the latest military models or even refurbished surplus jobs but slapped-together conversions from heavy cargo birds. Still enough to carry two full heavy companies of mecha and if those wouldn't be the latest and greatest either, there would still be a hell of a lot of them.

"Firing," Ford announced.

It was a formality; he could see it as clear as the primary star rising at dawn, hear it like the rumble of spring thunder. Smoke billowed out from their positions, engulfing the river and the machinery surrounding it in a shroud of white-grey, lit up from within by the missiles' rocket engines as they arced upward, two from each mech. The sunbursts shrank to faint glows in the night sky, the rumbles punctuated by sonic booms as they accelerated past the speed of sound and were lost in the starfield overhead.

The mecha stayed still, gargoyle statues guarding the land from the sky, as their pilots targeted the drop-ships manually, focusing a laser designator against their fuselage because they'd be able to jam a radar lock. His eyes flickered from the visual readout to the radar from the bunker to the thermal display and he began to see glowing clouds obscuring the drop-ships. It was ECM chaff, the same as they'd used on their nuke, cheap and easily fabricated and too damned effective.

Lasers scattered through the clouds of chaff and locks were lost. Missiles corkscrewed out of control and warheads self-destructed in fireworks-blasts, a punctuation of a symphony of chaos. And still the drop-ships descended, low enough now for the city's defenses to take over.

He couldn't see the coilguns firing, but he knew they would be. The drop-ships jinked and deked in response, winding random patterns across the sky. It wouldn't work forever but maybe long enough for…

"We have separation."

It was Lyta again, and it was unnecessary. He could see the flares of the jump-jets. Whatever mecha weren't equipped with them would have had quick-burnout, single-use rockets strapped on at hard-points just to get them to the ground. Those were as cheap and easy to make as the missile defenses.

"Do you want us to keep firing, Slaughter One?" Ford asked, her tone letting him know she'd guessed the answer.

"Negative, Arbalest One," he gave her the answer she'd been waiting for. "Hold fire and save your reloads for fire support. Take up defensive positions at the river." He switched frequencies to Paskowski's net. "Fourth, get your strike mecha in position to defend the Arbalests and act as a reserve."

"Roger, Slaughter One."

Paskowski sounded disappointed, but Jonathan wasn't going to leave the missile launchers hanging out there by themselves. They had no secondary weapons except a couple of grenade launchers to discourage infantry; they wouldn't last a second in a stand-up fight. And the strike mecha were slow and lumbering, most useful as stationary firing platforms for heavy weapons.

Which is why I let him have that damned Scorpion.

"First, Second, and Third platoons," Jonathan Slaughter said over the general net, "they're coming down on the west side of the city, two kilometers southwest of our position. Hit your jump-jets and get after them."

"Where are you gonna be, boss?"

That was Langella, and he glanced quickly at the communications readout to make sure it was on a private channel.

"You know where I'm gonna be, Marc," he told his friend, grinning tightly. "I'm going to be in the shit."

Jonathan clenched his teeth, hit his jump-jets and headed into the fight.

16

Who the hell did Magnus think he was kidding? "The Red Brotherhood" was a dumbass name, something a ten-year-old besotted with adventure stories might have come up with on the spur of the moment, and this attack was a stupid idea. Sungurlu had tried to warn the man—well, the half-a-man—not to make decisions when he was pissed off, but no, Magnus fancied himself a pirate and pirates "don't take shit from any two-bit colony world!"

Mehmet Sungurlu spat off to the side and tried to shed his anger and frustration with the gesture. He had a job to do, and the only way they were going to survive this was if he did it perfectly. Another piece of advice he'd given that Magnus wouldn't accept: if the Arachne colonists had risked shooting off a nuke at them, it meant they *wanted* them to get mad and come here, which meant they'd managed to prepare defenses. No, no, Magnus couldn't accept the idea. The colonists were sheep and he was a wolf and there the story ended.

Shut up. He forced his attention back to the deserted streets of the city, dark and humid and miserable and *why the hell do we want this place again? Ahriman give me strength...*

His shoulder rested against the limestone block of an office building, something about interstellar trade, he thought; he hadn't read the sign too carefully. It wouldn't matter much longer. In a few hours, the people they allowed to live would be slaves, either for them or for sale on the open market and that would be the only interstellar trade they'd have to worry about.

Hmmph. Might buy one myself. Been a while since that flakey Mbeki girl hung herself. Starting to get lonely.

"Back up, you moron," he growled at Rao. "If you want me to hold your fucking hand, you're going to have to buy me dinner first."

The wiry little exile from the Shang Directorate quickly backed away from him, scooting down the wall and gesturing for the line of men behind him to maintain their interval. Sungurlu scowled at just the sight of them. They were strung out and clumped up all the way from the front of this trade office back nearly a kilometer. There wasn't one of them with the makings of a good foot-soldier, but Sungurlu took what he could get. Everyone they recruited wanted to be a mechjock or a shuttle pilot, and he usually had to beat it into their heads they couldn't start at the top.

He pulled the radio off his belt and touched the key to send. It was cheap and easily fabricated and not much more secure than a child's toy, but they weren't dealing with a Dominion military unit here and it should be enough.

"Krieger," he said. The other sergeant was only a couple hundred meters down the street, but a residue of military training prevented Sungurlu from just yelling his name out to get his attention. Nothing for three seconds. He tried again. "Krieger, are you listening you fat son of a whore? You better have this thing turned on!"

"Calm down, Mehmet," the former Starkad Supremacy Marine said, always casual as if he thought feigning unconcern would make people think he was in control. "What do you want?"

"I want you to get your lazy ass up here along with that sorry bunch of rejects you laughingly call a platoon. We're only five hundred meters from their government center, their 'palacio' or whatever the hell they call it. You're going in first."

Another pause and Sungurlu began cursing under his breath, about ready to run back down the line of troops.

"Why us?" Krieger finally demanded, the affected cool replaced by a plaintive whine. "We went first last time."

Sungurlu's head popped up, eyes darting around behind him, trying to make out faces through the cheaply-fabricated infrared goggles, bringing his rifle up to his shoulder. He was going to kill the bastard, going to put a round right through his fat head in front of everyone just as a lesson not to screw with the senior sergeant. Krieger wasn't stupid though, for all he was a coward; he was blended in with his men, keeping his head down.

"Ahriman take his balls," Sungurlu murmured. He abruptly realized Rao was staring at him, the whites of his eyes visible because he'd taken off his night vision glasses again. "Rao, put those damned goggles back on before I shove them up your ass."

"I can't maintain my interval with them on," the man complained, hurrying to do it anyway because he was smart enough to be scared of his senior NCO. "It kills my depth perception."

"After we take this damn planet, I'll buy you the latest gear and you can fucking walk point instead of me." *Sergeant shouldn't be walking point anyway—just can't trust these idiots to do it right.* He keyed his radio again. "Krieger, you can either get your worthless excuse for a platoon up here in the next thirty seconds, or I'm going to come over there and execute you. And if you try to run, you'll just die tired."

"I'm coming, damn it."

Sungurlu shoved the radio back into its pouch, sniffing in satisfaction.

"Damn right you're coming."

"Sgt. Sungurlu," Rao ventured nervously, half raising a hand as if he were a child in a classroom. "Why aren't we going in first?"

Sungurlu favored him with the sort of pitying look one might give the slow-witted when they said something especially stupid.

"Because there's no way in hell I'm going to be first through the door, Rao! Shit," he scoffed, "a man could get killed doing that!"

Wilhelm Krieger was staring at the public, street-level entrance to the *Palacio* and planning ways he could get away with killing Senior Sgt. Sungurlu. It wouldn't be easy. Sungurlu was Magnus' favorite—some people even speculated they were lovers, but Krieger knew the thought was ludicrous. Sungurlu fancied himself a ladies' man and Magnus lacked the equipment to satisfy anyone, including himself, which was probably why he was such an ill-tempered son of a bitch. Magnus liked the hairy, greasy NCO for whatever reason, and had defended him from more than one challenge to his authority.

But Krieger was going to do it, he'd decided already.

If he lived through the next few minutes. He scanned the area around the street entrance carefully, searching for any obvious signs of a trap. These people weren't professionals and he remembered the lessons the Starkad Marines had taught him well enough to spot any amateurish booby traps or mines or ambushes they might set up. There were none. They were probably just inside the main entrance, maybe with barricades set up for cover and whatever their largest crew-served weapons might be, if they even had any left after the Brotherhood mecha had destroyed their pitiful attempts at gun manufacturing last time. The doors up front looked pretty sturdy, about three meters tall and no doubt a few centimeters thick. They probably figured they could hold up in there, dumbass civilians.

Still… he was at the last cover before the courtyard, fifty meters of open space between the brick and wood public restrooms and the entrance to the *Palacio*. He *liked* this cover and he didn't really want to give it up. Luckily, he was a good enough NCO to have actually trained his subordinates.

You have to delegate these things.

"Red," he said, pointing at the man he'd designated as a corporal, a tall, skinny, goofy-looking kid out of Modi. Long, jet-black hair stuck out from beneath the man's battle helmet and Krieger couldn't for the life of him figure out why people called him "Red," but it wasn't his job to ratify nicknames. "You got the explosives?"

Red nodded, the same dumb look on his face he always had whether he was eating lunch or putting a bullet into somebody. He pulled off his backpack, patting it demonstratively, as if Krieger would have thought he was carrying five kilograms of plastic explosives in his hip pocket.

"Then take Mortensen and Grundig and set me a nice, big door-busting charge over there," he instructed pointing at the double-doors at the end of the walkway, covered by a canvas awning for those days it was raining. *Which is probably like, every day here.* "Set it for three minutes."

He glanced over his shoulder and found the closest of his squad leaders.

"Dobrev, you take Tiger Squad and go cover him."

You couldn't just call them "first squad" or "third squad" with these doofuses. They thought they were badass pirates, so you had to call them something dangerous-sounding. "Tiger squad," and

"Wolf squad," and Mithra alone knew if there'd be a "Shark squad" someday if they kept getting more people. He wanted to laugh, but he wasn't dealing with disciplined soldiers here, much less Starkad Marines, but he did what he had to do to keep them motivated.

Dobrev looked doubtful, no matter what fearsome name his squad was called, but he did what he was told, undoubtedly figuring Red had the tough job. They jogged across the courtyard, likely would have run if it hadn't been for all the weapons and ammo and armor they were hauling around with them. He wanted to yell at them to use overwatch and move by teams, but in open ground like this, it didn't really matter. Speed was probably better.

He didn't watch their motion, instead keeping his eyes on the windows, the terraces, sure there would be sharpshooters there. It would be a shame if they took out one or two of Dobrev's squad, but it would reveal their positions and he could have them handled. And if Sungurlu got a few of his people killed, it would make it easier for him to justify fragging the man.

He was holding his breath, not wanting to miss the shot, not wanting to miss the muzzle flash. There was nothing. He frowned. Were these people cowards or just incompetent?

"Ah well, works either way," he mused quietly.

The squad was in place, sort of. Not exactly a textbook perimeter, but they were clustered around the doors in sort of a messy half-circle while Red directed his two helpers planting what was basically all the explosives they'd brought with them. It was overkill, but when it was his ass on the line, overkill was just enough kill. Maybe. He wished he had more explosives.

Red gave the set-up a last look-over, then flashed a thumbs-up back at Krieger… and stood there grinning like an idiot.

Oh, you got to be shitting me.

"Get away!" Krieger tried to mouth the words, waving his hand, but only received a confused look in return. He hissed a sigh and cupped his hands around his mouth. "Move away, you idiots!" he bellowed, the yell echoing off the cyclopean walls of the government center.

He ducked back slightly, trying to put more of the brick wall of the public bathrooms between him and any snipers who still might be watching. Again, nothing. It was quiet enough for him to hear the patter of light rain on the roof of the restrooms.

Had they evacuated the damn city? Was that their plan?

Red and Dobrev and the others were running back to cover and Krieger abruptly realized he hadn't been counting down the time. Red had just scrambled behind the wall and covered his ears, so Krieger did the same thing, not bothering to order the rest of the platoon to follow his example. If they were too stupid to cover their ears, maybe the ringing and the headaches would at least let them learn from their mistakes.

He'd sat there for over a minute when he began to suspect Red was as big of an idiot as he looked and had mis-armed the charges. He'd just let his hands slip out of the edges of his helmet and off his ears, just begun to straighten to sneak a look when the door-breacher blew. He was fifty meters away, but the concussion still knocked him off balance and the sound of the blast left a high-pitched whistling in his ears. Lights flashed in his eyes and he put out a hand to steady himself against the wall, too stunned to even muster anger at his own stupidity.

He shook his head and finally his vision cleared enough to see the cloud of dust and debris and smoke rolling out across the courtyard, billowing upward high enough to nearly mask the whole front wall of the *Palacio*. Not only were the doors blown completely off their hinges, but the awning over the walkway had collapsed and part of it was on fire.

Yes, perhaps he had used too much explosives.

"Go!" he yelled, motioning at the doorway with one hand and unslinging his rifle with the other.

He jogged just fast enough to not be the first one there, leaving that to Dobrev, who seemed to be more enthusiastic and bloodthirsty after the display of pyrotechnic prowess. He was yelling at his squad to follow him, waving his gun in the air like he was some action hero in a movie. Then he disappeared into the smoke and billowing dust enveloping the front of the building, Krieger clenched his teeth and kept running behind him even though it went against every instinct he had.

No one inside could have lived through that blast.

And he was right. No one inside *had* lived through the blast... because there was no one inside. The entrance hall was large, with a vaulted half-ceiling, half open to the landings of the upper floors, and all he'd managed to accomplish was the utter destruction of some nice looking waiting area furniture and a security/information kiosk.

He slowed from a run to a jog to a slow, scanning walk as he entered the vestibule of the government center. The interior lights were out, either left off intentionally or short-circuited by the explosion, and wisps of smoke teased at the green-tinted view in his night-vision goggles, but he couldn't see anybody, any *bodies*, any body *parts*.

"Shit," he said aloud. He turned to the rest of his platoon as they rushed through the smoke and into the lobby, waving for their attention. "They're hold up somewhere in this building," he told them, speaking loudly now, not caring about being overheard because there was no one around to hear but them. "They probably have some kind of bunker. Wolf squad, you're going to take the west wing of the building. Second, stop standing around like we're on a damned smoke break! Get..."

"Sarge!" Dobrev yelled. He was pointing up at the mezzanine between the second and third floor balconies, fumbling with his rifle one-handed. "There's somebody up there!"

Krieger's first thought was that Dobrev was just jumping at

shadows, but he brought his rifle up to his shoulder anyway, scanning along the railing and had just caught a hint of motion.

Somebody hit him. That was what it felt like, like someone had wound up and hit him right in the chest with a club, but there was no one near him. He staggered back, putting a hand to his chest instinctively. He wore gloves with the fingertips cut off, both because it allowed him a better feel for his equipment and because it looked badass; but now his bare fingertips felt a warm wetness on his chest. He held up his hand, frowning in curiosity, wondering what could have spilled all over the front of his tactical vest. It was too dark to see what color the liquid staining his fingers was; it seemed inky-black in his night vision goggles.

Maybe there was something wrong with his goggles, he thought, because his vision seemed to be getting blurry...or was something wrong with his head? He stumbled and suddenly, he was on his knees and didn't know how he'd gotten there. He was vaguely aware of the rest of the platoon running, yelling, shooting at something, but the sounds were muted, filtered through a haze of unreality.

I've been shot, he realized. The sniper he'd been worrying about had finally got him.

Not just a sniper, either. Dobrev was trying to take shelter behind the wreckage of what had once been an expensive-looking leather sofa, but bullets were slicing through the ruined furniture as if the wood and leather and stuffing weren't there. Full-auto fire from a machine gun, something crew-served. It took all the energy he had left, but he managed to tilt his head back and look up at the mezzanine.

Yeah, there it was. Pintle-mounted, screwed onto the railing up there with a quick-detach clip. Standard military issue for Starkad Marines or Spartan Rangers, but who the hell were these guys?

He would never find out. The full auto fire had raked through

Dobrev, leaving him lying sprawled out behind the sofa, blood pooling around his body. It walked its way backward and there was just a single half-second of bright, sharp pain before everything went black, leaving only one, last, fleeting thought.

Damn it, Sungurlu...

17

This was more like it. No screwing around in space with no gravity to speak of, no atmosphere for control surfaces and the only way you could tell how fast you were going was how much it hurt. Lt. Kathren Margolis took her assault shuttle through a banking turn, trying to come in behind the enemy birds. The four aerospacecraft had split up, two of them circling around the western edge of the town, and she'd left them to Lt. Lee and Sub-Lt. Gutierrez in the other assault shuttle.

She and Acosta were on the two swinging eastward, and for once, he was keeping his damned mouth shut. It might have just been the acceleration, but it sure made it easier to concentrate. The control yoke was an extension of her arm, the shuttle her own body soaring on the night wind, instinctive and liberating.

This was why she'd become a pilot, why she'd gone against her family and left for the Academy. This was why it was all worth it. She flicked up the arming switch for the lasers, snarling in savage joy. And this part was just gravy.

The targeting reticle blinked fitfully over the right-hand bird, not quite settling. The pilots weren't bad, not for pirate trash anyway. They rolled and yawed across the sky, doing their best to stay on their objective despite the maneuvers.

And their objective is to kill my boyfriend, so fuck them.

She fired, not waiting for a perfect target lock, and the night exploded with a flash of ionized air, heated to plasma by the laser burst. The actual laser was outside the visible spectrum, but she could see its passage clearly from the lightning flare passing only meters behind the enemy shuttle. It was a near miss, but the superheated air threw a wave of turbulence into the bird and it tumbled wildly, barely regaining control. But the pilot overcompensated, bringing the plane level and forgetting to keep maneuvering. The targeting system displayed a steady green and she fired again, draining the capacitors in one, long burst.

The shuttle didn't explode as much as it came apart, vaporized metal sparking burning gas in trailing jets of fire. Pieces of the bird tumbled forward, haloed by glowing red, slowly descending as gravity overcame momentum until it impacted with the ground. A half-dome of yellow flame rose above the jungle, the fusion reactor flushing in a shower of plasma, collapsing into a mushroom cloud towering hundreds of meters to merge into the midnight darkness.

Definitely dead. Not like last time, these guys are dead. You killed them.

Still nothing. Not a pang of guilt, not a single twinge of regret.

The other pilot gave up on his ground support mission, banking left into a desperate, rolling climb.

What is he thinking? she wondered. *Does he think I'll let him go if he gives up?*

That was the difference between a pirate crew and a military one; the military pilot knew the mission was more important than their life. And giving up on one wouldn't necessarily save the other.

G-forces pushed her against her restraints and tried to squeeze the blood away from her brain as she followed him. She heard Acosta's rasping grunt and wanted to tell him he'd better keep his mouth shut if he was going to puke, but she couldn't force the words out. Right now would have been a good time to pop off a missile, but she hadn't included any with her combat loadout for this mission, replacing their weight with extra capacitor banks for the lasers. It had been a tactical decision based on numbers. The enemy shuttles would have ECM and chaff and lots of other anti-missile defenses, and she could have only carried a half a dozen missiles at most. It had seemed more prudent to be able to cycle the lasers faster and have basically unlimited firepower.

No point in crying over spilt milk.

She pushed the stick further over and clenched her abdominal muscles to keep herself conscious against the massing gee-forces. It was a close thing—a black tunnel was closing in around her vision and her head was filled with a dull roar. Katy was sure if she passed out, there was no way in hell Acosta would be awake to take the stick. She had a vague sense of something wet striking the side of her neck and she just *knew* the worthless piece of shit had thrown up.

It took everything she had to pull back from the roll, to throttle back; her arms seemed to weigh a hundred kilograms, and her fingers were cramping up. The centimeters from the end of her armrest to the throttle control could have been kilometers. But the pressure eased off and when it did, she was on the pirate bird's tail, only half a kilometer back. The reticle was green and solid.

Lightning connected the two aerospacecraft for the blink of an eye, the visual side-effect of the laser's destructive energy, and the bandit shuttle ripped itself apart in a spray of white-hot plasma so bright it blanked out the view screens. Katy pulled up sharply, feeling the shudder of superheated air trying to swat her out of the sky.

By the time she leveled off, the remnants of the enemy shuttle were spread out over three square kilometers of fiercely burning jungle just outside the city. She sucked in a deep breath and risked a glance beside her. Acosta was shaking himself, something wet and bright green splashed over his flight suit. Katy sneered at the man and opened a line to the other bird.

"Lee," she broadcast, "splash two over here. How are you guys making out?"

There was no response for a moment, and she checked the sensor readout. The pirates were jamming as best they could, and radar coverage was spotty, but she had a laser line-of-sight link to the other assault shuttle. She could see it trying to make a tight turn far out to the west of the city. It was the kind of turn you'd be making if you were trying to get on someone else's tail, or if they were trying to latch onto yours.

"Katy." The word was gasped past g-forces she could almost feel through the radio. "Weapons malfunction. Going to need a hand."

"Shit," Acosta murmured, wiping a hand over his face to clear away the vomitus.

"Hold on, Francis," she told him, feeding power to the engine and pushing them into a tight turn. "The show's not over yet."

The city streets were tight and narrow and claustrophobic, and Jonathan couldn't see a damned thing except straight ahead. He approached the intersection cautiously, trying to find the Identification Friend or Foe transponder signals on his HUD and realizing with a sinking feeling in his gut that they were being jammed. The feed from the headquarters bunker was being jammed as well, and his whole commo board was nothing but a wide wedge of static... except for Marc Langella.

Langella's Golem was about a kilometer ahead of him, past

the next intersection, the streetlights glinting off the barrels of the Vulcan cannons on his flanks. His mech's upper torso swiveled from side to side, the long, cylindrical bore of his Electro-Thermal Chemical main gun scanning back and forth coaxially as he hesitated in the gap.

"You have any comms up there, Marc?" he asked over the the laser line-of-sight hookup.

"I got Prevatt moving parallel on my left down Fifth Street," Langella told him. His voice was tight, betraying nerves he usually didn't let on. "She's got a link to Second Platoon three blocks up at the intersection of Fifth and Corwin, but they haven't seen anything."

Jonathan hunted for the streets on the map overlaid on his HUD, trying to build a picture of what he had and where they were. He needed eyes in the sky, but there was no commo with the shuttles and any of his troops who went far enough to see the enemy might not be able to report back.

Fuck it.

"Marc," he said, "I'm going to take a hop a couple blocks to the northeast and try to get eyes on the bandit mecha. Start moving in that direction and picking up whoever you can. I have a feeling they're still coming in from that way."

"Log... ." Langella bit down on the name and corrected himself. "Jonathan, you're the damned company commander. I can do it..."

"I need to *see*," he cut his friend off. "I can't lead this company if I'm blind and deaf. Just start them moving and I'll try to get a clear shot to you when I spot the enemy."

He didn't wait around to let Langella continue the argument. The jump-jets pushed him into the cushioning of his "easy chair," and the featureless, grey walls of the business district blurred behind a wall of smoke and steam. His Vindicator cleared the rooftops in just over a second and he got flashes of the streets below, nothing clear enough to make sense, but enough for the interpolation in his passive sensors to let him know nothing as big as a mech was down there.

The turbines screamed, channeling all the power they could from the fusion bottle, but they were limited by mechanics and physics, and he was barely able to maintain enough altitude to clear a single city block. He let up on the foot pedals and guided the machine to a clear spot on the next block over, landing hard enough to crumble the pavement under the Vindicator's footpads. The turbines still whined their protest, huffing and puffing as they spun down, but he was already moving, running—as much as something weighing forty tons could be said to be "running." It was more of a ponderous, lumbering trot, but concrete spider-webbed with each stride and groundcars left parked in the road shuddered as he passed.

There was nothing. The city's civilians were safe in their shelters, but he saw no ground troops, no vehicles, no planetary militia, and no enemy mecha. It made no sense. They'd been heading this way the last time they'd been spotted, and the route he'd taken with the assault platoons should have cut them off before they reached the city center.

They couldn't have gone back around to the west, he reasoned. *They would have run straight into the strike mecha and the Arbalests and there wouldn't still be jamming because they'd all be scrap metal. But if they'd kept coming in from the east, he'd have seen them by now.*

He pulled the Vindicator up short and barely kept the machine upright, the footpads digging up long trenches from the pavement, sending fist-size bits of aggregate skittering down the street.

"Any Slaughter unit!" he yelled into his audio pickup, opening up to the general address net. "Any Slaughter unit that can read me, this is Slaughter One. The Gomers are coming in from the north! I repeat, the enemy mecha have circled around to the north!"

Nothing. He was trotting his Vindicator the way he'd come, but he stopped at the next intersection and swiveled to the right, heading north. He'd hoped he would have a line-of-sight link to one of his mecha from the intersection, but saw nothing, and he cursed impotently. They hadn't thought the enemy would try entering the city from the mud flats there—the footing was treacherous, the approaches steep up the outflow of the water treatment plant. They'd assigned a militia unit to watch for infiltration from ground troops and left it basically unguarded.

Swearing impotently, he hit the jump-jets again, rising on columns of shimmering fire above the broad, flat roof of a warehouse and barely clearing it. His left footpad caught at the edge of a ventilation fan near the front face of the building and a sickening emptiness opened up inside his gut as the Vindicator began to cartwheel forward. Desperate, he cut thrust to the left-side jet and the world swung back level, the ground approaching way too fast beneath him in the view from the posterior cameras. His heels dug into the throttle controls and the street blackened and fragmented from the thrust of superheated air, then everything was swallowed in billowing clouds of dust and debris and then impact.

Whiplash bounced his head off the easy chair's padding and his teeth clicked together hard enough that he thought he tasted loose enamel. It was all he could do to bring his right leg forward to turn a sure fall into a stumbling lurch, bringing the Vindicator into a kneeling position in the open yard around the cargo loading dock at the front of the warehouse. A tall, wire-topped security fence separated the yard from the broad lanes of the truck route circling around the perimeter of the city, leading to the spaceport.

On the other side of the fence was a column of enemy mecha.

There were two platoons' worth, if the bandits used anything like military organization, marching down the road, heading inward toward the city center. Six of them were Hoppers, slapped together with fabricated parts and bristling with whatever weapons the pirates could steal or salvage, but there were two assault mecha at the rear of the column. They were older models, designed just after the Fall, when everyone was scrambling for position, building whatever they could with what they had. They looked crude and awkward, an armored gingerbread man, whatever their official designation might have been was lost to two centuries of war. They were known colloquially as Reapers and they still carried enough armor and weapons to be dangerous.

Great. I found them, now what the hell am I going to do with them?

They'd seen him already—it had been hard to miss his landing. They were swiveling in place, moving almost in slow motion, cannons tracking and weapons raising, and there were just too damn many of them. He had to *move!*

One more jump, just as high as the overworked jets would take him; heat flooded into the cockpit as turbines already pushed to their limit went from red-hot to white-hot and he very nearly passed out. He couldn't think about the heat, couldn't even think about the cannon rounds, the bullets, and lasers ripping past his cockpit because his focus was on the tactical HUD, on the IFF display, hunting all around in the scant seconds he was airborne, searching for just one friend.

And there she was, just a kilometer away, paused in a T-junction between the government center and the edge of a shopping mall, Prevatt in her hunched-over Golem, more beautiful than anything he'd ever seen before.

"This is Slaughter One!" he said as clearly and quickly as he could, already feeling the Vindicator beginning to descend. "All Slaughter units to this position! I have found the enemy mecha!"

There was no time to repeat it; he was only thirty meters above the enemy column and falling fast. He targeted the Reapers and launched a flight of Fire-n-Forget missiles with a backward slap of his left hand, waiting till the last possible second to pound the jump-jet pedals to their stops. The turbines screamed in protest and vented their rage with another wave of waste heat, but it was all lost in another bone-rattling landing and something flashed red in the damage display readout on the far right side of his HUD.

Left hip actuator, he thought clinically. *Not a big deal; I won't live long enough for it to be a problem.*

He didn't panic, though he might pay for it later, somewhere in the dark with no one around. He was running scenarios through his head and grabbing at any possibility likely to work, yanking it out and implementing it as the selections scrolled by.

Chest-deep thumps rolled off the missile strikes, hardly able to miss at this range even with the jamming, and white, yellow, and red flashed just out of the range of vision of his canopy. He'd come down almost on top of the second Hopper in the column and he used the proximity and his Vindicator's superior mass to lunge forward and smash a shoulder into the side of the ostrich-legged machine. The Hopper's legs came out from under it, clawing at the air as it crashed on its back, an overturned turtle on the beach. Jonathan didn't flip it upright the way Logan had on the family vacation they'd taken to the shore when he was a boy; instead, he stomped a footpad down into the cockpit. Transparent aluminum crumpled under nearly forty tons of mass balanced on two meters of footpad and the man or woman inside was instant roadkill.

His stomach twisted; dying that way, with your cockpit crushing you inside it, was a mech pilot's worst nightmare. He couldn't bring himself to feel sorry for a bandit who preyed on innocent people, but he also didn't look back at the smashed cockpit. He pushed away from the wreckage and swung his mech's plasma cannon to the left, counting on the Hopper to his right, the lead machine in the patrol, not being able to get a clean shot off at him because he was right in line with the other mechs in the column.

Though the possibility of friendly fire certainly wasn't slowing down the other two Hoppers in the column—they cut loose a spread of missiles at point-blank range, two dozen of them, more than enough to strip away his armor and disable the Vindicator. Only two things saved him: distance and panic. He'd launched on the Reapers from about fifty meters away, which was as close as you could fire a standard mech-launched missile and have the warhead arm itself. The Hopper closest to him was only forty meters away. The missiles that didn't miss outright hadn't even had time to accelerate to their top speed when they hit, ringing off his Vindicator's chest plastron like a gong but doing no real damage.

The other enemy machine, the one just this side of the Reapers, was twenty meters farther out, just room enough for his warheads to arm, and they did. Unfortunately for him, half of them locked onto the bandit Hopper behind Jonathan, passing meters away from his cockpit and slamming into the Hopper, engulfing it in flame and smoke. The others managed to hit the Vindicator, stripping away a ton of armor beneath a chain of gut-punch explosions and a wall of searing heat.

But not before Jonathan fired his plasma cannon. The heat and light and concussion of the missile strikes faded to nothing beside the raw power of a star handed down to man, as if by some celestial Prometheus. He'd aimed at the further of the two Hoppers to his left, instinct or thought working faster than his brain could comprehend telling him it was the greater danger. At just sixty meters, the scintillating ball of sun-fire tore right through the Hopper's chest armor and incinerated the pilot inside it. The machine froze in place, the turbines still spinning but no one left at the controls.

He'd survived this long on surprise and violence of action, and he knew that advantage was fleeting, just like he knew the two Reapers hadn't been taken out of commission. He'd seen them striding forward with their stiff-legged, tottering gait even before the Hopper's missiles had struck his Vindicator and hidden everything behind a shroud of smoke and a wall of fire hot enough to blank out his thermal sensors. The Vindicator tottered to the left as armor was blasted off the right side of its chest, sending it off balance, and Jonathan shifted its weight, throwing the machine's left leg out at an awkward angle to catch it before it collapsed to the pavement.

Something shrieked, the tell-tale sound of ripping metal, and flashing yellow turned to insistent red on the damage display. The hip actuator had frozen and his Vindicator wouldn't be straightening up again without the benefit of a repair bay... which he would most likely not live long enough to supervise.

His left arm was down, keeping the Vindicator off the pavement, but his right shoulder was up and squared toward the Reapers, and the 30mm Vulcan mounted there was up and ready while the plasma gun was swung off to the side, thrown wide in an effort to keep his balance. He armed the gun with a flick of his left finger on the control panel at the end of the armrest there, fired it with a squeeze of the trigger on his joystick.

The rotary cannon roared, the barrels spinning faster than a human eye could follow. It would burn through the whole hopper built into the right side of the Vindicator's chest in seconds, but he held the trigger down just the same, knowing he wouldn't have to worry about running out of ammo unless he lived through the next two minutes. Hundreds of tungsten slugs the size of his thumb pounded into the chest plates of the closest Reaper—he wanted to aim at the leg, to knock it off balance, but he didn't have the luxury of precision targeting at the moment and the chest was big and close.

The Reaper had a universal weapons mount on its right arm, and it could have carried anything from an ETC cannon to a plasma gun to even a light coil gun, but these were bandits, and they made do with what they could find and feed and maintain. This one mounted a high-power laser, easily identifiable by the outsized focus crystal at its emitter, and the mech's pilot was firing the weapon even before he had it on line with Jonathan's Vindicator. Humid air, rich with vapor and particulates, lit up in lightning-sparks of plasma just above the right shoulder of Jonathan's mech, arcing downward until the 30mm rounds began chewing into the chest armor.

Armor splintered and cracked under the hail of slugs, the tungsten penetrators digging through the thick chest plates with dogged persistence. The laser slewed sideways to the left, not from the impacts of the rounds but from the panic of the pilot as he tried to spin the narrow transparent aluminum strips of his cockpit away from the incoming fire and forgot to let off the trigger. The laser bursts sliced into the luckless Hopper at the end of the column, nailing his left-hip turbine and blowing it out in a spray of plasma.

Jonathan would have laughed at the enemy's misfortune, but he had his own to think about. His Vulcan's barrels were spinning dry, his ammo supply gone, and he was still bringing the plasma gun back in line, and it wouldn't be soon enough. The second Reaper was already firing his own primary weapon and his laser was on-target. Jonathan's Vulcan cannon was swallowed up in an actinic flash of white, polarizing the canopy and blinding his external cameras, and he knew the next shot would spear right through his cockpit.

He triggered off a blast from his plasma gun even though it wasn't yet lined up with the Reaper and couldn't even hope to target him with his sensors blinded, hoping against hope the shot would distract the enemy pilot. He fully expected the laser to burn right through him before his canopy even had the chance to depolarize and let him see the shot that killed him, but... nothing happened.

And when his sensors came back online a second later, followed closely by his canopy clearing, he saw the Reaper was on the ground, its left leg blown off, power sparking from severed cables at the bare metal of the left hip. For just the barest fraction of a heartbeat, he was convinced he'd managed a miraculous shot with his plasma gun, but the notion was dispelled when something moving at hypersonic speeds, visible only by the faint trail of ionized gas in its wake, took the second Reaper in the center of the chest. The ETC round penetrated straight through to the fusion reactor and the pirate mech disappeared in a yellow globe of flushing plasma, most of the cockpit incinerated along with the pilot inside it. Thrown off balance, the Reaper toppled to the pavement, crashing heavily, metal and concrete impossibly burning from the heat of the liberated plasma.

Jonathan followed the round back to its source, saw the Golem ripping right through the security fence outside the cargo dock of the warehouse. His IFF display said it was Marc Langella, but he knew it already from the demon face painted over the mech's cockpit in subdued universal camouflage colors.

The disabled Reaper was still moving, its pilot trying to push himself up on the mech's articulated left hand in a futile attempt to stand on one intact leg. Jonathan lined up his plasma gun carefully and fired, the blast burning through the cockpit. The Reaper smashed to the ground, cracking charred concrete beneath its bulk. Everything was preternaturally still for a long second, until Langella's voice came over their private channel, the man's voice tinged with unmistakable disapproval.

"Dude," he said, "you're my CO and you're my friend... but you can't do this sort of shit anymore."

He wanted to argue with the man, but he shut his mouth on

the words, forcing down his pride and his ego and really thinking about it.

"You're one hundred percent right," he said instead. "Now give me a hand up. My left hip actuator is bad, but I think I can limp back if I can get this thing standing." He chuckled ruefully. "And I really don't want to have to wait for a ride again."

18

The first enemy plane went down easy. They'd both been so intent on staying on Lee's tail, neither of them noticed Katy's assault shuttle rising up from a nap-of-the-earth run only three meters above the jungle treetops. Not until it was too late.

"You're in range," Acosta told her, trying to be useful. She appreciated the attempt, but still hadn't forgiven him for puking on her.

"Yeah," she said, eyes locked on the targeting reticle, trying to will it to go green. "I noticed."

She touched the firing control and ionized air flared sparks in a line two kilometers long, connecting her shuttle to the enemy bird for just an eyeblink. It was enough. The armed lander folded in on itself, its starboard wing separating in a spray of white fire, sending the aerospacecraft tumbling out of control, pinwheeling into the river five kilometers outside town, steam exploding in a white cloud against the stars.

"Thanks, Katy," Lee said, his voice infused with a sigh of relief.

The last enemy bird cut and ran, but played it smart. He knew they would run him down if he just headed back to orbit, knew he'd never make it, so he headed down instead, straight for Piraeus. Katy muttered a curse and pushed the stick downward, following him in, knowing what he was trying to do.

"If he gets in over the buildings, we won't be able to shoot at him," Acosta warned her.

"Yes, thank you, Francis." *I will not lose my temper, I will not lose my temper...*

She had to get below him, she decided. If she could get a low angle on him, she could force him back up, unless he was suicidal.

The secret is to be just a little bit more suicidal than the other guy.

The nose of her shuttle dipped, her port wing tilting up as she banked east and dove, opening up the throttle. Acceleration peeled her lips back from her teeth and drove the breath from her chest and the stars disappeared above the upper camera view, the only lights still visible on the screens the street lights of Piraeus, sullen and subdued under the mists off the river.

"Make yourself useful," she grunted to Acosta. "Try to let them know they've got incoming."

Acosta didn't respond, and Katy couldn't afford to take her eyes away from the controls, not going this fast this close to the ground and the rooftops looming large ahead. She was about to repeat the order when he finally began to croak out a transmission, forcing air in past the acceleration.

"All Slaughter units, this is Cover One Bravo. Be advised we have an enemy bird coming in low over the city. I say again, we have enemy aircraft inbound. Cover One out."

There was no reply and she gave a mental shrug. The bandits could still be jamming their signals, either from their mecha or from the drop-ships, wherever they'd landed. Or it could be everyone down there was too busy to answer. Lacking further orders, she was going to take this guy down.

Maybe.

He was good, and desperate, and the combination was making him hard to pin down. Every time she went low, he went lower; she was only a half a kilometer back of him, but she still couldn't get a weapons lock. And the city was dead ahead, so close she could see the writing on the advertisements plastered across the entertainment district. Apparently, Polite's Shang-Style Barbeque had the best stir-fried gator in the Periphery; she reminded herself to give the place a try if it wasn't burned down.

She was as low as she could safely fly, only meters above the rooftop, and she swore the enemy bird was actually *below* her, his wings barely clearing the facades of the buildings on either side of it.

Crazy fucker, she thought, not without some admiration.

She was, she decided, going to have to chance pulling up and firing her laser down into him, despite the damage she might do to the city. She'd just begun to pull up when she saw the missile streaking upward from the streets below. Instincts yanked the stick to port in an evasive course, but the missile wasn't aimed at her. It described a precise parabola, guided by a laser designator from below, and speared through the bandit shuttle, consuming it in a fiery blossom of red and yellow. Burning debris rained down into the middle of the city and she couldn't help but wince at the damage it would do.

She throttled down the shuttle, pulling a tight turn around the area where the missile had originated, trying to give whoever had launched it a chance to establish a laser line-of-sight link.

"Cover One, this is Ranger One." She would have recognized Lyta's voice without the call sign. "The bandits landed dismounts and they tried to storm the *Palacio*, but we took care of them. I've had reports from scouts that the drop-ships are still on the ground northwest of the city, but they won't be there long once they figure out they're losing. Go take them out, then find Slaughter One and report to him. Ranger One out."

"Wilco, Ranger One," she told the woman. "Cover One out."

She eyed Acosta sidelong, offering him a half-smile, more because of satisfaction at the results of the day than for any good feeling she might have developed for the man.

"You heard the lady, Francis. Call Lee and tell him to scout for our forces." She turned back to the tactical display and opened the throttle, pushing the stick toward the northwest. "Let's go find some bad guys."

$$\oplus$$

More than anything, Lyta Randell wanted to walk point.

Used to be able to get away with it, when I was just a platoon leader.

Oh, sometimes the battalion commander would hear about it and give her a ration of shit, but Ranger platoon leaders were *supposed* to be a bit closer to the edge than your normal soldier. Even as a company commander, she'd been a bit closer to the front than she should have been. Now, though, she was a major, and their company was all by its lonesome without higher to send them a new CO if she bought it.

So, she swallowed her pride and took her spot in the formation between First and Second platoons, with the medic and a commo specialist attached to her hips like remoras on a shark. She'd left Top, First Sergeant Benitez, back with Third platoon at the *Palacio*, and he'd tried to talk her out of even that. She should be back with the civilians at the command post, he'd said, where it was safe.

Ha. The old man meant well, but she wasn't some wet-behind-the-ears CO still wiping the shine off her railroad tracks, and she wasn't intimidated by a First Sergeant, not at her age.

She felt the rough stucco of a storefront wall scraping against the body armor over her right shoulder and she glared through her visor at the medic, who was too damned close, and taking up more than his fair share of the sidewalk. She felt like telling him to go join Second platoon's squad on the other side of the street, but thought he'd probably be lost without an officer or NCO to tell him where to go. She hoped he was good at his job… and that they didn't have to find out.

She heard the gunfire about two seconds ahead of Lt. Crowe's warning in her helmet headphones.

"Ma'am, we have contact ahead, one hundred meters east of us."

Crowe sounded calm and analytical in the face of the enemy fire, which she'd expected. The man *should* have been a captain, but he'd given up a chance at the review board for this mission. The column had stopped and dropped to a knee at the upraised fist of Gironde, the Second platoon leader, and she mirrored the motion, making sure her parasites did as well.

"Roger," she confirmed. "I'm coming up." She pushed herself up using the butt-stock of her rifle as a lever, then raised a palm to stop the medic when he tried to follow her. "You stay here." She pointed to the communications specialist, who hadn't moved, enjoying the break from toting the heavy orbital communications gear she'd been carrying on her back for about three kilometers now. "You, come with me."

Gironde was motioning at his squad leaders as she passed him, giving orders in the privacy of his helmet, his voice held inside by the sound-proof visor. The enemy, the ground troops of this "Red Brotherhood," didn't use modern helmets with built-in light amplification and short-range radio. Theirs were basic, cheap, leaving the face and neck open and unprotected; they might be good for keeping out grenade fragments, but not for much else.

Well, if they weren't amateurs, they wouldn't be pirates, would they? They'd be mercenaries.

The shops gave way to the fabrication district at the intersection ahead, the street lights ending just as abruptly. Flashes of light and echoing peals of thunder teased at her senses from deep inside the rows of warehouses and factories and she knew the mech-jocks were fighting their own battle, totally oblivious to the "crunchies" below them. Her own struggle was more immediate and visceral, illuminated by lines of tracers arcing toward First platoon's positions.

Crowe had settled them into cover behind a row of delivery vans parked at the curb next to some sort of shop. She couldn't read what they sold because their sign had been shot out, bits of glass and plastic littering the sidewalk below, crunching under the soles of her boots. A stray round impacted the sidewalk less than a meter from her and the communications specialist threw herself down behind the wheel well of one of the delivery vans, nearly knocking over the Ranger already sheltered there.

Crowe was kneeling beside the company's mortar crew, which Lyta had attached to his platoon, directing them as they set up the base and tube for their weapon in the gap between two of the boxy delivery vehicles. Incoming gunfire smacked against the opposite side of the vehicle but failed to penetrate, and also failed to break Crowe's concentration.

Damn good soldier. I wonder if he isn't being wasted here when he should have his own company.

Oh well, it had been his choice.

"How many we got?" she asked, trying to get a look over one of the mortar crew's shoulder.

"Looks like about two platoons' worth of them, probably the group that hauled ass when they saw their people get slaughtered at the *Palacio*," Crowe told her. Another bullet pinged off the side of the truck only centimeters from his head. He paused and stuck the barrel of his rifle around the side of the truck, firing off a few short, controlled bursts before he continued.

"They're dug in down the street." He motioned past the edge of the line of warehouses, past an empty gravel lot to a line of dredging machines parked end-to-end. "They're using the equipment as cover and their backs are up against the canal running down to the fusion reactor cooling stacks."

"Your assessment?" she asked him.

"For us?" he shrugged. "It would be a hell of a place for a last stand. We could hold up there until someone called in an airstrike. For them, unless they feel like swimming in that shit, it's a deathtrap."

Her smile was far too broad for the circumstances and it was probably better he couldn't see it. It was considered bad form for a soldier to enjoy killing, but she made an exception for pirates and slavers. She'd seen the shattered lives left in their wake once too often to ever offer them mercy.

"Don't tell me, Marshall," she said, motioning toward the enemy positions. "Show me."

Crowe snorted a humorless laugh and slapped the gunner on the shoulder. The gunner was a junior NCO, an unlikely little man named Evans who didn't look as if he could lift his own weight, much less carry a mortar tube, but he managed somehow.

"Hang it!" Evans barked. It was a holdover from ancient times, as almost all mortars were magazine fed, just a signal for the assistant gunner to jack the charging lever and load the round for launch. "Fire!"

The "shoonk!" of the mortar firing was a homelike sound, comforting with the memories of years spent on firing ranges. The explosion of the round impacting only fifty or sixty meters away was less comforting, but the dredging machines contained the blast and the fragments, sending the concussion echoing out toward the canal and sending a mushroom cloud of dirt and dust and sooty smoke high into the air. Her instincts tried to force her to flinch, to duck behind cover, but there'd been no danger of a short round; Evans was guiding the shots with the laser designator in his helmet.

The enemy had figured it out as well and poured a hail of gunfire in the general direction of the mortar team. Evans and the rest of the crew dove away from the weapon, but not quite quickly enough. Lyta saw the blood spray and knew someone had been hit, but all four had gone to the ground and she had no idea which one was wounded.

"Covering fire!" Crowe yelled into the general platoon net. "Lay down covering fire, damn it!"

Nearly two dozen rifles spoke as one, chattering spitefully as if they resented the fact their machine guns had been left behind with the force in the *Palacio*.

We could use them now, Lyta admitted, *but it was a calculated risk.*

It seemed to be enough. The incoming fire was slacking off and Evans was pushing himself up, unhurt. The loader was scrambling to her feet, but the assistant gunner stayed down, clutching at her left arm.

Lyta knelt down over the woman, switching frequencies with a touch of her wrist computer.

"Medic!" she snapped. "Get up here, we got wounded."

The assistant gunner was a corporal and Lyta was ashamed to admit she didn't remember her name until she read it on her name tape.

"Steady, McClendon," she told the woman, squeezing her shoulder, more a symbolic motion than a meaningful one since she wouldn't feel it through her armor.

Evans was up and firing again, making slight adjustments

with a small joystick at the base of the mortar, walking the rounds up and down the line of dredgers, backlighting the machines with wreaths of fire. Yellow paint peeled away in charred and blackened flakes, and one of the machines crashed sideways, its left rear wheel blown completely off. Lyta let the barrage go on until the medic skidded in beside her and took over McClendon, then she tapped Evans on the shoulder and signaled "hold fire" with a hand waving up and down across her face, just in case the too-close concussion of the mortar hits might drown out her radio call.

"Marshall," she said to Lt. Crowe, "I don't want them swimming off and winding up someone else's problem. Advance."

"Sgt. Borgmier," Crowe snapped the orders out crisply, "stay here with Third squad and lay down suppressive fire along the right side of the line of dredging machines. First and Second, on me, Ranger-file."

On us, you mean.

She followed on Crowe's heels, ignoring protocol just this once. She sure as hell wasn't going to stay back and hide behind cover while he was chasing down the pirates. It was only fifty meters, after all.

The squad Crowe had left with his platoon sergeant was firing in tight, controlled bursts, which was a damn good thing as far as Lyta was concerned since she was one of the people running downrange and twenty meters to the left just wasn't quite far enough for her. The Rangers' gunfire was the only shooting accompanying their movement; from the enemy, there was nothing.

"Borgmier, cease fire! Cease fire!" Crowe yelled as he cleared the left edge of the left-most dredger.

The equipment was going to be a write-off, and she hoped the Arachne Council didn't take it out of their pay. The pirate ground troops were mostly a write-off, too. She slowed to a cautious walk, tracking each body with the barrel of her carbine and making sure not to sweep Crowe with her muzzle as he stalked just ahead of her. She couldn't see details of the corpses, not with all the smoke, but that was okay. She'd seen enough things in her life to haunt her dreams.

"Swimmers," the Lieutenant said, pointing out into the canal.

There were six or seven of them, splashing awkwardly in their body armor. They'd probably drown on their own, but she wasn't the type of officer to leave something like that to chance.

"No stragglers, no prisoners," she declared.

She targeted the one who'd gotten the furthest, a bulky, half-muscular, half-fat man with long, greasy hair and a full beard. The red reticle of the optical sight floated across his oversized, oddly-shaped head, shuddering slightly and then coalescing into absolute clarity as she held the weapon still.

He has to be an officer or senior noncom, she thought with wry amusement. *He ran first.*

The trigger broke cleanly beneath the pressure of her finger and the burst was a firm, welcome pressure against her shoulder. The crack-crack-crack of the bullets breaking the sound barrier was almost louder than the report from the integral suppressor. All three found a new home in the brain pan of the pirate trooper, blood merging with the dark, muddy waters as he sank from view.

Only after the job was done did she register Crowe and the others firing as well, their rounds sending up white sprays of water against the darkness until nothing alive moved in the canal. Behind her, an agonized moan from a wounded pirate cut off in the cough-snap of a rifle round discharging, and then there was silence.

"That's the last of them, ma'am," Crowe told her. "Should we head back to the *Palacio?*"

She shushed him with an upraised hand, focusing her external audio pickups back to the industrial district. The armor battle there was moving, heading toward the edge of town.

"Get me a vehicle, Marshall," she told him. "Night's not over."

19

Jonathan nursed the Vindicator along, keeping the left knee and hip joints locked and dragging the left footpad over the concrete, leaving an intermittent groove dug into the pavement behind him like a trail of breadcrumbs. It was frustratingly slow, but he knew what waited for him at the end of this road and the choice he'd have to make. He wasn't in any special hurry.

Langella had insisted on having his platoon escort Jonathan, and the four Golems surrounded him like guards around a prisoner, their ETC cannons pointed outward, swiveling back and forth watchfully. He thought it was a bit silly; the jamming had disappeared after Katy had found and destroyed the drop-ships nearly a half an hour ago. They knew where the remaining enemy mecha were, and none were waiting behind the trees beside the road to ambush him. But Langella had been right when he'd chewed Jonathan out for taking off on his own to find the main bandit force, so he'd given in and accepted the escort.

The city was two kilometers behind them, down the only road leading through the jungle. It had been cut with lasers and brute force centuries ago, and it was only kept clear of vegetation with constant maintenance and heavy machinery. Construction vehicles lay abandoned by the side of the road at intervals, some already sinking into the mud, left there days ago when preparations for the raid had begun.

How long, he wondered, would the people here be able to keep up the fight against nature? Would they go on with their lives if the Jeuta cut off trade with the outside? Would they ride out a war between the Dominions as they'd rode out the fall of the Empire, tucked into isolated hollows in the foothills of the mountain range, hiding from looters and raiders, then emerging timidly to rebuild what was left? Was that the future of all humanity?

The road passed on to the north, tracing a lonely trail on to the next town, kept open to haul cargo cheaply, in massive freight trucks powered by fusion reactors. There were only three of them on the planet and they circulated constantly, switching out drivers and loads but always moving. The bandit drop-ships had landed just to the east of the road, in a clearing created by what looked like a fairly recent fire, probably started by lightning. Black and blighted, the clearing rose in an island of solidity amongst oceans of mud and sand, stretching for a kilometer on a side until the tightly-packed foliage closed in on it.

The drop-ships were huge, bulky, ridiculous, lifting bodies kept in the air by raw power. Or they had been. Now, they were as charred and ruined as the land where they'd taken refuge, their engine compartments ruptured and molten where plasma had fought its way along the path of least resistance when weapons-grade lasers had pierced the reactor shielding. Flames still licked around them, pouring out steady, slender clouds of black smoke.

Clustered together between the wreckage and the encroaching jungle, about a kilometer from the road, were the broken corpses of what had once been eight mecha of mixed lineage and type. He saw the burning remains of four of the prolific Hoppers, torn apart and scattered back into the spare parts from which they'd been assembled. Two reapers had been there as well, both of them more or less intact but for the charred remnants of what had been their cockpits.

And two of the machines still stood, damaged and nearly immobile, the armor stripped off in chunks from missile hits. One was an Agamemnon assault mech, an older design but one still in service in the Dominions, possibly stolen or salvaged, or possibly pieced together from black market weapons vendors. The 'Memnon was missing its left arm and holed through in at least three different places, but still on its feet, standing in front of the other as if guarding it from them.

The last machine was a Sentinel, like the one Colonel Anders piloted, but for the hideous, bright-red and yellow paint job, and Jonathan cocked a curious eyebrow at it. Getting hold of a top-of-the-line mech like the Sentinel out here was an impressive feat, and he had no doubt whatsoever who was in it.

"Magnus is in the Sentinel," Hernandez supplied over the command net.

Her platoon was arrayed in a semi-circle around the clearing, lined up next to Kurtz and Second, looking like nothing so much as a firing squad. Above them, he could hear thje whine of the assault shuttle's jets as it circled around the area, keeping station in case they needed air support.

"We've been asking him to surrender..." A pause Jonathan knew was a shrug. "...mostly because that Sentinel would be a fair piece of salvage and I didn't want to order it destroyed without you here to make the decision, sir." Another hesitation, not a shrug but more an uncomfortable feeling about what she was going to say next. "He says he wants to talk to the commander before he surrenders. Face to face."

Jonathan sighed. It could be a trick, but she was right about the Sentinel. They were mercenaries as far as anyone else knew. Passing up that sort of salvage would look suspicious, if not reckless. He adjusted the frequency on his comms to a wide-band general address, something Magnus would definitely pick up.

"Captain Magnus," he said. It pained him to give the man the title, but you caught more flies with honey.... "This is Captain Jonathan Slaughter of Wholesale Slaughter Military Contractors, LLC. You need to surrender your mech and your weapons immediately or I'll have my assault shuttle take you out with a laser from five kilometers away and you'll never know what hit you."

The Sentinel stomped forward, ignoring the efforts of the battered Agamemnon to block its way. The mech's design dated back to the Empire, one of the few preserved past the Fall, and it seemed to retain something of the ancient Imperial nobility in its angular, sloping lines and oversized chest plastrons. Of course, Magnus had spoiled it all with a garish death's-head done up in red and yellow across the cockpit, but what else could be expected from bandit trash?

The Sentinel approached another twenty or thirty meters and stopped, its arms and legs locking into place with the unmistakable stiffness of the reactor being shut down and all the power leaving the joint actuators. The cockpit canopy popped upward, fitful and jerky as if the hydraulics had gone bad and never been replaced. A helmet flew out of the open cockpit, tossed with scornful disregard, striking the motionless right arm of the machine with a hollow clank and ricocheting off to hit the dirt and roll a few meters away.

Captain Magnus Heinarson pulled himself out of the cockpit and clambered atop the shoulder of his Sentinel with surprising agility for a man of his size. Jonathan knew the scale of a Sentinel and he could tell the bandit chief had to be two meters tall, though how much of that was natural and how much was due to his cybernetic replacements, he couldn't be sure. He was dressed in leathers rather than utility fatigues, dyed the same shade of red as the paint on the exterior of his mech and they were barely able to contain his barrel chest and the bulky mass of his bionic arms and legs. His long hair was a matching color and Jonathan was dead certain the shade wasn't natural. It was twisted into a braid reaching all the way down the man's back, tossing to and fro at each movement, pulled back away from the half-metal face as if in an effort to keep from concealing it. There was a large handgun holstered at Magnus' right hip, but he made no move toward it. Instead, he beckoned toward Jonathan, motioning for him to come closer.

"*Sir*," Langella said, stern warning in his voice despite the honorific.

"Keep an eye on the Agamemnon," Jonathan told his friend. He paused, smiling slightly even though the other man couldn't see it. "This *is* one of the things that comes with command, Marc."

He felt as if he were the one limping rather than the Vindicator, as if it had been his body beaten up in the battle rather than his machine's, and he whispered a soft apology to the mech for how badly he'd mistreated it. The left footpad scraped through the charred ash of the ruined plateau, exposing lighter soil beneath, an arrow pointing the way to the motionless Sentinel. He stopped the Vindicator about thirty meters from the bandit chief, locking it in place but not shutting down his reactor. The bandit chief might be trusting his good graces, but the feeling was not mutual.

He pulled his handgun from its chest holster before he hit the control to open the canopy, keeping it up and ready as the transparent aluminum raised on its BiPhase Carbide frame. The air outside was dryer and cooler up here, out of the valley, but only by comparison. It was still warm enough for him to start sweating almost immediately. He pulled his helmet off and set it carefully on the armrest of his easy chair, then grabbed at one of the handholds beside the cockpit and leaned out into the open air.

Magnus was above him, his mech taller by a good three

meters, and Jonathan found the height difference annoying. He scowled and clambered up the maintenance ladder to the top of the Vindicator's left shoulder, balancing himself against the bulk of the missile launch pod. From up there, he could see clearly the scars and scabs of the day's battle on his mech's chest armor; his gut clenched at the sight, whether from anthropomorphic empathy with the machine or from latent fear at what could have happened he wasn't sure.

He was close to level with Magnus now and he motioned at the pirate captain with his gun.

"You wanted to talk," he said. "I'm here, so talk."

"You're going to let me go," Magnus growled. It wasn't a literal growl, it was just the way the man's voice sounded, damaged, gravelly. His cybernetic eye glowed red, his natural one dark and nearly invisible in the flickering shadows of the fires surrounding them. "You're going to send me in a shuttle to my ship and let me go."

"Why the hell would I do that?" Jonathan wondered, blinking at the man's chutzpah.

"Because if you don't," the pirate warned him, "I'll make it my mission to tell anyone who'll listen all about how you used a nuke on a habitable world." The living side of his mouth sneered. "You'll never get another job anywhere in the Five Dominions, and that's if you don't wind up rotting in some prison cell."

"But if we let you go," Jonathan said, gesturing casually with the barrel of his gun, keeping it pointed toward the bandit, "*after* killing most of your people and destroying your mechs and shuttles, you'll be so fucking grateful you won't say a thing, right?"

He laughed, leaning against the missile launch pod. It was coated with soot, and he knew he was getting the stuff on the sleeve of his fatigues, but he didn't care.

"I know I must look young to you, but do I look *that* young?"

He tilted his head, eyeing the cyborg curiously. "Why do you think I just won't put a bullet in you from here?"

The sneer returned and the cyborg crossed his arms over his broad chest, eschewing any attempt to keep a steadying hand on the side of his Sentinel.

"You're military," Magnus accused. "I can smell it. You aren't one of these collections of losers who got kicked out of a half a dozen different armies. I've seen those morons." He grinned, and the teeth inside that mouth were metal and sharp. "I've kicked their asses. No, you people all trained the same place and I don't believe you're just some hired guns. And that means you don't kill prisoners." He shrugged, spreading his hands. "At least not without a trial."

Jonathan tried to keep a poker face, wasn't sure how successful he was. Jonathan Slaughter shouldn't have any problem killing a pirate, surrendered or not. Unfortunately, there was still just too much of Logan Conner left in Jonathan Slaughter, and the bastard was right; he couldn't bring himself to murder anyone in cold blood, much less order someone else to do it for him.

"I'll tell you what, Captain Magnus," he said, a decision firming up inside him, "I'll just have to take my chances on whether anyone will believe you over us." He motioned downward with the barrel of his pistol. "Why don't you just climb on down and give yourself up? And while you're at it, tell your friend in the pile of junk over there to surrender, too."

He watched the cyborg carefully, waiting for the slightest hint he was going for his gun. For all his bluster, the man was dangerous and ruthless. But he seemed content to carry through with his threat to inform on them, or perhaps confident Jonathan would change his mind, because the only move he made was toward the maintenance steps built into the side of his mech.

He gave Jonathan one last, leering smile as he bent down to

grab the first rung of the steps. It was frozen on his face when the top of his head disappeared in a spray of mist. The crack of the bullet breaking the sound barrier was still echoing across the field when Magnus' body pitched forward, tumbling off the side of the Sentinel and falling the fifteen meters in what seemed like slow motion. When he hit, it was with a strange, metallic thump, not what you'd expect to hear from a human body. The blood pooling beneath him seemed all too human though, staining the dirt dark red for just a moment before it was absorbed.

Jonathan's head whipped around, his gun coming up as if someone might be shooting at him as well, but he could see nothing but the lights coming off the mecha behind him. Then he heard the grinding of overworked and damaged actuators and remembered the Agamemnon. He barely had time to lunge back toward the first rung of the maintenance ladder, heading back to his cockpit, when the laser tore apart the night.

He was over five hundred meters away from the Agamemnon, but the heat washed over him like the tide, searing the breath from his lungs, and the concussion came damned close to knocking him right off the side of the Vindicator. He let his handgun drop, the dull finish still glowing in the explosion of light and fire from half a kilometer away, and grabbed at the rungs of the maintenance ladder. Metal bit into his hands, drawing blood, and still he held on, not daring to move as the hot wind buffeted him and deafening thunder rolled across the small plateau.

When it had passed, when he had secured a safe handhold and hooked a leg back inside the cockpit, only then did he allow himself to look back to where the Agamemnon had been. There wasn't much left of it, pools of fire burning fiercely, consuming things that shouldn't have burned. Overhead, the whining roar of the assault shuttle's turbojets rattled the sky.

Katy. She took out the mech. She was ordered *to take out the mech, which means the shot came from...*

He'd just slipped on his helmet when he heard Lyta's voice in the headphones.

"Sorry," she said in a tone with no apology. "I couldn't take the chance he'd go through with his threat."

He checked the transmission, made sure it was on their private, secure net before he replied. Except he didn't reply. He couldn't. The words raged inside his head, clawing their way up out of his throat, but he clamped his teeth shut against them. Instead, he turned the Vindicator, an awkward, hopping motion to keep the damaged joint locked. In the magnified view from the tactical display, he saw the groundcar, one of the government vehicles from Piraeus, open-topped and rugged. It was parked at the road, at the edge of the clearing, and Lyta Randell was standing in the backseat, her balaclava and night vision goggles pulled up, a sniper rifle tucked under her arm, the folded bipod resting on the vehicle's roll bar.

She'd fired the shot herself.

"I suppose if anyone asks," he finally responded, "you'll just say he was reaching for his gun."

Her face was clearly visible on the screen, the expression impassive, as if she'd just swatted a bug. "Something like that."

It was harder to bite the words back this time, so he chewed them up and spit them out instead. "Am I running this unit or are you, *Major*?"

Now the mask slipped just a millimeter, a twitch of the muscles on one side of her cheek. "You're in command," she told him, "except when your orders are contradicted by the last ones I was given by your..." Her lips pressed together for a beat and she corrected herself. "...by our superior officer."

Dad, in other words.

"And what was that?" he asked her, some of the anger transferring from Lyta to his father.

"Not to let you get yourself killed."

20

The sound was rhythmic, percussive, an amateur trying to play the drums for the first time. Lyta Randell's hand paused over the light switch to the *Shakak's* deserted gymnasium, head cocked toward the impacts, picking up a soft grunt with each of them. She threw her workout towel around her neck and paced silently past resistance machines and treadmills, past the hatch for the pool, used only when the ship was under steady boost as it was now, past the locker rooms to the last open hatchway before the circular compartment curved back around to the entrance.

The lights were dim inside the octagon, just bright enough to make her way through the equipment without switching on another. Inside, Terry Conner was losing a fight with a heavy bag. He looked ridiculously out of place in brightly-colored sweat pants and a sleeveless hoody, but at least he'd found the gloves. He was wearing them on the wrong hands, but it was the thought that counted. He smacked at the worn and ragged heavy bag with all the conviction of a three-year-old determined not to go to sleep early. His face screwed up with pain every time he connected, but the grimace was determined to push through the discomfort.

"You're going to break your damned wrist," she told him, stepping into the compartment.

The floors were mostly covered with padded mats, some of them still stained with what might have been long-dried blood. The cage was cheap plastic, but it was the correct shape. She wondered if Kammy had been able to sucker anyone into fighting him lately.

"Dad tried to teach me how to punch once," Terry admitted, resting a hand against the gently-swinging bag, sucking in air. His hair was shorter now than it had been back on Sparta, but what was left of it was matted with sweat and his face was pale. "I didn't pay enough attention."

She snorted a sharp laugh in agreement, grabbed his wrists and pulled the gloves off. His face reddened when she worked them back onto the correct hand and fastened the wrist straps. He was flexing his fingers as she walked around beside him, facing the bag, and fell into a fighting stance.

"Feet about shoulder-width apart," she instructed. "Squared off, but the left foot slightly forward so when you lean into a cross you won't go off balance. Bend your knees. Punch from the hips, that's where your power is, but start by stepping into it. Shoulders straight, arm at shoulder level, wrist straight if you don't want to break it."

She snapped a cross into the bag, the plastic stinging the skin over her bare knuckles, the cord securing it to the overhead yanking and vibrating as the bag shook with the impact. Terry's eyes went wide.

"Now, I'll show you slower."

She repeated the move at about quarter-speed, his eyes following her form... perhaps for more than combat tips. She'd always thought he might have a crush on her, despite their age difference.

"You try it," she invited, stepping back and waving at the bag.

His eyes set with what might have been anger and he stepped into the punch, his right glove crossing into the bag with a solid smack.

"Now jab," she urged him, tapping his left arm. He straightened it into a poke at his imagined opponent, weaker and more awkward but he needed more training for the speed the move required. "Jab again!" Better this time. "Cross!"

The cross was perfect and he followed it with another, left-handed, then another right and nearly fell over, crying out in frustration.

"Whoa," she said, putting a hand on his shoulder to steady him. "Are you okay?"

"No, I'm not okay," he snapped, brushing her support away and striking petulantly at the bag with a backhand. "You made me build a nuke and use it on a habitable planet, Lyta!"

"I did," she acknowledged. "And that's the sort of mission this is, Terry." She put a finger into his shoulder and turned him to meet her glare. "And *you* were the one who stowed away so you could come along. Or did you forget that part?"

"No, I didn't forget," he shrugged in grudging admission. "I want to help make this work, but…" He squeezed his eyes shut for a moment, as if he were trying to wipe away a memory. "I just want us to be the good guys."

She laughed and saw the hurt in his eyes, but she went on with the lesson anyway.

"There are no good guys and bad guys outside of children's stories." Her voice was harsh, but he needed to hear this. "Even that asshole Magnus was probably able to convince himself he was just doing what he had to do to survive. To people like him, anyone who gets in his way is a bad guy." She snapped a punch of her own into the bag, sending it swinging toward him and he stepped back, eyes flickering between it and her. "You think Declan Lambert didn't believe he was doing the right thing for

Sparta when he killed the Guardian and tried to seize control of the government? Oh sure, he wanted power, but people like him always think them being in power is going to be the best thing for everyone. I bet Starkad is just full of people totally sure they're the ones who can bring the Dominions together again and rebuild the Empire, and everyone will love them for it."

Terry's eyes went wide at the words and he spluttered a few syllables before he was able to say anything coherent in response.

"Then how do we know we're doing the right thing?" he finally managed to ask.

"I serve the Guardianship of Sparta," she told him. "I follow legal orders, and when I don't have clear orders, I do what I think will protect and defend the people of Sparta." She cocked her head at him sidelong. "Is what's right for Sparta what's right for Starkad? Or Shang? Or the Periphery?" She shook her head. "How the hell would I balance all that? The difference is, I took an oath to protect and defend Sparta."

"I haven't taken any oath," he protested. "I'm not in the military."

She advanced on him faster than he could back up and jabbed a finger between his eyes.

"If you're going to be on this mission," she said, each word the lash of a whip, "you had damned well better take an oath!" Her breath hissed out through clenched teeth and she tried to relax. "To yourself, if no one else. Because if you're not here to protect and defend the people of the Guardianship of Sparta, I will damn well find a way to ship your ass back to Sparta and to hell with operational security."

His mouth made an "o" as he seemed to finally realize the ramifications of the choice he'd made. There was still something of the overindulged and overprotected younger child behind his eyes, but she thought she saw something firming up inside them as well.

"How would..." He stumbled over the words. "I mean, do I need to join the military?"

She let her face slip into a grin. He was, after all, his father's son.

"No, but there's an oath we give to civilian researchers who agree to a term of employment with military agencies. I think that one would work fine."

He nodded, and she thought he might have been relieved he wouldn't have to enlist in the military... and maybe a little disappointed.

It's not what your father wanted for you, Terrin, she thought, but wouldn't allow herself to say. *Mithra knows, this is bad enough.*

"Did you know?"

Katy had been drifting in the drowsy twilight between sleep and wakefulness, and for a moment, she was sure she'd dreamed the question. She blinked against the glare of the light on the cabin's nightstand and saw Jonathan sitting up against the headboard, staring into the shadow across the compartment. His hair was matted with sweat, beads of it still glistening on his skin and she felt a purr of satisfaction somewhere in her chest. There was something so much more affirming about the sex just after combat.

She rubbed at her eyes and forced herself to concentrate on what he'd asked her.

"Did I know what?" she wondered, pushing herself up beside him, resting her head on his chest. She could feel his heart beating, steady and strong and she teased at his light-colored chest hairs playfully.

"Did you know Lyta was going to shoot Magnus?" he clarified. She looked up at the tone of his voice. He was deadly serious, even a little cold, and she gave up on being playful and teasing.

"She told me," Katy admitted. "When she ordered me to take out the Agamemnon."

"You should have warned me." The statement wasn't accusatory. It would have been easier if it had been; she could have just let herself get angry, argued with him. Instead, it was... disappointed. Which was so much worse.

Finally, he looked at her. There was hurt in his grey eyes, and she knew she'd caused it. Worse still.

"When you told me you wanted to come along, you said you understood you had to follow my orders. Mine, Katy, not Lyta's. Only one of us can be in command, no matter what she thinks."

Now she did want to argue, did want to be angry. Wanted to tell him he was being an idiot, that Lyta had saved his life, that he would have gotten himself killed going against someone like Magnus in some sort of half-assed, macho-bullshit, mano a mano fight.... But she didn't.

"You're right." The words dragged themselves out against her will, tasting worse than any medicine she'd taken as a child. "I was just thinking I wanted to protect you, to save you from yourself, but that's not my job. I'm a military officer and I should have followed your orders." She shrugged. "If you'd abandoned everything to run off and save me, I'd have been pissed. I'm sorry, Jonathan. It won't happen again."

He sat there in the dim light for a long minute, face creased with consideration, before he finally nodded.

"All right." He met her eyes and the corner of his mouth turned up, just slightly. "Lyta made it easy to pretend it didn't happen, publicly. And between us, well..." He shrugged and the smile grew. "I'm kind of glad you wanted to look out for me." He cocked his head toward her. "Just this once, though. It's only going to get harder and more dangerous from here on out, and the mission has to come first. Agreed?"

She pulled herself up his shoulders and kissed him, hands teasing once again.

"I agree it's going to get much more dangerous," she breathed in his ear. "And much harder."

"Damn it, Katy…" But at least he was laughing.

EPILOGUE

" ... And the latest reports from our sources at the Alcazar on Sevilla indicate the Imperium of Mbeki is proceeding with their initiative to expand their territory by trying to reclaim some of the Lost Colonies. Their researchers are convinced they can counteract the radiation on some of the more salvageable worlds with targeted asteroid strikes, but our analysts doubt the plan will prove practical and recommend allowing them to waste resources on the scheme rather than attempting to sabotage."

Kuryakin felt his attention drifting away and his eyelids drifting downward. It wasn't just the tedious nature of the intelligence briefing, it was Major Capron's monotone delivery. The man had the personality of a dead fish and the face to match, for all he was a loyal and hard-working officer. He'd never be anything but an intelligence analyst, though—he lacked that vital catalyst which could launch a staff officer into the command ranks, the ability to schmooze with his superiors.

"Yes, yes," Kuryakin said, making an underhand move-along motion with his fingers. "I believe I grasp the situation. I will make the recommendation to Lord Starkad when we meet tomorrow." *Though I'm sure Aaron will pay as little attention to it as I have. No one gives a shit about the Lost Colonies.*

Aleksandr Kuryakin glanced around the room at the three analysts clustered at his desk, eyebrows going up.

"Is that it? Because my wife would dearly love it if I could actually be home from work in time for us to have dinner together for once."

He'd actually braced his hands against the armrests of his office chair and begun to put weight on them when Captain Laurent cleared her throat and made a motion as if she were about to raise her hand like a schoolchild in class.

"Colonel…" she began hesitantly and he sighed, settling back into his chair. It creaked beneath him and he wasn't sure if that meant he should call maintenance or spend more time in the gym.

"Yes, Captain?"

He sounded, he knew, indulgent and condescending, but the woman was far too meek and retiring and while it had seemed cute at first, it was beginning to wear on him after three months of having her assigned to his analysis team.

"There've been a few reports out of the Periphery about a new mercenary unit." She chewed her lip, waiting for some sort of encouragement before she went on.

Deep breaths. Count to ten.

"Don't keep us in suspense, Ruth."

She nodded quickly and scrolled down on her tablet screen, reading notes he was sure she'd had memorized hours ago.

"They're called…" She seemed embarrassed to say the name. "…Wholesale Slaughter."

Kuryakin snorted an unwilling laugh at that.

"There's some truth in advertising for you," he said, leaning back in his chair, interested in spite of himself. "At least for the typical mercenary trash."

"Their commanding officer is a former Spartan mech pilot

names Jonathan Slaughter," she clarified. "According to our sources in Argos, he separated from the Guard after repeated disciplinary actions, mostly insubordination. He kept losing his temper at his superiors over what he perceived as..." She snuck another peek at the notes. "...official inaction on the problem of bandit incursions."

"He'll find plenty of bandits in the Periphery," Major Bhandaru remarked in his typical dry wit. Kuryakin eyed him balefully. He was one of the Schmoozers, a man who *would* be promoted, but Mithra knew he didn't deserve it. Bhandaru thought humor substituted for actual ability. "He'll break his damn teeth on them."

"Wholesale Slaughter recently had their first recorded client," Laurent went on, studiously ignoring Bhandaru. Kuryakin knew he'd been hitting on her, and while he didn't approve, he also didn't feel like stepping on the toes of the Generals and Admirals Bhandaru had been schmoozing so expertly with. "Arachne, a mostly agrarian world, hired them to go up against a pirate named Magnus Heinarson."

"The Red Brotherhood," Kuryakin acknowledged. "Small time, but ruthless killers."

"Not anymore, sir," she said with unusual temerity, apparently emboldened by his response. "They were wiped out to the last man, woman and scumbag. Their ship was destroyed and none of their usual brokers has reported any contact with them since."

Colonel Aleksandr Kuryakin raised an eyebrow.

"That *is* impressive for a young mercenary company. And they didn't even try to extort more money out of the Arachne government afterward?"

"No, sir," Laurent confirmed. "They even did the job at a bargain price. Apparently, they're trying to build their reputation."

"And they've succeeded." He rubbed the closely-cropped goatee that was as much of a beard as regulations allowed him, unfortunately. His wife was always saying he'd look good with a full beard. "Put a dedicated team on them, and get me eyes on, wherever they go next. I want a first-hand account."

"Me, sir?" she asked, a deer in the headlights.

"Yes, you, Captain Laurent." He leaned toward her across the desk and scowled when she flinched. "Unless you want to spend your entire career making reports like this, you need to get your hands dirty. *You* pick the team, *you* run the assets, and *you* are responsible for the intelligence assessment. I want progress reports every two weeks."

The woman was frantically tapping notes into her tablet, nodding absently to each statement he made. He was tempted to assign a capable NCO or warrant officer to hold her hand through the process, but he decided against it. This was probably nothing, and it was a good chance to see what sort of judgement she had in selecting her own people.

Wholesale Slaughter. He grinned. *That takes some balls.*

FROM THE PUBLISHER

**Thank you for reading *Wholesale Slaughter,* book one in the
series of the same name.**

W e hope you enjoyed it as much as we enjoyed bringing it
to you. We just wanted to take a moment to encourage
you to review the book on Amazon and Goodreads. Every review
helps further the author's reach and, ultimately, helps them
continue writing fantastic books for us all to enjoy.

If you liked *Wholesale Slaughter*, check out the rest of our
catalogue at www.aethonbooks.com. To sign up to receive a
FREE collection from some of our best authors (including one
from Rick Partlow) as well as updates regarding all new releases,
visit www.aethonbooks.com/sign-up

SPECIAL THANKS TO:

ADAWIA E. ASAD	EDDIE HALLAHAN	KYLE OATHOUT
JENNY AVERY	JOSH HAYES	LILY OMIDI
BARDE PRESS	PAT HAYES	TROY OSGOOD
CALUM BEAULIEU	BILL HENDERSON	GEOFF PARKER
BEN	JEFF HOFFMAN	NICHOLAS (BUZ) PENNEY
BECKY BEWERSDORF	GODFREY HUEN	JASON PENNOCK
BHAM	JOAN QUERALTÓ IBÁÑEZ	THOMAS PETSCHAUER
TANNER BLOTTER	JONATHAN JOHNSON	JENNIFER PRIESTER
ALFRED JOSEPH BOHNE IV	MARCEL DE JONG	RHEL
CHAD BOWDEN	KABRINA	JODY ROBERTS
ERREL BRAUDE	PETRI KANERVA	JOHN BEAR ROSS
DAMIEN BROUSSARD	ROBERT KARALASH	DONNA SANDERS
CATHERINE BULLINER	VIKTOR KASPERSSON	FABIAN SARAVIA
JUSTIN BURGESS	TESLAN KIERINHAWK	TERRY SCHOTT
MATT BURNS	ALEXANDER KIMBALL	SCOTT
BERNIE CINKOSKE	JIM KOSMICKI	ALLEN SIMMONS
MARTIN COOK	FRANKLIN KUZENSKI	KEVIN MICHAEL STEPHENS
ALISTAIR DILWORTH	MEENAZ LODHI	MICHAEL J. SULLIVAN
JAN DRAKE	DAVID MACFARLANE	PAUL SUMMERHAYES
BRET DULEY	JAMIE MCFARLANE	JOHN TREADWELL
RAY DUNN	HENRY MARIN	CHRISTOPHER J. VALIN
ROB EDWARDS	CRAIG MARTELLE	PHILIP VAN ITALLIE
RICHARD EYRES	THOMAS MARTIN	JAAP VAN POELGEEST
MARK FERNANDEZ	ALAN D. MCDONALD	FRANCK VAQUIER
CHARLES T FINCHER	JAMES MCGLINCHEY	VORTEX
SYLVIA FOIL	MICHAEL MCMURRAY	DAVID WALTERS JR
GAZELLE OF CAERBANNOG	CHRISTIAN MEYER	MIKE A. WEBER
DAVID GEARY	SEBASTIAN MÜLLER	PAMELA WICKERT
MICHEAL GREEN	MARK NEWMAN	JON WOODALL
BRIAN GRIFFIN	JULIAN NORTH	BRUCE YOUNG